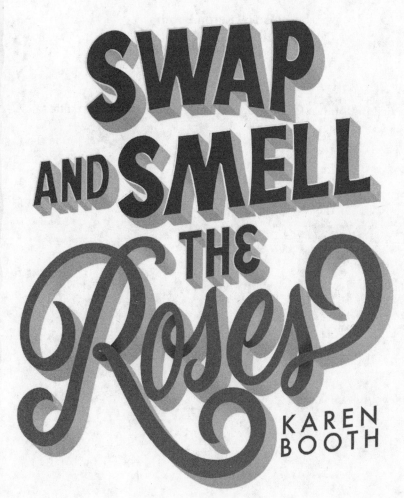

SWAP AND SMELL THE ROSES

KAREN BOOTH

Also by Karen Booth

Rancher After Midnight
Four Weeks to Forever
Their After Hours Playbook

Visit the Author Profile page at Harlequin.com for more titles.

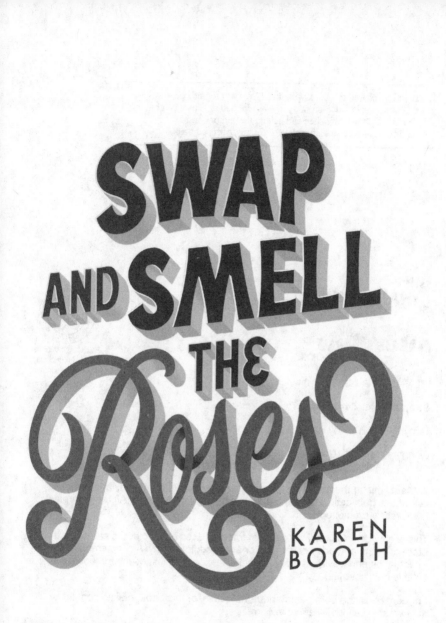

SWAP AND SMELL THE ROSES

KAREN BOOTH

HARLEQUIN

afterglow BOOKS

Recycling programs
for this product may
not exist in your area.

ISBN-13: 978-1-335-04164-7

Swap and Smell the Roses

Harlequin Enterprises ULC
22 Adelaide St. West, 41st Floor
Toronto, Ontario M5H 4E3, Canada
www.Harlequin.com

Printed in U.S.A.

For Katherine Garbera, Joanne Rock,
Reese Ryan and Joss Wood.
This book wouldn't have made it to the finish line
without your encouragement, and I love all four
of you amazingly strong and brilliant women.

AUTHOR'S NOTE

Reid, one of the main characters in this book, is coping with the loss of a parent. Although there are lots of light, fun and romantic moments in this story, just like in real life, grief is there and it sometimes cannot be ignored. I see this as part of talking about love in its many forms, and I hope it enriches the reading experience as Reid finds his way and finds love. But I also recognize that it's not always good or helpful to read something that might hurt. So I ask that you take care when deciding whether or not this book is for you.

All my best,

Karen

One

"What the hell, Bailey?" Willow Moore asked the question out loud, even though the only living being within earshot was a very skinny squirrel. Not to mention her best friend, Bailey Briggs, was hours away in Brooklyn at that very moment, now living in Willow's beloved apartment.

Willow tried again, bending over and poking another slate-colored stone with a stick, only to find a small patch of dirt and zero keys. "The key is under the gray rock by the front door? There are a million gray rocks."

When she straightened and wiped her hands on her jeans, she noted the flaking toothpaste-green paint of the arched front door and knew one thing for sure: she didn't want to be there. Like *really, really* didn't want to be there, alone on an unfamiliar cobbled walkway in front of a crumbling cottage in the middle of nowhere, Connecticut. She'd been gone from New York City for all of three hours and she already felt like her arm had been chopped off. Where was the noise?

The peculiar, sometimes unpleasant smells? Where was the rumble under her feet from the subway? It was quiet here. Too quiet. There was no way she'd survive it for sixty days.

Willow's phone rang. She frantically dug through her crossbody bag and pulled it out. The caller ID said it was Bailey. "I'm here, but I can't find the key," Willow blurted in lieu of *hello*.

"It's in my laptop bag. With me. I'm so sorry. I just found it."

Willow sighed. If it was anyone else, she might go on a tirade, but she could never be angry with Bailey. They'd been through so much in the twelve years since they were randomly matched as roommates, freshman year of college. They were always there for each other. Then again…it had been Bailey's idea to swap living situations for two months so that Willow could "start thinking straight" while Bailey took a coveted invitation-only screenwriting course. It was all Bailey's fault that Willow was keyless—and *clueless*—in Connecticut. "I'm telling you, this is a sign. This is the universe telling me that I shouldn't be here and I should come back to the city."

"This is a sign of nothing more than my general lack of organization."

"Just let me come back to New York while you take your class. It'll be fun. We can stay up late and drink cheap beer and eat too much pizza, just like the old days."

"That sounds like a midlife crisis. You're too young for that. And the last time we hung out, you could barely keep your eyes open past ten."

"I'm a morning person. So sue me."

"Will, I love you, but your apartment is tiny, you're unemployed, and I have to be writing every minute that I'm not taking this class. I'm sorry, but I need solitude to write. That's the whole reason I chose to live in Connecticut in the first place."

Solitude. *Ugh.* Willow hated being alone. She needed people. Human connection. At the very least, to hear the sound of others breathing. "Technically, I could evict you. It's my name on the lease."

"But you won't do that because you know how long I've waited for a break like this. Only ten people get to take this class every year. Ten. It's a freaking miracle that I got picked."

At least one of them had some glimmer of hope on the horizon. Willow certainly didn't. Her dreams had evaporated. Into thin air. "I know. And I'm proud of you for trying."

"Plus, you need some time away from New York. Get some perspective. Figure things out."

"There's nothing to figure out. I know what I want. And what I don't."

"I really don't think you do. One bad experience is not a reason to give up on your dream."

Willow felt ill. As in, *someone please pull my hair back because I'm going to yack.* That bad experience was painfully fresh in her head, being heckled offstage at the Hi-Life, a club she'd spent three years trying to get booked into. *You suck. Go home. Taylor Swift wannabe.* Even worse, her brother, Gabe, had witnessed every humiliating, soul-crushing moment. He'd even tried to fight the guys who'd hurled those unkind words. She loved him to the ends of the earth, but

Gabe greatly overestimated his ability to throw a right hook and he'd paid for it with one hell of a shiner. She'd never been so thankful for security guards in all her life.

Just thinking about that night made her eyes sting. She was done. She'd dreamed of being a singer/songwriter since she was eight years old. Possibly longer. She'd taken hundreds of piano lessons and practiced guitar until her fingers bled, which felt like such a cliché but was a real thing—those metal strings could rub right through tender skin if you gave them enough of a chance. She'd filled thousands of notebook pages with song lyrics, some terrible, others mediocre, and a few choice lines that sparkled with the slightest hint of brilliance, if she did say so herself. She'd climbed up on stage hundreds of times and put everything she had into sets where the audience only half-heartedly clapped. Sometimes, people talked through every song she played. Others walked away. Like she didn't even matter.

Sure, she'd had the opposite response, too. She'd had applause, adoration, and even a standing ovation once. Those were the moments that kept her going. But it wasn't enough. Not anymore. She was losing her joy. She was thirty now and her irrational stranglehold on her "dream" had become mentally and physically exhausting. Something had to give. It was time to pivot. Find an actual career. She couldn't send the minimum payment on her student loans forever, so it had better be something that could put money in the bank. If she was lucky, whatever she did next would nurture the remaining shreds of her tattered creative soul. "I've had enough rejection. I can't take it anymore. I need to move forward and I can't do it here. If I'm going to find a real job, I need to be in the city."

"Think of this as pressing pause. Taking a breath. Don't run down another path until you've had some time to think about it."

"I don't know…" Taking breaths and time and pressing pause…it all sounded so bleak. Somewhere off in the distance, thunder rumbled. It would've been easy to take it as a bad omen, but Willow found her heart fluttering in anticipation. At least something was happening.

"Look. If you really want to come back, then come back," Bailey said. "I know you're making a sacrifice for me and I love you for it. But I'll give up my spot in the class if you want me to. I just need you to tell me now. They can find someone to take my place before it starts."

Willow choked back another sigh. Their sixty-day swap wasn't about her. It was about Bailey. "Don't listen to me, okay? I'll be fine. I'll figure it out." *Somehow.* "Is there another key hidden somewhere?"

"Not that I know of. You're going to have to go find the owner. Reid." Bailey had previously described said owner as "odd and grumpy," which conjured images of a haggard troll living under a bridge. "Either that or I can try to rent a car and bring it to you."

"Don't do that. That's a total waste of money." They were both always scraping to get by. Willow hated that her generation had been made to refer to basic survival as hustling. "I'll find him. If I don't, I'll just smash in a window and let myself in."

"Do not do that. He will not be happy."

"Don't worry. I'll ring his doorbell a few hundred times before I resort to vandalism."

"Shouldn't be too hard to find him. I don't think he goes anywhere. Ever."

"He sounds more fun every time you talk about him." Willow took a few steps and peered around back behind the semi-charming dwelling that was to be her home for the next sixty days. Ahead, a swoop of green grass led to a long line of raised garden beds. At the farthest reaches of the property was another house. No expert on architecture, Willow was still pretty sure it was a Tudor, with the same creamy-white stucco of the guest cottage, but with thick dark brown trim and battens. "I'd better go find him. I think it might rain."

"He's a nice guy, but like I said before, don't take it personally if he's gruff. It's just his vibe."

Willow considered herself warned. "Good luck with your first day of class tomorrow. Don't forget the watering schedule."

"I don't know how I could. The seven-page dissertation you wrote about the care and keeping of philodendrons was enough to help me understand how much you love your houseplants."

"I don't have a pet or kids. They're my babies, okay?" Just thinking about it made Willow's chest hurt. How pathetic was that?

"Don't worry. I will take excellent care of them."

Willow needed to ward off her separation anxiety. Getting off the phone was probably the first step. "Thanks. I'll talk to you later. Love you."

"Love you, too."

Willow ended the call and stuffed her phone into her bag, then scooted her guitar case and roller bag well under the gabled roof of the front stoop. Not that she actually planned to play her guitar while she was here. She needed a break. Bringing it had been Bailey's idea.

Willow marched around the cottage, noting the patches of algae on the exterior and the peeling paint on the window-sills. Bailey had lived here for the last seven years, writing screenplays and working at The Tattered Page, a bookstore in town. Willow had lived a similar existence in New York, except she'd had so many jobs her resume was mostly a list of businesses within a twenty-block radius of her apartment.

Willow crossed a postage stamp of a flagstone patio and tried the back door, jiggling the old brass knob, hoping to get in and avoid talking to Mr. Odd and Grumpy. The dead bolt was latched. It was officially time to find the mysterious Reid.

She started across the grass, ducking out from under the tree cover surrounding the cottage and entering a yawning expanse with nothing but an open stretch of stormy gray sky above. She walked along rows and rows of garden beds, more than she'd possibly ever seen, which was saying a lot since she'd grown up in a small town in Ohio, where pastimes like gardening were a very big deal. It was the first of June, and the beds were already bursting with baby to-matoes, yards of cucumbers, and splashes of brightly colored peppers. It forced her to take a beat—it might not be *completely* terrible here. She did like smelling the earthiness of soil and freshly cut grass. She felt the warm dampness of coming rain. Being nowhere might be okay.

As she got closer to the house, she saw something move. Or more specifically, *someone*. A man practicing Tai Chi in the shade of a massive oak. She came to a stop. Mostly to catch her breath. Holy hell...he was hot. Apparently, Bailey had chosen to gloss over that particular fact? He was not a troll. Oh, no. Tall and lanky—Willow's exact brand of catnip—with a chaotic case of cocoa-brown bed head, no shirt, and gray sweats hanging low on his hips. It was more than his spectacular body that kept her entranced. The way he moved mesmerized her—his impossibly long arms sliced and swooped through the air, while strong legs kept him steadily anchored to the earth. Willow bit her lower lip. A man who could command such fluid movements...well, she could only imagine that he might be able to extend those talents elsewhere. She shook her head. *Don't even think about it.* Her ill-fated music career wasn't the only jumbled mess she'd created. Her love life had a similar flair.

"Hello?" she called.

No response came. He simply continued with his practice, moving from left to right with his back to her, showing off the deep channel of his spine, the sharp contours of his shoulder blades, and the most heartbreaking dimples near his butt.

"Hello? I'm looking for Reid. Is that you?"

Nothing. Not even an acknowledgment of her presence.

She took several strides closer, then noticed his earbuds. No wonder he wasn't responding. He was in his own little world. She found it strangely endearing. It wasn't like there were crowds to avoid in the backyard of this old house. He didn't need to escape here. For a lot of people, *this* was the escape. "Hello?" Now she was probably only twenty feet away. She waved her arms wildly, and still he didn't notice her. This was going to require a more direct approach, so she bustled closer, calling out as loudly as she could. "Hello? Hello?"

She hesitated again, little more than an arm's length away. How could he be so unaware? Frustrated, she reached out and tapped on his bare shoulder.

He whipped around and yanked out one of his earbuds. "What the?" His dark eyes blazed. "Who are you? What are you doing here?"

Willow jumped back. "I'm sorry. I'm, uh, Bailey's friend, Willow," she stammered, trying to ignore the way his chest rose and fell.

"You scared the crap out of me."

"I'm sorry. I'm staying here. I can't get into the cottage."

His brow wrinkled in dismay. His lips turned to a scowl. "She left a key for you."

"She accidentally took it with her." Willow's heart thundered, a toxic cocktail of embarrassment and adrenaline rushing through her veins. "So you're Reid?"

"Uh, yeah. Nobody else lives here."

Gruff? Epically so. Which, to her great annoyance, she didn't hate. "I'm sorry. I didn't mean to scare you." She clasped her hands behind her back, reminding herself that she was not going to touch him again.

All he did was glare at her. If his annoyance was a bonfire, she could've stuffed her face with s'mores for her entire two-month stay. She narrowed her eyes, as if that might help her figure him out, but that only made her focus on the many features that made him so hot, like the smooth and glistening skin of his chest. *Dammit.* Her shoulder-tapping finger tingled from the memory of that split second. "I was hoping you could let me into the cottage. Preferably before it starts to rain. Please."

He grumbled and stalked over to the base of the tree, plucking a T-shirt from the ground. He threaded his arms through the sleeves then tugged the garment over his head. As he covered up, it was like watching a candle being snuffed out.

"Come on." He started for the cottage, leaving Willow standing there.

She sighed, then started to stumble along behind him, dreading what came next—she was going to turn on the charm. She just knew it. She was going to get chatty and make jokes. She couldn't stand it when people didn't like her. And sixty days was entirely too long to live next door to someone who was so clearly not her biggest fan.

Reid Harrel had been promised that Willow Moore would be zero trouble. That he *wouldn't even notice she was there.* He should've known better. Nothing was ever as easy as advertised.

"There's another key. I'll show you." He stepped up onto the flagstone patio behind the guest cottage and beelined for the kitchen window, reached under one of the shutters, and removed the spare from a tiny hook.

"Dang. I wish Bailey had known about that," Willow said.

"My dad was her original landlord. I guess he never told her about it."

He turned and dared to look at Willow. She nodded slowly, her head tilted ever so slightly to the side, making her thick fringe of blond bangs drape across her forehead and highlight her pale blue eyes. She was… Well, it was hard to not stare. Something about her silently insisted, *look at me*. She was beautiful, but in a broken sort of way.

"I heard about your dad," she said. "Bailey told me. I'm so sorry. She really liked him a lot. She said he was wonderful."

"He was."

"She said he was a chef, too. Was he the reason you became one?"

He was ready to hand her the key and get the hell out of there. That was his usual reaction any time someone struck up a conversation about his father, and now she'd had to go and add in the topic of the profession he'd left behind. What was next? Was she going to ask him about his worst breakup? His most embarrassing moment? "I'm not a chef. Not anymore."

"Oh. Then what are you doing?"

Good God, how he despised that question. "Existing."

"Gotcha. Sorry I asked." She smiled softly and turned back to survey the garden. It only gave him the opportunity to eye her up and down. In curve-hugging jeans, a black tank top and Converse low-tops, she read as casual and carefree, qualities Reid did not possess. "You've obviously been gardening. Your crops look amazing. I'd love to help out while I'm here. I'm kind of a plant nerd. And I like to stay busy."

"I don't need any help. I've got it under control. I have a system."

She turned back to him. "Okay, then. Sorry."

"No need to apologize for everything, okay? People quit their jobs. People don't need your help. People die. It's just the way the world works."

Her perfect eyebrows arched into two waning moons. "You're up to your eyeballs in pleasant thoughts, aren't you?"

He shrugged. "I'm a realist. Not everyone can handle it."

"I can get real. In fact, I think I just did."

Not knowing what to say, he instead grunted. This was getting messier at every step. All the more reason to keep it short and make a quick exit. He unlocked the back door, then drove his shoulder into it, anticipating the sticking point at the upper corner. It swung open and he stepped back. "There you go." He handed her the key. "Use this for now. I'll get it from you at some point and make a copy."

"I don't get a tour?"

"It's a cottage. Pretty self-explanatory. Kitchen, bathroom, bedroom."

"Bailey mentioned your family has owned this property for nearly thirty years, right? I guess I figured you might want to show me around. Since there's so much history."

He supposed she had a point, although he wasn't happy about it. "Fine."

He led the way, Willow trailing behind him. Once they were inside, he closed the door behind her, leaving him with enough of a whiff to stop him dead in his tracks. He would've pegged her as a flowery girl, but her fragrance was a blur of evocative scents—woodsy like cedar and summery like rain. That coupled with the overwhelming sense of nostalgia he felt whenever he stepped into the cottage had him even more unsteady than he'd been outside. This was where his parents had lived when they were newly married. It had been Reid's home until he was six years old.

"Kitchen is cute." Willow ran her hand along the old Formica countertops, then stepped to the white enamel sink. A vision of his mom flashed in his head. Willow peered out through the window that overlooked the yard, gardens, and even had a glimpse of the main house. "I love the view. I can stand here and do dishes and spy on you while you do Tai Chi."

He fought so hard against the smile that wanted to spread across his face. He wasn't going to give in to it. No way. "Please don't."

She turned and rolled her eyes, then stepped over to the original Frigidaire, peeking inside. "I'm kidding. I'm not a creeper. Well, not much of one."

"As long as you don't sneak up on me again, I'm good. In fact, I'm guessing I'll live several years longer."

She closed the fridge. "People die. That's the way the world works, right?"

He appreciated her cheekiness a bit too much. So did his dick. It had already been keenly aware of her presence, but now that she was throwing his own words back at him, it was really sitting up and taking notice. *I like her. She's feisty*, it said. "Right."

She laughed quietly, seeming quite amused with herself. "I

know you think I apologize too much, but I *am* sorry about that. I should've known better than to tap you on the shoulder when you were off in your own little world."

Some people might've taken issue with her suggesting he was a daydreamer, but she wasn't wrong. He craved the escape. "It's okay. It's not entirely your fault, anyway. I get very into it. I can't meditate. It's too quiet. So I do that instead."

Willow reached out and lightly swatted his forearm. "Oh, my God. So it's not just me. I can't meditate, either. My brain kicks into overdrive. It's like it's actively trying to not calm down."

That was his experience as well, but he didn't need to connect with her on another level. He wanted to keep his distance. She wouldn't be here long, and she was already upsetting the natural order of his life, where he kept to himself and left everyone else alone. "I'll show you the rest of the house. Then I'll get out of your hair."

Willow followed as he headed for the living room, opening the small utility closet on the way out of the kitchen. "Laundry?"

"It's a small machine. Don't overload it."

"Aye, aye, Captain."

Reid wanted to laugh. She had this way of catching him off guard. "Here's the living room. Not much to see. A sofa, chair, and a TV."

"Perfect. It's all I need." She stepped ahead and poked her head into the room to their right. "Bedroom?"

He remained in place, imagining his feet were glued to the floor. There was no way he was going in there. Not with her. That room was tiny. It was basically *all* bed. One misstep and someone would fall on it, and then where would he be? In deep trouble, that's where. "Yep. Bath is attached."

Just then, a sudden roar engulfed the room with white noise from above. They both raised their sights to the ceiling.

"Whoa. Is that rain?" Willow asked.

"It's really coming down." The raindrops hammered the roof. Louder and louder. His pulse picked up. He needed to leave. He couldn't be cooped up in the house with her because of the weather.

"Oh, crap. My stuff. It's still outside." Willow scrambled for the front door and flipped the latch, then rushed out onto the landing. She jerked a black guitar case inside. "Wait. Where's my suitcase? It was right here."

Reid hurried to help. Out on the stoop, the rain was coming down in sheets all around them, but he quickly spotted the problem. Her bag had rolled down the front walkway and was lodged in the holly bushes. "I'll get it." He stepped past her.

Willow grabbed his T-shirt. "Wait. You'll get soaked."

He turned and looked at her hand grasping the soft fabric. For a fleeting second he wanted her to push him up against the cottage door, rip his shirt from his body, and kiss him into oblivion while Mother Nature unleashed her fury. Bolts of lightning and claps of thunder. Willow could take away his misery for a few moments. He was reasonably sure of that. The trouble was, it always came back.

"No. I'll do it." He broke free of her hold and flew down the cobbled path as he was pelted with fat, warm raindrops.

He grabbed the handle of her roller bag and raced for the front door.

Willow rescued her bag from him and whisked it inside. "Thank you so much. Come in. Please. Dry off," she pled.

A tiny part of him wanted to step back across that threshold more than anything. The rest of him, the pragmatic part, knew what logically came next—he'd need to shed his wet clothes. Common sense would dictate he get into the shower—let the warm water roll over his shoulders, down his belly and back, bring his body to life, all while he was keenly aware that beautiful, intriguing Willow was in the next room. When he was done, he'd have to walk through her bedroom, clutching a towel around his waist, all while his dick reminded him that a rainy afternoon was the perfect time to get lost in a woman he hardly knew.

"No. No. It's okay. I'll just track a bunch of water inside. It'll be a big mess. The hardwood floors are old. They really shouldn't get wet. I'll just head home."

She reached for him again. "Are you sure? I feel bad."

He froze. What was it with Willow and touching? She did it all the damn time. It was really starting to grate on his nerves. He'd had a perfectly acceptable, quiet existence before she arrived. Now she was stirring up far too many sensations. "I'm sure."

She let go of him. "Okay. Be safe. Don't get too wet."

"I'll be fine."

"Thanks for your help."

"Just try to stay out of trouble, okay?" He wasn't even sure why he'd said it, and he didn't offer more. He didn't say that he'd be happy to be of help any time. Or that she should let him make her dinner sometime. Instead, he turned and jogged away in the rain. As soon as he was sure he was out of her sight line, he tore off, around to the back of the cottage. The rain was coming down so fast he could hardly see, but he knew the way, down the grassy slope and past the garden beds. He traveled as fast as his feet would carry him. It wasn't that he was worried about getting wet. He was already doused. He was trying to get away. Away from Willow. Away from any chance of getting close.

Two

Willow got up with the sun after her first night in Connecticut. Not that she was much of a sleeper to begin with, but she hadn't had much at all—the quiet kept waking her up. It didn't seem to matter that the bed was squishy and soft, or that Bailey's sheets were cool and crisp and a little bougie, smelling vaguely of lavender. Apparently, Willow couldn't reach a deep sleep unless there were police sirens at 3:00 a.m. The Reid situation wasn't helping, either. She kept replaying the events of their meeting in her head. So she hadn't had the key. So she'd tapped him on the shoulder and made him jump out of his skin. *Get over it.* Neither of those facts were reasons to run away in the rain like she was a serial killer.

She put on a pot of coffee, stoked that Bailey had left her a bag of Kenya French from a place in town called The Bean Machine. In true best friend style, she'd also bought a carton of half-and-half, a necessity Bailey was well aware of because she absolutely refused to put so much as a drop of cream in her own coffee. Willow learned this on their first morning as roommates, in the cafeteria at Denison University, a school Willow had only been able to afford because her mom worked there. Bailey took her coffee black. Like she'd grown up during the Great Depression or something. Willow liked hers the color of chocolate milk, creamy and delicious and only very vaguely tasting like actual coffee. Up until that point, she'd assumed that every person her age liked theirs the same way. Not so, it turned out.

Bailey had also left a lengthy note about the idiosyncrasies of the cottage—how to make the fridge stop emitting its loud grinding noise, and something about the paltry size of the hot water heater and not expecting to wash dishes if you'd just taken a shower. At the bottom of the note was Bailey's parting thought: *find Reid if anything breaks*. Yeah, that was not going to happen. She'd take a course in hot water heater repair before she'd give Reid one more reason to think of her as a pain in the ass.

Willow flipped the dead bolt on the back door and tugged on the knob, then stepped outside onto the flagstone patio. The hard uneven surface was cold beneath her bare feet, a stark contrast to the morning air that was already warm and nearly as comfortable as her worn-out pajama pants and tank top. She held on tight to her coffee mug and took a long sip, then almost spit it out when Reid popped up from behind one of the garden beds. Her breath caught in her chest. Even from this distance, she was drawn to him. His hair was a mess again, but this morning it was full-on bed head. Why was it in any way appealing that he clearly did not glance in the mirror often? She knew she shouldn't stare, but she couldn't stomach the idea of *not* staring, either. And then he looked up. His dark eyes narrowed.

Fuck. "Morning!" she called, following it up with a wave, and it wasn't just a casual wag of her hand, either. It was like she had a flat tire and was flagging down a tow truck.

He pulled out one of his earbuds. "What?" he shouted.

"I said good morning! What a beautiful day!" Willow tiptoed to the edge of the patio and stepped into the soft and dewy grass.

"Morning," he grumbled. He waved, too, but it was really just a flip of his hand. If he'd had all but his middle finger folded down, it wouldn't have shocked her.

"What are you working on?"

"Weeding."

"Oh! Fun!" *No it isn't.*

Reid then popped the earbud back in and returned to his task. What kind of music was he listening to? Something dark and emo was too easy a guess. Hip-hop? Indie rock? Scream metal? Or was she thinking about this all wrong and was he instead listening to a podcast or an audiobook? She was dying to know. Of course, fixating on this totally meaningless question gave her an excuse to ignore the larger overarching problem—why didn't he like her?

She needed to give it time. He'd come around eventually. Or he wouldn't, and she'd spend the next fifty-nine days feeling hopelessly lonely from lack of human contact. For now, it was time to get dressed, visit whatever constituted the town of Nowhere, and find a job to hold her over for the next two months. She and Bailey had traded rent as well, and although it was far cheaper to live there in Connecticut, Willow needed something to keep her busy. And money, or lack thereof, was always an issue.

After a super-quick shower, lest she use up all of the hot water, Willow drove along narrow, winding, tree-lined roads toward town in Bailey's car. That was another part of their swap—Bailey had driven her rusty old baby blue VW bug into Manhattan, moved her stuff into Willow's apartment, then Willow packed up and trekked back to Connecticut.

On the outskirts of town, she was greeted by a sign welcoming her and pointing out that Nowhere had an actual name—Old Ashby. Of course, Willow had always known the name of the place where her best friend lived. It just hadn't fully settled in her brain. She wondered if there was a New Ashby, and if so, why she didn't get to be there instead.

As she turned onto Rosemary Street, which was the main drag, it felt like déjà vu. She slipped through a time warp and landed in the tiny Ohio town where she'd grown up. An uncannily similar procession of storefronts ticked by—a quirky gift shop, rainbow-hued ice cream parlor, and rustic brewpub on one side of the street and a cozy bookstore, fine dining restaurant, and charming bakery on the other.

She was overcome with the strangest case of nostalgia as she pulled into an available parking spot. Small-town Willow's life had swung back and forth between dreams that were unfathomably huge and the nagging sense that she would never be good enough. Her relationship with her family only added to the latter. Her brother was the golden child. The handsome straight-A student with the easy smile. The brilliant mind who did everything right. Willow was the adorable do-nothing. Her parents thought it was "cute" that she wanted to pursue music. They'd only ever humored her dreams.

And despite all of that, she wouldn't have traded her up-bringing for anything, because her family was also rock solid. They were always there for her, with unwavering love and support, especially Gabe. She didn't take any of that for granted now. When she'd gone to college, she'd naively thought everyone's family must be like that. Then she met Bailey and discovered that was very much not the case. That was part of what made her failure in music so painful. She'd do anything to make her family proud, and she hadn't come anywhere close.

The worst was that she had nothing to show for the years and years of gigging and writing. Even when she got a break, like a big show, and even if she did well, it was never enough to make a difference somehow. There was always disappointment waiting on the other side—a gig she didn't get, or one where her friends and family were the only people there. There was nothing worse than being alone on a stage and seeing that mix of disappointment and pity on the faces of people she loved. If she gave it up, she could save herself and everyone else so much heartache.

As Willow passed the various businesses on Rosemary Street, like The Bean Machine, the place her morning coffee had come from, she weighed her employment options. Bailey had encouraged her to apply at The Tattered Page, the bookstore where she worked, but Willow already had a problem with quiet. If she was going to spend two months in this place, she needed something upbeat and completely new. Which was what brought her to a stop at the brick-clad storefront right next door to the restaurant—a bakery called Flour Girl. A handwritten help-wanted sign was perched in the window. Aside from being an actual sign, could this be a figurative one? The prospect had Willow tingling with possibilities.

She pulled on the door, and a tiny bell overhead rang. Straight ahead was a long line of glass cases stocked with pretty pastries and massive cookies. Behind, on the wall, were baskets brimming with loaves of fresh bread. Heavenly aromas swirled, but there was a slightly off-putting odor hanging in the air. Was something burning?

A woman with dark curly hair popped her head out of the back. She had a silver-gray streak that was epically cool. "Sorry. I'll be right with you. I have a bit of a situation." Just like that, she disappeared.

"Is everything okay?" Willow inched closer to the cases, peeking around the corner where the woman had gone. The acrid smell became stronger.

"It's okay. I think I've got it," the woman replied. Metal clattered. "Oh, shit. Shit. Shit."

Willow couldn't take it. She had to help. She bustled into the back room. The air was heavy with smoke and the woman was on her knees, picking up what looked to be charred croissants and tossing them into the trash. "Is there an actual fire back here?" Willow heard the frantic edge to her voice.

"No. I burned a batch of *pain au chocolat*."

"Let me help," Willow said, stooping down and lending a hand.

"Thank you. You're an angel. I'm short-staffed and I was on the phone taking an order from one of my commercial customers. I guess I lost track of time." The woman appeared to be in her late forties or early fifties, with exceptionally kind eyes. She blew her hair from her forehead and cast her gaze in Willow's direction. "What a waste. I hate throwing these away."

"I'm sure they were delicious." Willow examined one of the nearly black pastries. "At one point."

The woman laughed and picked up the now empty baking sheet. She stood and wiped her hands on her white apron, which had all sorts of streaks and smudges on it. "Hi. I'm Faith."

"I'm Willow. Nice to meet you."

"This isn't normally how I like to greet a customer. But thank you for the help." Faith slid the baking tray into a sink. "Come on out front. Whatever you want. On the house."

"Actually…" Willow started, following Faith out into the front of the bakery. "I saw the help-wanted sign in the window. I'm looking for a job."

"If you tell me you're a baker, then I'll have no choice but to believe you're an actual angel."

"Well, not exactly. On either count." This felt uncomfortably familiar—wading into waters she had no business being in, trying to talk her way into a position she wasn't qualified for. She'd done this a zillion times over the last eight years since she'd graduated from college and moved to New York.

"So what kind of experience do you have?"

"As far as *eating* bakery items, pretty extensive. I once downed seven donuts in one sitting. Now, in my defense, they were really, really good donuts."

Faith laughed, tossing back her head. It felt good to make someone happy. To make someone *smile*. "Donut-eating ability is strong. Duly noted."

"But if you want actual baking experience, I'm afraid to say that aside from occasionally helping my mom make cookies, my skill set is basic. You sure you don't need someone to work the front counter?"

"Actually, no. I've got two students that work for me. Ella and Isaac. Ella's home from college for the summer. She was supposed to be here this morning, but she had a dentist appointment. Isaac handles the afternoons."

"Hmm. Okay." Willow didn't offer more, waiting for Faith to decide where that left them.

Faith pressed her lips together and nodded slowly, seeming deep in thought. "I mean, that's not necessarily a deal-breaker. How do you feel about coming in early every morning? Like really early. I get here at five."

"Yes. No problem. I'm a total morning person. And I don't sleep a lot to begin with. The only downside is that I'm only here in town for two months."

Faith drew in a deep breath and blew it out slowly. "You know, Willow. I really need the help. So if you want to be here at five for the next two months, you're hired. We'll start with the basics and see how you do."

"Sounds great."

"We're closed Sundays and Mondays. The pay is sixteen an hour, but you can take home fresh bread every day."

"Awesome. I'll take it."

"Really? You sure? It can be grueling."

"Really. I've got nothing else to do while I'm here."

Faith tossed her hands in the air. "Perfect. Let me get your info." She flipped through a file folder propped up against the cash register. "What brings you to town for only two months? Visiting family?"

"I swapped living situations with my best friend. She's in my apartment in Brooklyn taking a screenwriting class while I'm here living in her place."

"And where's that?" She slid a generic job application across the top of the bakery case, along with a pen. "Just put in your name and contact info."

Willow began filling in the form. "I'm staying in the guest cottage of a guy named Reid Harrel. He lives on the outskirts of town. Not sure if you know him. I get the impression he keeps to himself." When Willow looked up, she saw the most wistful look on Faith's face, like she was on the verge of tears. "Are you okay?"

"I knew Reid's dad. Graham. Quite well, actually." Faith nodded eagerly, forcing her sad expression into a smile. "It still doesn't feel real that he's gone. He was an incredible man. Just so friendly and warm. He was one of those people who you liked from the moment you met him."

Willow couldn't help but wonder about genetics and personality because Reid was nothing like the man Faith was describing. She might've guessed that he reserved "friendly and warm" for people other than Willow, but even Bailey had described him as gruff. "I wish I'd had the chance to meet him. He sounds like a really special guy."

"He was." Faith wiped a tear from the corner of her eye and took in a deep cleansing breath. "So, can you start tomorrow morning? Be here at five a.m.?"

"Yes. Absolutely."

"Great. I'll make a big pot of coffee. Just wear jeans and a T-shirt. Or whatever's comfortable. You'll get dirty. And sweaty."

"Got it." Willow hitched her bag up on her shoulder. "Is there somewhere in town where I can get a key made?"

Faith leaned against the glass case and pointed to her right. "Hines Hardware. Another block down. On the opposite side of the street. Ask for Carlos. He'll hook you up."

"Perfect. Thank you. I'll see you tomorrow morning." Willow strode to the door and opened it. She noticed a few plants in the window that were in need of tending. She'd have to get to that tomorrow.

"Hey, Willow," Faith called.

She turned back to look at Faith. "Yeah?"

"Welcome to Old Ashby. I think you'll like it here."

Willow remained unconvinced, but she'd take any reason to have her attitude turned around. "Thanks. I'll try to make the best of it."

Reid wiped sweat from his brow with the back of his hand. The sun was particularly punishing today, so fierce that it was wringing every ounce of energy out of him. He was spent, but this was what he needed. Every day he made a point of working himself as close to the brink of physical exhaustion as possible. It made it easier to sleep. And staying busy during the day made it easier to be awake. Easier to quiet the ghosts in his head.

He'd been working in the garden all morning, pulling weeds, taking suckers off tomato plants and staking eggplant he'd started indoors weeks ago. It all made him hot and hella thirsty. He bent over, grabbed his water bottle from its resting place in the grass, and took a long drink before dumping the rest over the top of his head to cool down. Caring for the garden and the rest of his parents' property wasn't exactly a labor of love—more like penance. He'd never forgive himself for staying away from this place for so long.

"You're hard-core. Hours later and you're still out here," a now familiar voice said behind him.

Reid turned and was confronted with the vision of Willow, standing only a few feet away. His pulse picked up, just like it had that morning when she'd waved at him from the back patio of the guesthouse. He hated that his body reacted to her in this way. It felt like a betrayal. Maybe he would eventually get used to Willow and his heart would calm the fuck down, but becoming accustomed to her presence would require a degree of familiarity he wasn't going to explore. He didn't invest time in other people. Especially not ones who weren't sticking around. "There's a lot to do."

Willow dug into the bag that hung across her body and inconveniently drew attention to her curves. She wasn't busty. Like not at all. But everything about her was so damn inviting. He could only imagine how warm she must be. How soft. "I brought you a surprise." She held up a silver key that was nearly as bright as her eyes. "Now you don't have to worry about having this done."

Damn her. That was thoughtful. He wasn't about to say it out loud. He didn't want to encourage her to do kind and generous things for him. He already had the feeling she was inclined to do nothing less. "You can keep the new one and put the old one back on the hook." Reid waved it off in case their fingers brushed and left him with even more conflicted feelings.

"Oh. Okay." She frowned, which made him feel like an ass, a punishment he whole-heartedly deserved.

"Thank you. For doing that. It was nice." He swallowed hard and looked away. Birds swooped from the mighty trees that skirted the property. An early summer breeze ruffled the branches. Those oaks had probably been there hundreds of years—silent custodians of this land, marking time with a new ring of bark every year. The greatest irony of Reid's existence was that life was going on all around him and he still felt so...*not* alive...inside. Willow's presence was making him far more aware of this cognitive dissonance. It had to be the reason she put him on edge.

"It's the least I could do," she said. "Plus, I was already in town."

"Right," he said by way of small talk.

"I got a job. At the bakery. I start tomorrow morning."

"That was quick."

"I need money. So I can do fun things like eat and pay you rent."

"Sure." He tried to remember what Bailey had told him about Willow and her vocation beforehand, but he couldn't recall if she'd said anything. His interactions with Bailey had been brief and minimal. "Are you a baker?"

Willow bent down and tugged on a weed he'd somehow managed to miss. "Nope. Big fan of baked goods, but I have zero experience."

"Please don't do that," he said, pointing to the unwanted plant in her hand. "I would've gotten it eventually."

"Sorry. Would you like me to put it back?"

He shook his head. "Don't be ridiculous. Just don't do it again."

"I like weeding. I like being in the garden," she countered, tossing it into his pile of yard trash, then wiped the dirt from her hands. "I told you that yesterday."

"And I told you that I have a system and don't need your help."

"But you missed that one, so clearly your system could use some fine-tuning."

"Sometimes I miss one. I spend enough time out here, I'd eventually pull it."

She shrugged and sat down, perching herself on the edge of the raised garden bed. "Anyway, Faith, the owner, said she'd teach me. About baking."

In Reid's experience in the culinary world, bakers and pastry chefs were often unsung heroes. They worked long, odd hours and it took years to perfect their skills. "You're only here two months. I doubt you'll be able to pick up much in that amount of time."

"I appreciate the vote of confidence."

"Look. I know how much there is to learn in that realm. From my days as a chef. It isn't easy. You'll probably just be starting to get the hang of it when it's time for you to leave."

"I told Faith up front that I was only here for eight weeks, but she still offered me the job. I guess we'll see how I do." Willow reached behind a tomato plant and yanked yet another weed he'd missed. He was torn between being amused and pissed off. She just couldn't help herself, even when he'd asked her to stop. "Faith said she knew your dad. Pretty well, it seemed like. She was definitely sad about him passing away. She teared up when she talked about him."

"I've met her a few times. She brought bread to the house when he was sick. She came to the funeral. Then she came by the next day to express her condolences." That had been one of many grueling conversations he'd had to endure, where he had to soak up exactly what his dad had meant to a stranger, then somehow go on with his day as if nothing had happened. Meanwhile, every bit of remorse expressed was nothing but another reminder that Reid had made a huge mistake. "I think that last visit was just an excuse to ask for help with some garden project at the high school. I guess her sister teaches there."

"Huh. She didn't mention that. She doesn't seem like the kind of person who would need an excuse to ask for a favor." Willow uncrossed her legs, then crossed them in the opposite direction. She was always moving. Rarely still. "Did you help her?"

"I gave her some money."

"Was that what she wanted? Or did she want actual help? Like physical labor?"

"I don't know. She didn't really say and I didn't ask."

Willow looked to her left and then her right. "Seems to me like you kick ass with a garden. Anyone can write a check."

"I don't get involved with what's going on in town." There were too many unwanted conversations waiting, from countless people like Faith who'd known his dad and were torn up over his death. Reid was already well aware how amazing his father was. He didn't need to have the concept reinforced by others. Plus, he knew that people would naturally expect him to be like his dad, and he simply wasn't. He wasn't that good. He wasn't that pure of heart.

"Not at all?"

"Well, there's one thing. I'm going to be selling at the farmer's market on Saturdays. But that's new. Another vendor dropped out." The prospect of his weekly face time with the locals made his stomach lurch, but there were only so many vegetables he could eat on his own, and although he had a fair amount of money socked away from years of working like crazy and making zero time for anything fun, he did need to bring in something. Maintaining his family's property was a costly venture. The house and land were paid for, but there were taxes and upkeep to worry about.

"It sounds to me like you're doing more than merely existing. That's practically a job, Reid."

"It's not all-consuming," he said, hearing the defensiveness in his own voice.

Willow bounced her foot. "Really? How long have you been out here today?"

"It's therapeutic to be outside and dig in the dirt. Being a chef gave me time for nothing other than sleep."

"I can think of one other reason your new job is better than being a chef. Now you have time to chat with cute women who wander by to do unwelcome weeding."

Heat rushed to Reid's face so fast he thought he might pass out. He literally had to avert his eyes. Look away.

"Oh, my God. Are you blushing?" Willow hopped up from her perch and grasped his arm.

"No," he barked, a bit more forcefully than he wanted to.

Willow dropped her grip and stepped back. "Oh. Sorry."

"It's okay," he countered in a tone that was in no way convincing, not even to him.

"I should go."

Reid felt like such a jerk. "No. Sorry. I just…"

"You just what?"

He swallowed hard, searching for the right words. He wanted to explain himself, but not share too much. "I'm not used to having someone around. That's all. Bailey keeps to herself. I rarely see her. I guess I've forgotten what it's like. To have someone in my space."

She sighed and silently considered him with her pale blue eyes, which were so beautiful they were like the physical embodiment of her spirit. Being met with her appraisal only made him feel more unsettled. "It's okay, Reid. I don't bite. In fact, I think I'm pretty easy to get along with."

That's what I'm worried about. "I'm sure you are."

"I should go. You have a system to maintain and everything."

His deepest impulses told him to stay on the path he'd chosen for himself and let her walk away. But something inside him hated that she'd offered so much and he'd given virtually nothing in return. He might be a guy who kept to himself, but he wasn't selfish. "Well, hold on. You didn't tell me anything about you. Other than your lack of baking skills." He knew how that sounded—like a genuine attempt at friendship. When he saw the way she lit up like a Christmas tree, he regretted it. He should've known better.

"Oh. Sure. Yeah. What do you want to know?"

He had a whole lot of questions tumbling around in his head, none of which were things he might actually utter. *Why do you seem so damn happy? What makes you radiate sunshine? Why are you so fucking earnest?* "What's the deal with the guitar?"

Willow turned away slightly and started absentmindedly tugging on the strap of her bag. "Bailey made me bring it," she mumbled.

He waited for more of an explanation. They hadn't known each other long, but in every conversation they'd had thus far, there'd always been plenty from her side of things. "And?"

"And nothing. I brought it with me to get her to stop talking about it. I don't plan to play it."

"I don't understand. Are you learning? Did she buy you the guitar? Why would she care?"

She looked at him like he was quite possibly the most ridiculous person on earth. "It's a long story, okay?"

He'd touched a nerve. Possibly a deep one. And he couldn't help but be pleased with himself. Virtually everything she said to him hit one of his soft points. It was nice to level the playing field ever so slightly. "I'd like to hear you play sometime."

All the rosy pink drained from Willow's face. "Uh. No. No way. That is *not* happening."

"Why? It's a guitar. Who cares? I don't know how much you think you suck, but you can't be that bad."

Willow stood frozen, jaw slack and mouth agape. "Wow."

"I mean, how bad could you possibly be?"

"You don't know anything."

"So educate me."

Her jaw shifted to a tight and rigid line. "You're just a big jerk, aren't you? That's all this is. You act like an asshole and that gets people to leave you alone."

"Probably." He shrugged. In some ways, it felt good to be called out on his shit.

"Probably?"

"Definitely."

"Good. I'm glad we agree on something." Willow blew out a long breath and shook her head. "Well, this has been super fun. I'm going to go now."

"You don't want to talk about the guitar. Got it."

She narrowed her vision on him for what felt like the hundredth time. A flamethrower would have directed less heat at him. "Proving a point?"

"I don't think I have to."

"No. You definitely do not." She turned and started to walk away.

"If you ever want to share your general lack of talent, I'm around." He could hardly believe the words when they came out of his mouth. It might have been one of the most insensitive things he'd ever said. But maybe it would do the job. Keep her away.

"Thanks for the great offer. I'll let you know."

"Good luck at the bakery," he muttered, but she was already out of earshot. And that was for the absolute best.

Three

At the end of Willow's third day at the bakery, she was comforted by the fact that she was kinda *sorta* figuring out what she was supposed to be doing. "The sourdough loaves are shaped and ready to rise overnight," she called to Faith. Willow slid a tray into what she'd learned on her first day was a commercial bread proofing box.

Faith was putting some finishing touches on a batch of fancy French macarons. "Great. Thank you."

Of course, Willow had made so many mistakes in her first few days that it was a major triumph that she'd successfully shaped loaves of bread. The first time she'd tried, they'd all turned out looking like deformed footballs. She'd also made the world's toughest batch of white chocolate macadamia nut cookies by overmixing the dough, and baked some remarkably flat layers of red velvet cake by undermixing. Baking seemed to be about precision, but it was also a lot about timing and feel. She saw a few corollaries with music—enough to give her a glimmer of optimism that she'd ultimately get pretty good at this—but she didn't dwell on the similarities. Hopefully, her baking career would turn out better.

"Oh, gosh. It's already two," Faith said. "How did that happen? You should go home."

Home. That was laughable. That cottage on Reid Harrel's property did not feel like home, and it was really dragging Willow down into the depths of a dark mood. Having a neighbor like Reid was lonely. He was not only distant— he reveled in it. He flaunted it like it was some great personality trait. The one and only time she'd gotten him to talk, he'd had to go and ask about her guitar. It was like he had a metal detector for uncomfortable subjects and her music was a freaking pirate's treasure buried two inches under the sand.

Why couldn't he just be nice? Or maybe let her help him in the garden? The entire situation was so confusing and frustrating—not that long ago, she would've written a song about it. It would've helped her process her feelings or at the very least get them out. She would need to find a different outlet.

"I'm good. I'll help you finish cleaning and then I'll head out," Willow said.

"Are you sure? Isaac will be here in an hour. He and Ella can clean up, too, if you need to go."

Willow smiled to herself, happy to have found this job. Faith was amazing—kind, patient and always thankful. "It's okay. I'll work a little bit longer."

"Thanks. You're the best."

Willow knew that wasn't true, but she sure appreciated that Faith was willing to say it. Willow washed a whole slew of baking trays and mixing bowls, then took a minute to go up front and tend to the hanging plants in the window, a task she'd been meaning to tackle since her first visit.

"Hey, Ella. How's it going out here?"

Ella was perched on a barstool behind the counter, hunched over with her nose in a book. Her pin-straight jet-black hair was tucked behind her ears. She was wearing jean shorts, a pink Flour Girl T-shirt, and bright white sneakers. "Fine. It's pretty slow today."

Willow took down an emerald green and white trailing pothos from the window and brought it back behind the counter. She snipped away some dead leaves, wiped the healthy foliage down with a damp rag, and gave the plant a nice long drink of water. "I guess I haven't been around long enough to know what's busy and what isn't."

"I think it might be the weather. When it's warm out, people don't necessarily think about things like bread and cookies."

"Makes sense." Willow went to return the plant to its original spot and grab the other two remaining—both trailing philodendrons. "Faith says you're home after freshman year of college. Princeton?"

Ella closed her book and hopped off the barstool. "Yep. Civil engineering."

"Wow. That's impressive." Willow went to work on the other two plants.

"Not if you ask my parents. They want me to be a doctor. They're still holding out hope that I'll change my mind and shift to premed."

Willow could hardly imagine such lofty aspirations. She'd never been a very good student. Math and science in particular made her nothing but frustrated. "You can't live to make your parents happy." Willow had no problem rolling out that little gem, even though it was advice that sounded easy to take and nearly impossible for her to follow.

"I know. It just makes it really hard to come home for the summer. You'd think they'd want to shower me with affection, especially since I got straight As, but they're disappointed."

Willow rinsed off the scissors she'd used on the plants. "Just do your thing and give them time to come around. I'm sure they will."

"Thanks, Willow. You're pretty cool. For, you know… somebody older."

Willow nearly burst out laughing. She was only thirty, for God's sake. Ella might think that made Willow wise, but deep down, she felt like she and Ella were in the same spot— starting out, trying to find their way. "Thanks. It's good to know I've still got game."

Just then, two women walked into the bakery and Ella greeted them. "Welcome to Flour Girl. What can I help you with today?"

Willow ducked away from the conversation, returned the plants to their usual homes, and made her way into the back room. "*Now* I'm going home."

Faith looked up from her phone. "Actually, I have a question for you."

"Sure. What's up?"

"How would you feel about manning the Flour Girl booth

at the farmer's market Saturday morning? It's just for a few hours. Pretty easy. Selling bread and pastries."

Of course, Willow's first thought was Reid. He would be there. Hopefully it was a huge market and they could have a football field between them. "Sure. I'm game."

"That would be awesome. I hate doing it myself."

"Why?"

"Actually, *hate* is a strong word. It's more exhausting for me. I end up chatting so much that I'm even more tired than I am on a regular day."

"Well, don't worry about it. I'm in."

Faith unleashed a wide grin. "Sounds great. See you tomorrow. Thank you for today."

Willow bid goodbye to Faith, went out the back door, and climbed into Bailey's car. She sat still for a moment, staring at the old brick wall of the back of the building and a stack of plastic bakery crates leaning against it. Despite the non-picturesque view, she couldn't bring herself to put the key in the ignition. It was the thought of going back to the cottage. That was where her new lonely life happened. And she hated it.

Her old remedy for boredom or loneliness had always been playing or writing music. It had been her constant companion for as long as she could remember. A song or an idea for a song had always been running in her head. Even when she was a little girl. But the soundtrack of her own music stopped the night she flopped at the Hi-Life. She hadn't even realized it until the next morning when she woke up and heard nothing more than the ambient noise of Brooklyn and rumble of a garbage truck on her street. She'd lost more than her ambition that night—she'd lost the actual music. There was a part of her that wondered what might bring it back. Perhaps returning to her old ways when she got back to the cottage? Pick up the guitar, play a few chords and see what happened? The thought of looping the strap over her head or feeling the smooth wood of the neck made her stomach twist into knots. She couldn't go there. She wouldn't scratch open that wound.

No, the only cure for the way she was feeling right now was to talk to someone who knew how to cheer her up. She pulled out her phone and found Bailey in her starred contacts. Then she started the car and headed back to the cottage.

"I can talk, but only for fifteen minutes," Bailey answered. "We got a massive assignment for class today and I really need to dig into it."

Willow's heart sank with disappointment. She'd been hoping for one of their epically long BFF phone calls. "We can chat later if that's better. I just wanted to touch base. See how you're doing."

"No. No. I'm going to be busy then, too."

"Oh. Okay."

"I'm sorry, Will. That sounded horrible. I'm just so amped up about this class. I feel like I've learned more in the first three days than I learned in the last three years. It's just crazy busy and I don't want to miss a single minute of it." The frantic lilt of Bailey's voice was impossible to mistake—she was stressed. But she was also happy about it.

"Oh, wow. That does sound amazing. I'm glad it's working out so well." Willow came to a stop at one of the few traffic lights on Rosemary Street, then made a left turn.

"Did you find a job?"

"I did. Actually. At Flour Girl."

"Oh, cool. Faith is super nice. I've met her a bunch of times."

"I adore her. She's been super patient with me."

"Are you actually baking? You don't have any experience, do you?" Bailey asked the question much like Reid had—as if it was the most ludicrous idea ever.

Willow was only vaguely offended. "I am actually baking, but I was hired on the basis of my sparkling personality."

"I mean, it doesn't really matter, does it? Two months is your usual max with a job. By the time you're feeling restless, you can come back to Brooklyn."

Willow was starting to wonder why she'd ever thought she could expect to have her mood lifted by her best friend. "Maybe I won't feel restless." Except that she knew she would.

"Oh. Shoot. I forgot to tell you the most exciting part of my class," Bailey started. Apparently they were right back to her life and her fabulous opportunity. "Our instructor is bringing in a few film directors and producers from LA. Right around the end of the term. We get to pitch them on our scripts, Willow. I'm so nervous I think I'm going to throw up. I'm dying."

Willow had to take several deep breaths. She didn't want to be jealous of her best friend. Bailey had worked so hard. She deserved every shred of success she could get. But Willow couldn't help but feel that she also deserved some success. Or at least a little less abject failure. "Wow. That is so epic. You're on your way. I'm psyched for you."

"Will. You can't fool me with that tone of voice. What's going on? Are you sad?"

Just a blip of concern from Bailey and Willow already felt better. That's how suggestible she was. "I'm fine. Just feeling a little lonely. And exhausted. My new job is a lot." What she really wanted to say was that she wanted to be social, and she stupidly maybe wanted to be social with Reid, but the only time he'd taken any interest in her, it had to do with her guitar.

"You'll settle in. It's just a different pace of life up there. That's all." In the background, ambulance sirens blared.

"I miss that sound," Willow said. "Sirens."

"Why?"

"I guess I just miss the city." Willow pulled the car into the cottage driveway. Down the slope, she could see Reid, working in the garden. Her stomach soured. She wasn't sure she wanted to be here anymore, but she owed it to Bailey to stick to their plan. "What can you tell me about Reid?"

"Reid Harrel? The owner? Why?"

Willow killed the engine, undid her seat belt, and relaxed against the driver's seat. "I don't know. I've talked to him a few times. It's hard to figure him out. He's not very nice. Most of the time, it feels like all he wants is for me to go away."

"Honestly, I have no clue. He's only ever been aloof with me. Maybe it's because of his dad passing away. That seems like a pretty obvious answer considering it's only been since December. But you tell me. It sounds like you've already talked to him way more than I ever have."

Maybe Reid was lonely, too. Not that Willow had the

slightest clue how to break through to him. "You know how I am. I can't handle it if someone doesn't like me."

"You are perpetually thirsty for friendship." Bailey laughed, then Willow joined in, and for an instant, it was like they were in the same room. How she loved this unspoken reminder of the strength of their bond. It was healing. "But seriously. I wouldn't put too much stock in how nice he is to you. He's not the reason you're feeling lonely, is he?"

"It's not the primary reason. But it's definitely not helping. I want to work in his garden, but he won't even let me do that." Willow opened the door and climbed out of the car. Holding her cell phone to her ear, she dared to wander alongside the cottage, back to the patio and the spot where she had the best view. Reid was oblivious. In his own little world. Again. "It'll be fine. I'll be fine. And I'm so glad things are going well with your class."

"Speaking of, I'd better dig into our new assignment. Love you."

"Love you, too."

"Oh, and Will? It would be better for me if you texted me before you call. I really need to focus on my class, but I also want to be sure I have time to chat with you when we're able to catch up."

"Okay. Sure." Willow respected anyone's need to put boundaries in place, but it still didn't feel good. "I'll text you later."

"Perfect. Bye."

Willow ended the call and took a few steps closer to the back patio. Reid was pushing his wheelbarrow to the end of a garden row. By the looks of the load, he was headed for the compost.

"Need any help?" she called, but only half-heartedly. Her ego couldn't take another rebuke.

He kept on walking. *Damn those earbuds.* It was for the best. Willow was starving and needed time to think.

Willow went inside and foraged for what she had dubbed *linner*—not lunch, and not dinner, but the big meal she had to consume late afternoon because of her new bizarre schedule. She tossed some leftover spaghetti into the microwave and hit the reheat button. Just waiting for that gave her enough downtime to consider a nap right then and there. Who was she kidding? She probably didn't have the energy for a social life right now.

After she ate standing up in the kitchen, she changed into leggings and a tank and managed to do some yoga in the living room, which did serve to wake her up a little. After that, she took a shower, tossed in a load of laundry, and climbed into bed to watch Netflix on her laptop. Willow quite literally groaned in ecstasy when her head hit the pillow. She'd never make it through even part of a movie or show. She set aside her computer, closed her eyes, and allowed herself the luxury of a few passing thoughts…her best friend's new exciting life… Reid and the question of loneliness…the garden…and her guitar…and what it might be like to not feel like a total failure.

For some reason, Reid's head was pounding. He rolled over in bed and punched his pillow to fluff it up. The pounding came again. *Bap bap bap bap bap bap bap.* Hold on a minute—

was that actually his head? Or was it something else? He managed to pry open one eye to glance at the clock. The glowing blue numbers were slow to come into focus in his pitch-black room. 4:36. *Bap bap bap bap bap.* What in the hell was that sound? A tiny voice seemed to answer. *Reid? Wake up! Hurry!* Confused, he sat up straight in bed. Someone was at the front door. Was it Willow? Was the house on fire?

He grabbed a T-shirt from the chair near the bed and threaded it over his head, then stumbled across his bedroom floor. He thundered down the creaky old stairs, barely holding the bulky wood banister and creating a sound only slightly louder than the pounding. As he jumped the last few steps to the foyer, he heard his name again.

"Reid! Reid! Please wake up!"

He flung open the front door and there was Willow, eyes wild and hair a complete disaster. She looked like a feral cat. "What's wrong?" he blurted.

"The cottage. Water. There's too much. I can't get it up fast enough on my own." She started back down his front steps. "Come on!"

"Hold on. Water? Where?"

Now she was at the bottom of the stairs, flapping her arms and frantically pointing in the direction of the cottage. "The floor. The kitchen. And the hall. And a bit in the living room."

Oh, God no. He wasn't going to panic. Even when adrenaline was surging so forcefully through his veins that it made him sick to his stomach. "Towels. We're going to need a ton of towels. Come on. I'll need your help." Back up the stairs he went to the linen closet at the top of the landing. He yanked on the old door and it popped open, then he began grabbing as many towels as he could.

Willow arrived at his side, breathless. "Give me some."

He loaded up her arms, then he dropped to his knees and started emptying the bottom shelves, making a pile on the floor right next to Willow's feet. She was wearing her black Converse low-tops. "Your shoes are untied," he said as he scooped out the last of the towels. "You're going to trip and fall and kill yourself on the stairs."

"I'll be fine. Just hurry."

He peered up at her, past the towering mound of towels in her arms. She bugged her eyes, telegraphing impatience. He grumbled and started tying her shoes.

"What are you doing?" she asked, obviously wiggling her toes.

"Saving you from yourself."

"I don't need saving."

"Well, maybe you do." He finished the second bow with a strong tug, then got to his feet, plopped a few extra towels into Willow's waiting arms, and took the rest for himself. "Let's go."

Willow started down the stairs and he followed. "I'm sorry. I didn't want to wake you up, but I just figured that time was of the essence. You know. Two sets of hands would be faster than one."

They arrived at the foyer and Reid didn't bother with shoes as they rushed out the door and down his front steps. "What happened?" he asked as they bustled across the lawn in the dark. Ahead, the cottage was all lit up.

"I think it was the washing machine."

"I told you not to overload it."

"I know. I know. But I had a ton of dirty clothes from working at the bakery and I was so tired, I just threw in the laundry and went to bed."

"How long has this water been sitting on the floors?"

"I don't know, exactly. Since eight o'clock?"

He stepped up onto the cottage's flagstone patio. The back door was wide open. He paused and turned to Willow. "Eight o'clock last night? And you didn't notice it?"

"Not until I got up. I passed out last night. I was so freaking tired." A deep furrow formed between her eyes. She felt bad. He could see it.

He didn't have time to feel sorry for her. He had to see exactly how extensive the damage was. He crept up to the doorway, then froze. The dinged-up original checkerboard linoleum of the kitchen was covered by a shallow lake. Ahead, in the hall, water was standing on the hardwood floors.

He stepped into the kitchen. The water was nearly over the tops of his feet. He sloshed his way to the counter and plopped down the towels. He began unfolding them. "Come on. We'll just sop up as much water as we can. We can toss the towels out on the patio when they're saturated." He dropped the first one, a pale blue bath towel that was probably as old as he was. His mother never threw anything away. The color quickly changed from light to dark as the terry fabric soaked up the moisture.

Willow joined in his efforts. "I'm so sorry. I feel terrible that this happened."

Reid felt terrible, too, but he couldn't be mad at Willow. Part of him wished he could let anger take control. Right now, he felt nothing but an urgency to fix what was wrong. "Let's just get the water out as quickly as possible."

She followed his instructions, and he shouldn't have been surprised, but she worked quite quickly, sopping up water and tossing the wet towels outside. "Really, Reid. I am so sorry. I will pay for whatever damage there is."

"With what, Willow? Your hourly job at the bakery?"

"Hey. That's not nice. Don't make it sound like that. I work hard."

He grumbled. Deep down, he wanted to scream. Why was he being such a dick to Willow? He kind of liked her. But he really didn't want to. That's why he was being a dick. "I know. You're right. I'm sorry." He picked up a soaked towel from the floor and was presented with an image of Willow's ass, probably about two feet away as she bent over to sop up more water. Now his dick was being a dick. More than he wanted to admit. "And don't worry about it. I can probably fix whatever damage there is."

"Well, materials and supplies aren't free. You should at least let me pay for some of it." She tossed yet another towel out onto the patio.

"I don't know. We'll see how it goes. It might not be much more than sweat equity."

Once the supply of towels was exhausted, Reid tiptoed to the laundry closet, which ironically was where the mop was kept. This had actually happened once before that Reid remembered, when he was still in high school and his parents had a tenant named Don living in the cottage. Don had been the first one to make the washing machine overflow. Maybe it was simply time to get a different washing machine. Not that Reid had time to think about that now.

He grabbed the broom and handed it to Willow. "Use this and push as much water as you can into the kitchen from the hall. The hardwood floors need the most protecting."

Reid started mopping, but it was slow and ineffective. Maybe that was because he couldn't stop thinking about what this cottage meant to his family and the memories of both his mother and his father. When his mom died and Reid came home from culinary school for the funeral, he'd stayed in the cottage while the rest of the extended family stayed in the main house. It should've been lonely, but he felt comforted by the memories he had of the cottage. Being a little boy and pestering his dad while he made dinner. Or Reid and his mom catching fireflies in the garden until all hours. Their little family had started in this place. They'd brought Reid home from the hospital to this cottage. His entire origin story was contained within these four walls. And now a whole lot of it was underwater.

Eventually, Reid and Willow switched jobs and he used the mop to push the water from the hall into the kitchen, while she used the broom to flick it out into the backyard. Reid did everything he could to avoid looking at Willow. She was wearing a baggy pair of pajama pants and a tank top that left nothing to the imagination. Actually nothing. He had to avert his eyes. Looking would buy him so much more trouble than it would be worth.

About twenty minutes later, they'd gotten up a good deal of the water. "Oh, shit," Willow said with panic in her voice. "I completely lost track of time. I have to call Faith and tell her I'm going to be late."

"Aren't you already late? Just go to work. You can call her on the way. I don't want you to get fired on account of this."

"Faith is amazing. I really don't think she'll fire me. I'm sure she'll understand."

"I'm sure she is, but it'll be better for both of us if you go to work and let me finish up in here on my own."

"Why will it be better for both of us?"

"Because you need your job and I work better when I'm by myself."

Willow twisted up her lips in a bunch. "Fine. Suit yourself." She turned on her heel and marched off in the direction of the bedroom.

Reid sighed. *It's better if she hates you.* He went back to work.

A few moments later, Willow appeared in jeans, a T-shirt, and a different pair of sneakers. "I'm heading out. I'll help with whatever you need as soon as I get home from work."

"Hopefully, everything will be back to normal by then."

Willow's head dropped to one side in disappointment. "Can I give you a hug before I go?"

"No," he blurted. If she touched him, his brain would short circuit. It happened every time. "I mean, it's fine. I don't need a hug." He cleared his throat. "I'm a grown-up."

"I just feel so bad. I really am sorry." She took a step closer and it occurred to Reid that Willow might be the one who needed a hug.

"You don't have to apologize. Really."

She pressed her lips together tightly. It was like she was fighting back a deluge of words he might need to brace himself for. "Okay. Fine. See you later."

Apparently she'd decided to spare him. "Yeah."

Reid listened to the sound of her car starting, then stood there for a moment, trying to process what had just happened. Amazingly, the sun was rising. His day had started, whether he liked it or not.

He decided to make himself a pick-me-up in the form of a pot of coffee, although he did make very sure that he was not standing in any water when he turned on the coffee maker. A few hours later, the water was out, every door and window was open, and the coffee was long gone. He inspected the flooring. There was no way around it—the old hardwood floors had started to warp in a few spots, and it would likely only get worse as they dried. Then there was the question of the subfloor beneath. There was easily the potential for rot. Or mold.

Time in the garden wasn't happening today. He needed to head straight to the hardware store, get some supplies, and see if he could rent some industrial fans. The thought of going into town filled him with absolute dread, and then he realized he probably needed to make more than one stop. He might also need to stop by the bakery to talk to Willow. If he was about to rip up everything in the cottage, there was no way she could continue living there. It wouldn't be safe. But as to where she would now be residing, he greatly disliked the most obvious option. He did not want a roommate. No way, no how.

Four

Willow's fifth day at the bakery was too much like her first—a dumpster fire of mistakes.

"Is everything okay with you? I don't think this bread is done." Faith picked up a loaf, flipped it over, and tapped the bottom. "Definitely not done."

Willow rushed over to help Faith slide the pans back into the still-hot oven. "I'm so sorry. Everything I do today is wrong. First the flood in the cottage, then I got in late, and now this."

"It's okay. The bread is salvageable. It's only been out of the oven for a minute." She closed the oven doors then turned and planted both hands on Willow's shoulders, plaintively peering into her face. "Deep breaths. It's not the end of the world."

"But I want to do a good job and I'm messing everything up." With that sentence Willow could have titled her memoir, surely destined to go to the top of exactly zero bestseller charts.

"We all have bad days. Cut yourself a little slack."

"That's the last thing I need. I'm made of slack. I am the human embodiment of it." It was the truth. Willow needed to get her act together.

Faith shook her head slowly, exasperated. "Girl. Just wait until you get to your fifties. You haven't even touched on the amount of grace you're going to need to grant yourself to get through life."

Willow wondered if that was really true or if Faith was merely trying to make her feel better. It didn't seem like Faith ever did anything requiring grace. "I'll try. I'm not very good at stuff like that."

"It takes practice. A hell of a lot of practice."

Isaac ducked into the kitchen—quite literally. He was so tall he had to crouch to clear the doorway. The scary thing was that he was still in high school and likely still growing. He was wearing a sunflower-yellow Flour Girl T-shirt that beautifully complemented his dark skin and warm brown eyes. "Hey, Willow. There's a guy named Reid here to see you."

"Reid? Seriously? He's here?" This was both strange and entirely unexpected, especially since Reid claimed to never go into town.

"He's outside. On the sidewalk." Isaac took a few more steps into the room. "And he's *hot*," he whispered. "Who is he? I've never seen that guy in my life and I've lived here for seventeen years."

"He's my landlord. And he's kind of a hermit. He also didn't live here for a long time."

"Isaac, do you remember Graham Harrel, the chef from Oak and Ivy?" Faith asked.

The corners of Isaac's lips pulled into a very sad expression. "The guy who died right before Christmas?"

Faith nodded. "Exactly. Reid is his son."

A look of recognition crossed Isaac's face. "I got it. That's Reid. It's so sad about his dad. He was such a nice person." Isaac scrubbed the back of his short-cropped hair with his hand. Willow had only worked with Isaac once before, but this seemed to be his trademark nervous habit.

Willow glanced at Faith, who countered with an arch of both eyebrows. "I guess I should go talk to him."

"Yes. Go. I've got everything covered," Faith said. "And tell him I say hi."

"Hopefully he's not about to evict me. I could see him doing that. Actually, I could imagine him showing up with all of my stuff in a moving van. Maybe he's already left it out on the sidewalk."

"Really?" Faith asked. "His dad was so easygoing."

"I think I've disrupted the flow of his life. He doesn't seem too happy about it."

"If you need a place to stay, I'm happy to put you up. My place is tiny though. And I have three cats, but I'm sure we could make it work. Of course, you might get sick of seeing me all the time."

It made perfect sense that Willow's one other option for housing had to be life-threatening. That was the direction her world was spinning. "That's generous, but I'm super allergic to cats. I love them, but I'll puff up like a balloon."

"Definitely not a good idea."

Willow took a deep breath and braced herself for the

worst, then waltzed through the bakery, pushed open the glass door, and walked outside. Reid was standing next to a rusty old Chevy pickup she'd never seen. It was mint green with a white pinstripe, white top, and chrome trim. She tried to ignore how good he looked in jeans and a T-shirt. Focusing on his scowl helped. "Didn't want to stay inside the bakery to talk? Did it smell too delicious?"

He glanced at the Flour Girl storefront. "No. I just... I didn't want to have to talk to Faith."

"Why? She's a total sweetheart. In fact, she says hi."

"I'm not here to discuss the personality traits of your employer, okay?"

"Right. You probably want to get straight to the part where you kick me out of the cottage. I get it."

He narrowed his stare on her. It was icy cold. And white hot. Thereby making parts of her body infuriatingly warm. "That's your first assumption?" he asked.

She dared to step a little closer. A warm breeze blew past them, ruffling the trees lining the street and lifting his hair back from his face. She noticed a scar high on his forehead, near his hairline. She was of course curious about where it had come from, but she wasn't going to ask. Not under these circumstances. Or possibly any. "Well, yeah. You'd have every reason, right? Between the shoulder-tapping incident, the unauthorized gardening, and the laundry flood, I'm guessing I've used up my three strikes." She crossed her arms, if only to shore up her defenses. Part of her wanted to collapse on the sidewalk before him and beg for mercy.

He stared down at his feet, leaving her to guess at what

he might be thinking. Nothing going through her head was good. "I do have to kick you out of the cottage."

Willow's stomach became like a sieve—it felt like it had a million holes. Now what was she supposed to do? "Of course. I understand."

"I had to pull up a big section of the hardwoods. It had to be done right away. I was worried about rot and mold."

"Oh. Of course."

"And I had to pull off baseboards and cut away some of the old drywall behind that."

With every new word out of his mouth painting the picture of the mess she'd made, Willow felt a little worse. "I'm so sorry."

"And of course the water ended up seeping into the subfloor underneath. I'm going to need to cut out some of that. I just came into town to go to the hardware store and get some supplies and rent a couple of industrial fans."

"Did Carlos help you? He's such a good guy."

His eyebrows sharply drew together. "Carlos?"

"Yeah. The owner of Hines Hardware. He bought it from Patty and Joe when they retired and moved to Florida? Orlando, I think."

Reid stared at her like she had a third head. "How do you know all of that?"

"That's where I got the extra key made."

"Which takes all of two minutes."

"It only takes one minute to be nice and ask someone their name."

"I don't know who helped me. I paid and left." He shook

his head and stuffed his hands into the pockets of his jeans. "I have to figure out what to do about the kitchen floor. That linoleum has to be fifty years old or more. There's no way I can match it. I'll have to start over."

Willow felt like the human embodiment of a hurricane. She was a Category 4. The kind they talk about for days on the Weather Channel. "I'm serious about paying you back. And I'll help with the repairs, too. I'm super handy. In fact, if you want me to do all of it myself, I can try." She started to think about what that would entail—working all day at the bakery, then heading straight to the cottage for a few hours of carpentry, which would undoubtedly mean watching a few tutorials on YouTube. She was going to have to learn to live on way less sleep.

"The more important part right now is sorting your living situation."

She'd known this was coming. It didn't make it any less disappointing. Willow pointed over her shoulder with her thumb. "Faith told me I can move in with her."

"Is that what you want to do?"

No. *What I really want to do is go back in time to several days ago before I made a mess of your life and my life and maybe just figure out a way to not flood your guesthouse.* "She has cats though and I'm super allergic. I can get an EpiPen, I suppose."

"You'd rather risk your life than live under the same roof as me?"

Willow wondered if she needed to have her ears cleaned out. "*That's* what you're suggesting?"

"Never mind. It's a stupid idea." He turned and started to round the back of the truck.

Willow practically launched herself across the sidewalk, grabbing his arm. "No. Stop."

Reid turned back and stared at her hand on his arm. "Please. Willow."

She let go and raised both hands in the air. "I'm sorry. I just wanted to say that I don't think that's a stupid idea. I think that's a great idea. Very generous of you."

"It's not generous. You've already paid rent. And it's only until I do the repairs, which I plan to finish as quickly as possible so you can move back into the cottage and we can forget that any of this happened."

"Right. Of course." He really couldn't have made it any more obvious how much he disliked the notion of proximity to her.

"And we'll have to set some ground rules."

"No messing around in the garden. No more grabbing your arm. Stuff like that."

"No overloading the washing machine."

"That's the most important one."

"There's more…" He sighed and combed his fingers through his thick, chaotic hair, turning and glancing down the street. The twist of his torso lifted his T-shirt and revealed perhaps a half inch of his stomach, territory she'd already glimpsed more than once. And still, the sight zapped her with electricity. Why was she like this? Why was he like that? So beautiful and perfect and grumpy and frustrating.

"But I can't remember what is is. I have too much on my mind right now."

Silence fell between them, and Willow was desperate to lighten the mood. To create some blip of levity. "Maybe make a list."

"A list."

"Sure. My mom always told me to make a list when I was worried about forgetting something."

"I don't think that's necessary."

"But then you'll have everything in writing. For later. I mean, this is probably going to end up in a lawsuit of some sort. We should keep a record."

"There will definitely be lawyers involved. At some point." He nodded and the slightest smile crossed his lips, an expression he was so quick to erase that it made her wonder if it had actually happened. But it had. She knew it.

"So that's settled?"

"For now. Yes."

Willow could hardly believe this was the situation she'd carved out for herself. She was thankful for the lifeline, but this was such an ill-fated idea. He hated her. It was so freaking obvious. And being around him was only going to make his dislike and disdain all the more potent and palpable. Once again, she thought about writing a song. The old Willow would've been racing to scribble lyrics on a scrap of paper.

Instead she said, "Good. I'll move in as soon as I get home."

Reid left Willow and the bakery, but not before she brought him a loaf of sourdough bread and a dozen assorted cookies, items she'd insisted he take. As his dad's truck rumbled along back to the house, the aroma of the baked goods filled the air and his stomach angrily reminded him that he hadn't eaten a single thing yet today. He glanced at the box of cookies. They were so tempting, neatly stacked beneath shiny cellophane. They reminded him of Willow. They reminded him of everything that wasn't good for him.

"Fuck it." He flipped up the lid and grabbed one from the top, then took a bite so big it felt reckless. Crumbs tumbled down his chin and onto his lap as the crispy caramelized edges and the chewy, gooey, chocolate chunk–filled middle practically melted in his mouth, thanks to what was probably an entire pound of very good-quality butter. It was the most delicious thing he'd tasted in quite some time. He downed the rest in three more bites, then licked chocolate from his lips and fingers. *Damn you, Willow.*

He pulled the truck into the cottage's driveway and unloaded the supplies he'd bought at the hardware store—nails, drywall screws, Spackle, and a new blade for his circular saw. Lumber would be delivered tomorrow, so he was limited as to what he could repair right now. He set up one industrial fan in the kitchen and was just plugging in the second in the hall when he heard Willow's car in the driveway.

She walked in through the front door a few moments later. "Hey, roomie."

"I'm not your roomie. I'm your landlord."

"Setting boundaries. Good. Just add it to the list." Willow's gaze fell to the floor behind him. She clasped her hand over her mouth and crept closer. "Oh, God. It really is bad."

He turned back and looked over his shoulder at the patchwork of holes that was now the hallway. "Please stay away from this. I don't need you falling and hurting yourself."

She inched even closer, forcing him to raise his hands to keep her at bay. He could feel her breathing, smell the sugar and flour that were all over her clothes. In her hair. Cookies weren't the only things that were sweet and vexing to resist. "I feel horrible. Truly horrible." She took another step.

"Willow. The words literally just came out of my mouth. Stay. Away." Reid knew this was good advice for him to take as well. He knew it down to his bones. "Go pack up the stuff in your bedroom. I'll deal with whatever you have in the kitchen."

"Okay." She slowly backed away.

"And don't forget your guitar."

"I don't need it. It's just one more thing to carry back and forth. I'll leave it."

She really was determined to keep her distance from the guitar. Reid shook his head. "No. I'm going to be working in here. There'll be all kinds of sawdust and drywall dust and dust from Spackle…"

"Sounds like a lot of dust."

"There's going to be a big mess, okay? And I don't want to be responsible if anything happened to it."

One side of her mouth fell into a grimace. "Fine." She turned and stalked toward the bedroom.

"Good." Reid headed for the kitchen via the obstacle course that was now the hall. He grabbed a paper grocery bag from under the sink and packed up the contents of the refrigerator. He couldn't help but be amused and somewhat appalled by her culinary choices, which mostly seemed to revolve around dairy. Store-brand neon-orange cheddar cheese and skim milk and yogurt with all sorts of artificial sweeteners and flavors. He would have to teach her the ways of decent food…or maybe just leave it alone. He didn't need to make plans with Willow. She wasn't a project. They were going to coexist in the house together. That was it. Full stop.

Plus, he hadn't cooked for anyone other than himself and his dad since he'd left the restaurant world. Even then, the things he'd prepared for his father had been a far distance from culinary achievements. It'd been smoothies and hamburgers and anything else that had struck his ailing dad as appealing. One night, about ten days before his father passed away, Reid decided to prepare a serious meal for the two of them—seared grass-fed ribeye steak with a Madeira and shallot pan sauce, roasted garlic mashed potatoes, and garlicky green beans. His dad had only been able to stomach a few bites before he started to feel ill. And Reid was struck by one thought—that he'd never figured out when something was too much. He'd always been an all-or-nothing sort of person. It defined his career as a chef. Hell, restaurant reviewers and foodies and bloggers lauded him for how intensely he lived for absolute perfection in his food. There was always another way to innovate. More to create. More steps to take toward perfection. More, more, more.

Until one day, there wasn't. And he woke up in a hospital bed with a gash on his forehead and a speech from a doctor about how he was lucky to be alive. He wasn't going back to trying to impress anyone with his food. Not ever again. Especially not Willow.

"I'm all packed up," she called from the other room.

Reid stuffed the last of Willow's things into the grocery bag. "Go out the front. I'll go out the back."

"Got it."

They met up on the grassy slope behind the cottage and walked down to the house, Willow pulling her suitcase behind her and toting her guitar in the other hand.

Reid's mind immediately flew to logistics. "There's only one full bath in the house, so we'll have to figure that out," he started. "We could do a schedule."

"Since I'm at the bakery all day and tend to get super sweaty, I shower late afternoon or right before bed. When do you like to take a shower?"

He drew in a deep breath to steady himself. He hadn't thought through this topic. He hadn't bargained that she'd immediately plant a seed in his imagination of her showering. His mind swirled with visions of soapy suds and steamy air, Willow's curves and bare skin. "I, um… Don't worry about me. I'll figure it out." They arrived at the bottom of the steps up to the house. "Give me your suitcase."

"I've got it." Willow lugged the guitar and her bag, step by step, having to practically bend her torso at a forty-five-degree angle to accommodate the size of the suitcase.

He shook his head and trailed behind her. "You sure about that?"

"Yes." She plunked the roller bag down at the top of the

steps, breathing hard. "But I won't be mad if you carry it the rest of the way."

He handed her the groceries and opened the front door, then picked up her bag. "You can leave those on the table inside." He waited for her, then closed the door behind them and started up the stairs.

"Oh, wow. The house is so nice," Willow said from behind him. "Cute. Quaint. Now that I can see everything because I'm not running up the stairs to help you grab towels."

"At four thirty in the morning." He reached the top of the landing and went left. His room—his parents' old bedroom—was in the opposite direction, thank goodness.

"I can't believe that was this morning. That seems like a lifetime ago."

"It's been a day. For sure." He placed Willow's bag just inside the door of the room where she'd be staying. "Here you go. This was my mom's sewing room. It was my bedroom before that. She took it for herself when I went to culinary school. She kept a bed in here because she liked to take naps."

"Wait. Is that your childhood bed?" Willow asked.

"No. It's not. That's long gone."

Willow wandered inside and put down her guitar, then went right to the window. "Wow. What an amazing view of your garden. You can really see the full scope of it from up here."

Reid brought her suitcase into the room and parked it near the bed, then stepped closer to the window. He didn't necessarily want to stand right next to her, but it was the only way to see her point of view. He'd spent hours of his life peering out this window, watching the seasons go by and the garden change accordingly. Funnily enough, he hadn't taken the time to look down at the current incarnation of the garden from this vantage point. He'd worked his ass off. And it showed. "I guess it's pretty over-the-top."

"I think it's amazing. Really." She breezed past him and sat on the end of the bed. She spread her hand across the quilt on top of it. "Nice. Soft."

All he could think was that *she* was nice. And soft. Or so it seemed. And he needed to get the hell out of there. Every promise he'd made to himself when she arrived had already been broken. He could only imagine how quickly things would fall apart now that they were living in the same house—he had to keep his guard up. He had to keep his distance. "You already know where the linen closet is. I'm afraid there aren't any extra towels right now, but there should be in an hour or so. The first load is in the dryer now." He walked out of the room.

"Reid. Wait." Willow followed him and stood in the doorway. "Thank you. For everything today. For being so cool about all of this. Anyone else would've blown their top after what I did."

Reid realized that with anyone else, *he* might have blown his top. If Bailey had flooded the cottage, he probably would've gone ballistic. But there was something about Willow that always had him backpedaling just a little bit. "You don't need to thank me. I'm just doing what my dad would've done. He was a generous guy. I'm not, but he was. I figure I should try to be at least a little bit like him."

"I'm thinking that you're probably a lot more like him than you realize."

And just like that, tears stung his eyes. He would never live up to what his dad had been. He could try like hell every day to be a better person and he'd be lucky if in the end he was only half as good. His dad had been perfect—sweet, generous, and understanding. Reid had wasted so much time away from him. And he'd realized it far too late. "Feel free to use whatever you want in the kitchen. I'll put your groceries away."

"What if I want to use you in the kitchen?"

Reid nearly choked. "Excuse me?"

"Get you to cook for me? Maybe dinner?"

"I don't cook for other people. Not anymore."

"That seems like a waste of talent. I read some reviews of the restaurant you used to work at. Online. It sounded pretty epic."

"Why would you do that?"

"What? Look you up on the internet? Doesn't everybody do that?" She shrugged. "I was curious. You don't talk about yourself. It was my only way of finding out anything."

It was funny, but it would have never, *ever* occurred to Reid to look up Willow online. Now he was curious. Or at least wanted to level the playing field. "Please don't do that. If you want to know something, just ask me."

"Okay. What time are you going to the farmer's market tomorrow? Maybe we can carpool. Oh, yeah. And where did the truck come from? I hadn't seen that before. Did it belong to your dad?"

Reid's head was reeling. He could only handle one topic

at a time. "Why do you want to know what time I'm going to the farmer's market?"

"Faith asked me to run the Flour Girl stand. So I guess we'll be farmer's market buddies."

Fuck. How was he supposed to keep his distance from Willow when his one activity away from the house was also going to involve her? "I'm leaving at seven, I guess. But I doubt I'll see you there. It's a pretty big market. And it's busy." His only hope was that he would be so preoccupied that he wouldn't even have time to remember that she was there.

"Okay. Well, I'll be sure to stop by and say hi."

"You don't need to do that. I'm going to see you plenty."

"Right. I mean, we *are* sharing a bathroom."

Five

Annoyingly, Reid was up before his alarm went off. He'd spent much of the night not sleeping, repeatedly shaken awake by the squeak of the bed in Willow's room. The bedsprings announced her presence every time she rolled over, reminding him that a) she was in the house, and b) probably wearing those maddening pajamas, and c) he was going to feel perpetually frustrated every day and night until he remedied the situation and fixed up the cottage. Willow seemed to roll over quite a lot, probably because she snored. From anyone else, the buzz saw would've been insufferable, but Reid found it oddly charming. It was cute. Almost musical. How was that even possible?

He dressed in sweats and a T-shirt, put on a pot of coffee, and as soon as daylight broke harvested his veggies for the market—baby cucumbers, the first wave of early-season tomatoes, radishes, lettuce, spinach, and herbs like parsley and cilantro. He loaded everything into waxy cardboard produce boxes and filled up the bed of his dad's truck, then went back inside to change into something slightly more presentable.

As he ascended the stairs, the light from the bathroom beamed into the hall. He could hear humming and the sound of water running in the sink. A few steps before he reached the landing, Willow came into view. Jean shorts and a pink T-shirt. Bare legs and feet. The humming stopped when she spotted him, but her eyes lit up while the toothbrush jutted out of her mouth. For an instant, he questioned his turn-ons. Why was this particular vision in any way enticing? He had zero clue. He only knew that if things were different in his life, or in his brain for that matter, it would've been nice to sidle up behind her, place his hands on her hips, and kiss her neck.

"Good morning," she mumbled through toothpaste foam, then bent over and spit in the sink.

He had to keep moving. "Morning." He lurched into his room and quickly shut the door. "Just get dressed and get out of here," he muttered to himself as he shucked his grubby garden clothes.

"Did you say something?" Willow's voice was so close. She was right there on the other side of his door.

And there he was in his underwear. Only a few feet away, nothing more than a slab of old wood hanging on squeaky antique hinges to separate them. "Just getting ready."

"Okay. Well, I'm going to head to the bakery, but I'll see you at the market."

"Yep. See ya." He pulled a fresh T-shirt out of the drawer and threaded it over his head.

"Reid?"

He laughed quietly under his breath as he fetched a pair of jeans from his closet. There was *always* more Willow had to say. "Yes?"

"I know you don't like to interact with everyone in town, but I want you to know that I think you're going to do great today. Don't be nervous, okay? You're going to kick some major ass."

He felt like a kid getting a pep talk from his mom on the first day of school. "I don't know what kind of farmer's markets you've been to, but there's not really a lot of ass-kicking to be done in Old Ashby. But thanks." He buttoned his jeans and drew up the zipper.

"You know what I mean. I don't want you to be on edge about it. You grow beautiful produce and I know it'll be a big success."

He grabbed his phone from the bedside table, then opened the door. "Willow. I'm not five years old. I'll be fine. Go to the bakery."

She pressed her lips together and peered up at him with those pale blue eyes. Fucking A. They got him every damn time. "Okay. See you later." She turned and ducked back into her room.

For a moment, he considered going after her. Maybe he should say thank you for the things she'd said. Maybe he should ask her if she wanted to hang out that night. Or maybe he should stop gulping the lingering traces of her perfume like it was secondhand pot smoke and get on with his day.

He hurried downstairs, hopped in the truck, and drove into

town, to the far end of Rosemary Street, near the building that was once the post office but was now an Old Ashby museum. The market itself was built on what had been an abandoned lot for some time, with an L-shaped stretch of concrete and a dark green corrugated metal roof. Vendors could back right up to their stalls and unload, but it wasn't quite time for him to do that yet. His first task was to check in with the market coordinator.

He parked in the lot and found the information table, where a gangly man with a white beard, black-rimmed glasses, and baggy overalls was presiding over a clipboard.

"I was told to speak to Sandy," Reid said.

"She's not here today. Can I help you?"

He drew in a deep breath, realizing how ill-equipped he was for even a single obstacle. "I'm a new vendor. I guess I need my stall assignment."

"Last name?" The man flipped through the pages before him.

"Harrel."

The man's vision flew to Reid. "Are you Graham Harrel's boy?"

"Yes, sir. Reid."

The man removed his glasses and pinched the bridge of his nose while shaking his head, then stood and offered his hand. "It is so nice to meet you. I'm Lewis. Your daddy was one of the finest people I have ever met in all my life."

Reid swallowed hard, reminding himself that this could easily happen a bunch today and the sooner he learned a rote response and adopted it like a mantra, the easier his day would go. "Thanks. He was amazing."

"I knew him from when I grew microgreens for Oak and Ivy. I don't farm anymore, my back can't take it, but I sure did love talking to your dad. He knew a little about everything. Baseball, music, wine. Of course, he knew everything about food. I don't think there was a single thing he couldn't cook."

All of those things were absolutely true. And wonderful. Leaving Reid to wonder why it had to be so fucking uncomfortable to hear them said out loud. He simply nodded. "Yes. I know."

Lewis hesitated, staring at Reid, then he pushed his glasses back up along his nose. "Well, I'll let you get set up. Sandy gave you a real good spot. Stall number fourteen. You'll see the numbers painted along the roofline. You're right across from Flour Girl. They're one of our top vendors. Have you been to the bakery? Faith makes some mean cookies."

Reid laughed quietly, only because it wasn't going to do any good to get pissed off about it. "I had one yesterday, believe it or not."

"Be sure to get you one today before they sell out."

The Flour Girl stand would not be one of his stops. He was going to be head-down, staying busy, hopefully selling out and making a quick exit. "Thanks for your help."

"Sure thing."

Reid moved his truck, backing into the spot at number fourteen, between Old Ashby Creamery, purveyor of local cheese, and Chicken Bridge Farm, which sold fresh eggs. As he climbed out and approached his stall, it was impossible to miss the Flour Girl stand directly across from him, and Willow, who was busy artfully arranging cupcakes and cookies on wood displays painted in pastel shades along with loaves of bread in wicker baskets. She was so consumed by her job that she didn't notice him, and he took that as a good sign. Perhaps they could coexist without getting in each other's way.

Determined to focus on his own tasks, Reid began unloading his boxes, removing the lids and simply lining them up on the long wood table provided by the market. His extra inventory sat in the bed of his truck. With a wad of small bills in his pocket and a stack of paper bags for packing up orders, he pulled out the folding chair that had been left for him and took a seat to wait for the first customers. But that left him with two options to stay occupied—either chat with the people in the stands next to his, which he most definitely was not going to do, or...watch Willow.

The latter was easier and more pleasurable, even when he knew deep down that it was a dangerous pursuit. It was fascinating to watch as she organized and fussed with the stand and its products. She was not a person who took her job lightly, which definitely tracked since she seemed prone to overthinking everything. She finished just as the first customers were filling up the parking lot and starting to filter into the market.

She walked up to her table and set both hands on her hips, then finally looked up. When her eyes landed on Reid, it felt like the sun coming up in the morning. She waved and unleashed her warm, sweet smile. The one that made her entire face come alive. "Hey there, neighbor."

"Hey." He stood up. It seemed rude to remain sitting. "Ready?"

He shrugged. "As ready as I'll ever be."

A split second later, Willow had her first customer. Then another lined up. And another after that. In a matter of moments, there was a sizable line. Reid focused on his own business, but that was an awkward proposition, having to make eye contact with people as they walked by and slyly surveyed his produce, but didn't actually stop, or if they did, it was to scrutinize a bundle of radishes, then move on. He figured that Willow was so busy because they were the only bakery at the market, while there were dozens of growers selling produce. But those facts didn't make it any less uncomfortable to stand there, and it certainly gave him pause about this whole idea in the first place.

About fifteen minutes after opening, a woman with a large bag of items from Flour Girl walked over to him. "I heard you have the best produce here," she said.

He immediately pointed his gaze in Willow's direction, hoping to make eye contact. She was the likely culprit, but she was busy helping another customer. "Looking for anything special?"

"I'll take a pint of cherry tomatoes, three cucumbers, and a bunch of parsley."

It was a bit silly, but it felt good to have a customer and something to keep him busy. "You got it." He bagged up the woman's items and made change when she paid with a twenty-dollar bill. "Thanks. Come back." He could hardly believe that string of words had come out of his mouth, but thus was day one at the farmer's market.

"I will. Thank you."

The woman left, but just as quickly, a man took a loaf of bread from Flour Girl, then headed over to Reid. He arrived with a similar comment about how he'd heard Reid was an excellent farmer. After he left, there was an eager family of four who said they'd been told his tomatoes were the best, then an older couple ferrying a Flour Girl box. They'd been hyped on the virtues of Reid's spinach, which was hilarious since to his knowledge, Willow hadn't actually eaten his spinach, unless she'd been sneaking it when he wasn't looking.

Next was a young woman, who was quite possibly still in high school. "The lady from the bakery told me to come over here."

There it was. His suspicions, confirmed. "Hmm."

"She told me I should be nice to you. That seemed a little weird."

Reid shot a look over at Willow, who just happened to glance over at him. She smiled, then directed her attention to a customer. "She's weird. Don't listen to her."

"I told her I didn't want any vegetables. I told her I just wanted a cupcake for my friend's birthday. But then she gave me a free cookie to come over here."

Bribery. Willow had resorted to bribery. "You don't need to buy anything. You've earned your cookie."

"Well, she was right about one thing. You *are* pretty cute. You know. For an older guy." She shrugged. "See ya."

Reid's cheeks went dry and hot as she walked away. This

was ridiculous. And embarrassing. Sure, he needed help getting his footing, but he didn't need Willow to spoon-feed him customers. And he certainly didn't need her to use his appearance as a selling point.

Willow felt like she hardly had time to breathe, but she loved working the Flour Girl stand at the farmer's market. She'd never felt so popular or appreciated, even if the flurry of business was all because of Faith and the incredible following she'd built in Old Ashby. "That'll be twenty-seven dollars," she said to a customer, who handed over their credit card. Willow waved it over her handheld card reader and gave it to the patron for a quick signature. "If you're shopping for veggies at all, you should check out the guy across the aisle from me. He's got great stuff."

"I'm good. But thanks."

Willow saw out of the corner of her eye that Reid was beelining toward her. Much to her dismay, he did *not* look happy. Luckily for her, he was forced to stand in line behind two people, which at least gave her a moment to gather herself. Had he figured out that she'd been trying to help? If so, he had zero reason to be angry. Every new business could benefit from word of mouth.

He crossed his arms over his chest, telegraphing his anger. Typical Reid. He had her bracing for the onslaught when he reached the front of her line. "I'm going to need you to stop." There was a tremble in his voice that said he was more than mad. He might be furious.

Her only option was to feign ignorance. "I don't know what you're talking about. Is business going well?"

He planted both hands on her counter and leaned closer, enough so that her pulse picked up. Erase the pissed-off expression and this might be what he'd look like if he was about to bestow a kiss. "You know exactly how business is going because you've been the sole source of it."

"Sir, can I help you with something?" she asked loudly, looking beyond him.

He dropped his head to the side and delivered the sternest look she'd ever seen. Willow actually went weak in the knees. "Stop doing what you're doing," he growled.

She smiled wide. "I'm so sorry, sir. We're all sold out of sourdough. You'll have to get here earlier next week." She then turned to the next customer. "Can I help you?" She expected Reid to walk away.

To her great surprise, he slipped around behind her counter and spoke straight into her ear. His breath was curiously hot. "Cut it out, Willow. I'm serious. I don't need your help."

Willow became impossibly still, afraid to turn her head, lest her lips get too close to Reid's. Still, the idea of kissing him did cross her mind. "Oh, stop. You love it," she muttered out of the corner of her mouth as she bagged up some lemon poppy-seed scones and tried to ignore the way her hand was trembling. All this closeness to Reid was doing something to her. "And by the look of things, you needed the help."

"What does that mean?"

"Your total is sixteen dollars," she said to the customer, who thankfully paid with exact change. She turned to Reid.

He'd given her a bit of room. This was a good thing. Probably. "Your stand needs some serious work."

"Why? I sell vegetables. I have vegetables."

She pointed across the way. "First off, you don't have a name. Or a sign. Your merchandise is all displayed at one level. Look at the way my stand is arranged. It's eye-catching. It's interesting. It's no accident that Faith is so successful. She knows what she's doing when it comes to presentation."

"Well, good for Faith."

"I could help you make your stand better. We just need a name." She tapped her fingers against her lower lip, scouring her brain for ideas. She probably shouldn't tell him some of the first thing that sprang to mind—Hot Guy Farm.

"There is no 'we.' And I don't need your help."

"But you do. No one is even in charge at your stand right now. That's a fail."

"That's because I had to talk to you."

"But did you? Really? You could've kept your thoughts to yourself and been thankful for my help."

He grumbled under his breath. "Just let me do my thing, okay? And stop telling high school girls that I'm hot."

"I said cute, not hot. And don't be so hetero about it. I told men, too."

Reid shook his head. "You are ridiculous."

"Ridiculously successful. Now, go back to your stand. I have customers to help."

Reid stalked away and Willow went back to work. She didn't have time to argue with him. Even if their give-and-take was so hot it was bewildering. He really knew how to push her buttons. And she could think of one button she possessed that would love to be pushed. She closed her eyes to center herself, but the thought of him touching her there... and then kissing her... It overheated her cheeks and made the rest of her tingle.

The stand quickly became busy again and she stopped sending people Reid's way. He had a few customers, but not nearly as many as he should have, so after a half hour of staying quiet, she returned to her old tricks. "If you're shopping for produce today, please give the stand across the way a look. He's new here and still building up his customer base."

The woman regarded Willow with kind eyes. "That's very sweet of you to help out someone else."

"We all need help sometime, right?" *Even if he doesn't want it.*

"That's so true."

Willow watched as the woman wandered over to Reid and spoke to him. Moments later, he looked over at Willow and shook his head in dismay. She was so tired of this dynamic. No, she wasn't very good at following someone else's orders if she found them to be baseless. She was good at helping, dammit. If he would simply let her do that, everything would be fine. He could sell his produce and go home. She could feel good about having done a good deed. And they could peacefully coexist.

An hour or so later, the stand was nearly sold out. In fact, all that remained in Flour Girl's inventory was a single cupcake with pink icing. Faith had told her that as soon as she ran out of product, she should pack up the truck with the displays, bring them back to the bakery, and then she could be done for the day. That sounded like sheer heaven. She could sit down. Take a nap. Maybe drink a beer. But that one pathetic cupcake was standing in her way. Who was going to buy a single cupcake? No one.

Which gave her an idea. She could give away said cupcake and perhaps it would help bring a little peace to her world. She did realize that Reid still had some reason to be angry with her, and it might have a little to do with her farmer's market shenanigans, but likely far more to do with what had happened at the cottage.

She opened up a box of random supplies Faith had given her, which had a few spools of ribbon for tying up bakery boxes, some birthday candles, and a book of matches. She popped one of the candles into the pink frosting, then walked it across the way to Reid, who was finishing up a sale. Like he had, she took the liberty of slipping around the side of his stand and behind his table.

"Happy Birthday," she announced, presenting the cupcake.

A deep furrow formed between his brows. "My birthday is in February."

"It's not for you, silly. It's for your farm stand. It's your farmer's market birthday."

"Thanks?" He tucked some cash into his pocket and rearranged the bundles of his remaining cilantro.

Willow did not think of herself as a person with a short fuse, but she was absolutely losing her patience with Reid. Why did he have to be such a freaking jerk about everything?

This cupcake was a peace offering and he wouldn't even take it. "I thought you might want to mark the occasion."

"Why?"

She drew in a deep, cleansing breath, willing herself to calm down. "Isn't this a milestone for you? You've turned your family's property into a business."

"There's no need to make a big deal about it."

"I'm not making a big deal. It's a cupcake. A few bites and it's gone. You'll hardly even remember it." She held up the cupcake until it was at her eye level and stepped a little closer to him. "This is a special cupcake, too. It has fresh strawberries and pastry cream on the inside. You'll regret it if you don't eat it."

"Stop trying to make me do stuff, Willow."

"Why are you so resistant to everything I suggest?"

"Because." He started to walk back to his truck.

"That's not an answer. I want to know the actual reason."

He abruptly turned back and marched toward her. "Because my life was just fine before you came along and decided that it needed changing. Or disrupting. Or improving. In fact, I'd go so far as to say you've done the opposite since you've been here. So maybe you just need to stop. Okay?"

Willow stood frozen, but her brain was off to the races. White-hot anger and deep, seething frustration bubbled up inside her so fiercely that she didn't know what to say. There were no words that could adequately capture exactly how pissed off she was. Reid always had the upper hand. He always had the last word and it was always delivered with an unmistakable air of superiority. He not only *had* to win every argument, he had to make her feel stupid for having bothered to participate. And she was, quite frankly, over it.

Over. It.

"Nothing to say?" He stepped closer. So close that they were nearly toe-to-toe. "I can't believe it. I actually managed to quiet you down."

"Quiet me down?" she asked, with incredulity dripping from every syllable. The fucking *gall* of him. The smug arrogance. The misogynistic assholishness…it had reached new heights.

"You heard me."

Words would never work with Reid. She needed action. She needed to show him in no uncertain terms that he was being a royal jerk and deserved to be treated as such. So she took the cupcake. And flattened it in his face.

Frosting first. Right against his lips. Right up his nostrils. Cake and strawberries and cream smooshed against his cheeks. And she just held it there. Neither of them moved. It was just Reid blazing his eyes at Willow, while all she could hear was her own pulse in her ears. Her immediate and intense satisfaction with her actions was swiftly replaced with regret. Why did she have to let her emotions get the best of her? She considered her escape. There were a lot of moving parts to this scenario she'd just created, including her genuine concern that he might murder her in her sleep that night. He'd have more than enough opportunity. "I…uh…" Willow let go of the cupcake and the remnants plopped to the ground.

"Don't say it." Reid took one step back and lifted his

T-shirt to wipe off his face, leaving her with a magnificent view of the contours of his abs. Any thoughts she'd ever had of touching his stomach were now ruined.

"Don't say what? I'm sorry? I am." She stepped closer.

His jaw drew tight while he held his shirt in his fist. "Leave me alone, Willow."

She swallowed hard. "Okay."

"I'm serious."

"I can tell." She blew out one more breath, endlessly exasperated with herself, then turned and scurried back to the Flour Girl stand to pack up. She'd learned something. A valuable lesson. There was no way she and Reid could peacefully coexist. Ever.

Six

Willow's life in Old Ashby might be a disaster, and she might have had an emotional hangover after the farmer's market, but the main house was an upgrade. She was willing to concede that much on Sunday morning. Her new room was pretty and cozy, with a patchwork quilt made of pink-and-green calico. There was celery green on the wall, and mismatched flea market furniture tucked in all corners, and old framed photos taking up the space above the vintage sewing table. She was just now looking at the pictures in earnest for the first time. It was partly a diversion tactic. She was too scared to leave her room. Somewhere in the house was Reid, and even though nearly a day had passed, there was no way he had forgiven the cupcake incident.

The photos were filled with smiling people, including a few she did not know, although she ventured some guesses. The ethereal woman with flowing strawberry hair and freckles, who wore floral skirts she'd likely made herself, had to be Reid's mother. She had his eyes—soulful and complicated. The tall and lanky handsome one with chaotic hair was certainly Reid's dad. He and his son were practically the spitting image of each other, with one striking difference. This version of Reid smiled in every picture. In some, it was as if he couldn't possibly contain his happiness. That wasn't present-day Reid at all, but he was grinning in these family photos—as a young towheaded boy and even as a gangly teenager. There was a light in there, somewhere. But it had been snuffed out.

Willow looked closer to see if there were any clues in the photos as to why Reid was the way he was—distant, defensive, and unwilling to cook for anyone other than himself, even though he was apparently a genius in the kitchen. That was at least what she'd learned when she'd stalked him online. He'd been head chef at a very fancy restaurant in Boston. He'd not only won awards and accolades, he'd worked his way up from the bottom rung on the ladder in that kitchen. His staff seemed to both respect and fear him. His customers had nothing but praise.

But then he left. With no explanation. It was a mystery she might never know the answers to. Reid was that closed up. And she didn't dare ask. Especially since she'd made things between them so much worse yesterday.

Some of the photos in her new room included the garden as a backdrop. It seemed to be a fixture in the story of this family, but it had been much smaller in years gone by. Judging by the bright and untarnished wood of the current raised beds, the garden had received an overhaul in recent months.

Maybe it was part of Reid moving on after the death of his father. And maybe that was why he was so protective of it. Maybe that was why he didn't want her help.

Her stomach rumbled and her head begged for coffee, so she put on a sweatshirt and padded out onto the landing. "Reid?" she asked in a voice loud enough that she hoped he would hear. She stood still for a moment, sort of like she was waiting for lightning to strike her down. Or perhaps he might answer. But neither happened, so she decided to get on with her day.

But first, it seemed reasonable that she shouldn't go downstairs without at least poking her head into Reid's bedroom. She crept across the hardwood floors like a cat burglar, hoping she'd escape detection. His room was much larger than hers, nearly three times as big, but it was much more spartan—a big bed with a navy blue and white quilt, a dresser and a chair in the corner. That was it. There wasn't even much in the way of artwork, just a few framed posters that looked like they were from events at the farmer's market— the annual tomato festival and a summer potluck for charity. Had this room been his father's? And logically, his parents' before that? Not that it mattered much. If she'd thought his room would hold clues about the mystery of Reid, she'd been mistaken.

She made her way downstairs and called for him again. "Reid?" No answer came. She wandered into the kitchen and was happy to see that the coffeepot was half full and the burner was still on. So maybe he didn't want to actually murder her after the cupcake incident. He might be distant and standoffish, but something in him was considerate enough to be mindful of the fact that they were living in the same house now. She was thankful for that. She found a mug in one of the cabinets, then poured herself a cup and went to the fridge in search of cream. All she could find was milk, which didn't do nearly enough to mask the taste of the coffee. This cup would have to be purely medicinal.

Willow next checked out the living room, which was full of more flea market furniture, none of it from the same era and none of it overly fancy, but the furnishings were not what caught Willow's eye. It was the upright piano in the corner that she immediately zeroed in on. It had been a long time since she'd played a piano. They'd had one in the house when she was growing up, but there was no room for one in her apartment. Hell, there was barely room for a *bed* in her apartment. She stepped closer and she could've sworn that her fingers twitched with electricity. Music had been so much to her—a love, an obsession, a pursuit, and, ultimately, a heartbreaker. It would be one thing to pick up her guitar again. It would be something entirely different to peck away at a keyboard.

"Reid? Are you here?" she called one more time before she had the courage to pull out the wood bench and sit down. She smoothed her hand across the dark wood fallboard and took a deep breath, then flipped it open, revealing eighty-eight keys—fifty-two white and thirty-six black. She tapped on an A, and the sound reverberated not only through the body of the instrument and in Willow's ears—she also felt it in her chest. It did something to her heart.

She hit the key again, then again, and matched the note with her own voice. That was another thing she hadn't done in quite some time—sing. To her delight, it didn't make her quite as queasy as she'd imagined it might. She played a few other keys with only her right hand. The piano was nearly in tune. She pulled back her hand and let it rest in her lap. Inspiration wasn't exactly bubbling up inside her, but she could feel it swirling in the vicinity. Music had always been a huge part of the way she processed her feelings. And, oh man, did she have a whole boatload of jumbled-up emotions right now. But music had hurt her, too. So she wasn't ready to go there. Not yet. But she could close the lid and know that this piano was sitting there waiting for her if she wanted to chase after a song any time soon.

As soon as she got up, she heard the buzz of an electric saw. So *that* was where Reid was—working on the guest cottage. Of course. She was tired and very much in the mood for a day of reading a book and taking a very long nap, but she also knew that she should make another attempt at an apology then offer to help with whatever repairs were necessary. So she ran up the stairs, pulled on a pair of jeans, stuffed her feet into her sneakers, being very careful to tie the laces, lest she get a lecture from Reid, then went outside and hiked up the hill to the cottage.

It was strange approaching from that vantage point, knowing she wasn't living there at the moment and she might not ever again, depending on how long the work took. Up on the patio was a stack of building supplies, and the back door was wide open, so she stepped inside.

"Reid?" she managed before she took pause. The devastation seemed even more significant in the bright light of day. This was not a small amount of damage.

"Don't come in," he replied from somewhere off in the belly of the cottage. "It's not safe. I tore up more of the floor."

Again, he was putting her off. Keeping her at a distance. It was exhausting. "I'm not wearing a hard hat, but something tells me I'll be okay." She stepped around the holes in the kitchen floor and made her way to the hall entrance. And then she saw Reid. *Holy hell.* There he was, on his knees and one hand, bare-chested and glistening with sweat while holding a hammer, for God's sake. He couldn't have been any hotter if he tried. How was he so effortlessly beautiful? So perfect in every way.

He sat back on his haunches. Apparently gardening and Tai Chi got a person in insanely good shape. "You're not great at following instructions, are you?" A single drop of sweat trailed down his abs.

Willow found it hard to swallow, thinking about the happy life of that tiny bead of perspiration. "I'd go so far as to say I suck at it."

He shook his head and laughed ever so slightly. It wasn't a *real* laugh. It was basically just *ha ha.* But it felt like a way in. "What do you want?"

His harsh tone made her flinch, but she knew she deserved it. "You might not want to hear it, but I wanted to apologize. For the cupcake incident. It was childish of me. And stupid. And I'm sorry."

"I don't want to talk about it."

"That's your response to 'I'm sorry'?"

"I don't want to talk about it." He picked up a nail and started hammering away at the floor.

Willow's jaw tightened. Why did he get to her like this? She wasn't an angry person. She thought she was pretty easygoing. There were people who had referred to her as happy-go-lucky. There were some people who thought she was goddamn delightful. "So you're not going to accept my apology?"

He grabbed another nail. "Why do I have to accept anything? You said it. I heard you. End of story."

"You are so infuriating."

"And you're a complete pain in my ass, so we're even."

She leaned down, planted her hands on her knees and stared at him. "I was trying to be nice."

"By assaulting me with a cupcake?"

"Before the cupcake. And after. Also, right now. Or one minute ago."

"Just go, Willow. Let me get this work done so you can move back in here and we can never speak to each other again."

Willow didn't want to cry, but tears were stinging her eyes. It would've been so easy to do exactly as he'd asked. Turn around and leave. Just run out the door. She could hide away in her room and daydream about the day when she could finally go back to New York. But something told her that if she and Reid didn't hash this out, things were only going to get more miserable for her in Old Ashby. And that was something she simply wasn't willing to accept.

"Why are you like this?" she asked, standing up straight again.

"You don't want to know."

"No. I *do* want to know. Why did you leave the restaurant in Boston, Reid?"

What in the hell was Reid supposed to do with Willow? She just kept showing up everywhere in his life. And with each new appearance, things between them got messier and messier.

"I'm not answering that question. Leave. Please." He got up from the floor. Unfortunately, he needed to get past Willow in order to reach the supply of lumber on the back patio. He took a step, but she didn't flinch. "Excuse me. I need to get through here. You're in my way."

She stood her ground. "Why did you leave the restaurant?"

He wasn't going to stand there and listen to that, so he braced his hand on the wall and took an extra-long stride, traversing one of the gaps in the floor. Clear of Willow, he ran the obstacle course that was now the kitchen, dodging holes until he could hop outside onto the patio. He bee-lined for a piece of plywood and pulled out a piece of paper, where he'd scribbled down some dimensions. He fished his metal tape measure from his pocket and stretched it out to map out the piece he needed to cut.

"Why did you leave the restaurant?" Willow asked. She'd followed him outside. "Why won't you let me help you in the garden? Is it because it meant so much to your dad? And your mom? Is your mom the pretty woman with the red hair in those photos in my room?"

The tape measure snapped shut. It took everything in Reid not to scream at the top of his lungs. *This is why I want to be by myself.* But it was turning out to be an utter waste of time and energy to respond that way to Willow. Every time he told her to go away, she stayed. She was unrelenting. Which left him with only one logical answer—he had to turn the tables on her. "Why are you so touchy about your guitar, Willow?"

"Oh, no. We are not talking about me. We're talking about you."

Reid tossed his pencil aside and walked right up to her. "One of us assaulted the other with a cupcake yesterday. And it seems to me like the person who *received* a nose full of frosting deserves answers way before the person who *delivered* it."

She crossed her arms over her chest. Wearing an oversize sweatshirt and a ratty pair of jeans, and smelling like honey and bread, she had this preposterous pull on him. It felt like someone was cracking his chest open. Damn her. It would have been so easy to plant his hands on her cheeks, smoosh her face ever so slightly, and kiss her. Taste her lips. Possibly bite them. Then get a hint of exactly how much heat they might create together. He was thinking they might set everything around them on fire.

"If I tell you about the guitar, you have to tell me about the restaurant. And the garden."

He opened his eyes wider. "You think we're going to negotiate? Because I have a hell of a lot more leverage than you do right now." That was the only thing he could be thankful for. He was on solid ground and he wasn't about to give that up. Being vulnerable and honest with Willow was only going to create more problems. "I blew my nose before bed last night and it was pink. Plus, don't forget that I'm putting a roof over your head."

She blew out a breath. "Fine. You know what? Fine. I'm *fine* talking about myself because I'm not a human armadillo. I don't roll up into a ball every time someone asks me something personal."

Reid wasn't about to argue. "I'm waiting."

She paused to blow out yet another cleansing breath. It was like she was about to unpack something. "I've been playing guitar and piano and writing music since I was a little kid. I started performing live when I was eleven. I thought that I was really good at it, and I dreamed of it being my career. And it's been total agony and heartache wanting something so bad and feeling like I was good enough but that didn't matter. Everything I wanted was always just out of reach. So I decided I can't do it anymore. It's not worth it. I was killing myself for nothing. That's why I don't want to play my guitar."

"But Bailey thinks you shouldn't quit. That's why she made you bring it with you."

"She thought I'd get 'inspired.'" She made air quotes. "She thinks I'm being 'shortsighted.'" The air quotes returned.

"Maybe you should listen to her. It takes a long time to become successful."

"So says the guy who won a million awards as a chef. You were getting unbelievable reviews when you were twenty-five, Reid. People waited months to eat at your restaurant. It's really easy for you to say that to me. You already made it to the top of your game."

Mere mention of his past life made him want to bend over and retch. "I made sacrifices. I gave up more than you can even imagine. Sometimes that's what it takes."

"And you're saying that I haven't?"

"I'm not saying anything other than facts. You have to be willing to give up something."

"You don't know shit about what I've given up. You don't know a single thing about the sacrifices I've made or the things I've been through." Her voice told him that she was rattled. Down to her core.

"You're right. I don't."

She walked away to the edge of the patio, looking down the hill at the garden. "I bombed, okay? I got an amazing opportunity at a club I'd been trying to get into for years and I was booed off the stage. I had to stop playing in the middle of a song and walk away with my tail between my legs. I was publicly humiliated. For my music. And then, just to make it super fun, my brother, Gabe, got in a fight with the guys who booed me, he ended up with a black eye, and my parents blamed me for the whole incident."

"So you failed. You lick your wounds, get over it, and try again."

She turned back. "Oh, my God. Have you even been listening to me?"

He wanted to be understanding. He really did. He had nothing but empathy for what he was sure had been a very traumatic experience for her. But she was letting one bad thing defeat her. "I'm not trying to be mean."

"You hate me. That's what's really going on. Admit it."

He didn't hate her. That wasn't what was going on. But he didn't want to get close. He didn't want to forge a friendship. She would be gone in seven weeks and if they had a connection that went beyond the one they already had, it was going to hurt like hell to watch her leave. He was going to feel left behind. Again. At thirty-five, he was smart enough to know that purposely putting himself in the pathway of hurt meant he was asking for his life to fall apart. He needed to be in the business of putting his life together. Not the other way around. "I don't hate you."

"And yet everything you do says that you do."

"It's not my job to make you believe me, Willow."

"Are you going to tell me about the restaurant?"

He shook his head. "Not today."

"Are you serious right now?"

"I am."

She tossed her hands into the air. "Of course not. I rip open my heart and tell you about my trauma and you just shrug it off and give me some bullshit speech about pulling myself up by my bootstraps and toughening up. And then you won't take two seconds to be even the slightest bit vulnerable with me."

"I never said bootstraps."

"I'm not going to argue word choice. I'm done with this. I'm done with you." She started down the hill.

He watched her every stride, partly because he was sure

she was going to turn back at some point. Argue with him some more. She always had more to say. But she didn't stop. She trudged past the garden, up the steps, and slammed the front door forcefully enough that he swore he could feel it in the ground beneath him.

He looked at the stack of lumber, knowing he needed to get back to work. Even though finishing the cottage would fix the Willow situation, he was exhausted, mentally and physically. She drained him. There was no more gas in the tank. He would just have to get back to working on the repairs later.

He grabbed his circular saw and took it back inside to recharge it. The rest of his tools were mostly put away and he didn't have the energy to do more. He headed back outside and covered up the lumber with a tarp. As he wandered down the hill and the house got closer, he dreaded what came next—seeing Willow. Another argument. Hopefully she was out of cupcakes.

When he arrived at the front door, he came to a stop, doubting at first what he was hearing. Music. A sparse and winding tune. Was Willow playing his mom's piano? He turned the knob slowly, going only a millimeter at a time, not wanting to make a noise and announce his arrival. As the door opened and he crept inside, the piano music filled his ears. It was a pretty, languid melody, with just an edge of melancholy. Then came Willow's voice. Reid became impossibly still as he tried to wrap his head around this improbable sound she was creating. *That's why her snore is cute.*

Willow's voice was the perfect expression of her—soft and

warm and light. And sexy. She wasn't singing decipherable words—it was more her harmonizing with the tune she was playing. He closed his eyes and leaned against the wall in the foyer, just listening. It had been so long since he'd heard someone play music in the house. His mom used to sit at the piano nearly every day. It had been as much a fixture of their home life as the garden. In fact, his dad took lessons after she died, just so he could feel closer to her. His father never achieved her level of musical prowess, but it wasn't about achievement. It was about love.

Willow's musical syllables turned into words and he inched closer to the entry to better hear the lyrics. *A handsome jerk, wound too tight…as mean as can be…he argues, he fights…and I'm just being me.* It took no time at all to compute who she was singing about. He wasn't sure whether to be offended or flattered. The answer was probably somewhere in the middle. He stepped just inside the room. Willow was in the far corner, with her back to him. He slow-clapped a round of applause.

Willow stopped playing and turned around.

"Good song. Is it about me?" he asked.

She rolled her eyes. "Typical guy. Thinks everything is about him."

"Well? Is it? Handsome jerk. Wound too tight. Sounds like maybe it's me."

With a clunk, she closed the piano, then got up from the bench. "The guy in that song is pretty smart. I think he can figure it out for himself." She patted him on the shoulder and walked out of the room.

"Well, I guess I'm flattered. I never thought I'd inspire someone to write a song." He soon heard stomping up the stairs.

"Don't get a big head. It's not a compliment."

Seven

It had been the strangest, most frustrating week with Willow in the house. Her anger after she and Reid had talked on Sunday wasn't fading. Oh, no. It was growing. On Monday, Willow had the day off. Reid wasn't sure exactly how much time she spent at the piano that day, but he did know that every time he returned to the house after working on the cottage or tending the garden, she was filling the space with her achingly beautiful voice and a fresh batch of lyrics about what a big jerk he was. He took his lumps, thinking she'd go back to work on Tuesday and be too tired afterward to continue sharpening her barbs.

That was not the case. If anything, ruminating over Reid's many character flaws seemed to invigorate her. She spent several hours at the piano that night, and Reid stayed in his room, doing his best to ignore her while sticking his nose in a book, an approach that was a magnificent fail. Every time he'd manage to focus on reading, she'd yank him out of the story by coming up with a clever turn of phrase about what an asshole he was. By Wednesday, Reid decided that however annoying, this was the best possible scenario. Willow could stay pissed off, he could steer clear, and it would keep his life as close to normal as possible. By Thursday, he'd learned that it was impossible to ignore someone when they were playing music that filled your entire living space and that music happened to be about you. On Friday, he ordered a pair of noise-canceling headphones and had fleeting thoughts of selling the piano, or perhaps dragging it to the curb and letting the trash collectors take it away.

But he'd never do that. That piano had meant too much to his parents. He hated the thought, but it was true that in this case, he might be defeated by sentimentality. Plus, as much as he and Willow argued and disagreed about everything, he didn't have it in him to stomp on anyone's creativity. He understood down to his bones what it was like to be consumed by an idea or a need to make something. That song she was working on might show him in the world's worst light, but it was Willow's creation and he wasn't going to stop it. Plus, she'd more than proven her point—he was a jerk. He knew this.

Of course, that didn't mean that he could continue to endure everything else, like Willow's openly hostile attitude. By Saturday morning, he'd grown tired of it. Giving each other space didn't have to mean every interaction was horrendous. "Morning," he muttered to Willow as he came upstairs on his way to change clothes for the farmer's market. It was part polite greeting and part experiment. Would it make her mad if he was nice? He wanted to see.

Just like last week, Willow was in the bathroom brushing her teeth, this time wearing white shorts and a mint green Flour Girl T-shirt. As always, she looked impossibly cute, albeit a bit pale. Perhaps she was spending too much time indoors at the bakery or at the piano. She shot him a dagger-laden glance, grunted, spit out her toothpaste, then slammed the bathroom door.

Reid nodded. Experiment concluded. Nice did not make a difference. "Willow, are you going to be long? I have to pee."

She replied by clicking the lock.

He knocked. "You're being a child, Willow. I know I'm not your favorite person, and I know we've had our share of disagreements, but keeping your housemate from using the bathroom seems unusually cruel."

She opened the door a crack, stuck out her hand, flipped him off, then closed it and clicked the lock again. Apparently he hadn't made his case. And he was going to have to pee outside.

"Suit yourself. I'm heading to the market. See you there." He could hardly believe he'd been the person to utter those words. A week ago, she'd been the one who was all rah-rah about seeing each other and acknowledging each other's presence at the market, a concept he'd found superfluous and unnecessary. But after a week of ice-cold stares and chilly receptions, he wondered if he might have taken the whole notion of keeping Willow at bay too far.

By the time he got set up at the market, Willow was backing into her space with the Flour Girl van. He glanced at the time on his phone. It was already a few minutes past seven thirty. The first wave of customers would be arriving at eight. Willow was late, and he knew from last week how much time and attention she put into her setup. She was going to need help and he had nothing to do for the next half hour. Did he dare do it? She might literally bite his head off. Then again, things between them couldn't possibly get worse.

He proceeded with caution up to her stand, keeping an eye peeled for stray cupcakes. "Hey," he started. "Can I help?"

She rolled her eyes, turned around, and bent over to pick up a basket of bread. Unfortunately for him, her shorts were not super long and only served to show off the perfect curves of her backside. "No. I have a system."

Reid forced himself to look away. Otherwise, he wasn't going to be the only one who needed roomier shorts. "No, you don't. You haven't been doing this long enough to have a system."

She set the basket down on one of the display tables. "I just want you to understand how ridiculous it is for a person to say they don't want help."

"Point taken." He didn't enjoy self-reflection, but he was more than capable of it. "So? Do you? Want help?"

She shook her head like she was hoping he'd just give up. "Faith is on her way. Since I'm late."

"Late because you were too busy preventing me from peeing."

She pressed her lips together tightly. "I did stay in there for an extra ten minutes just to spite you."

He laughed. He couldn't help it. "I'm glad you're so honest."

"I rearranged your bathroom vanity. You had some expired condoms I threw away."

He snorted. If ever there was a more telling sign of how little life he'd been living when he was a full-time chef, it was that. He hadn't had a girlfriend or a need for condoms in years. "Thanks for looking out for me."

"Wouldn't want you to go around getting the women of Old Ashby accidentally pregnant."

"No danger of that happening."

She looked over at him, seeming tired. "Fine. You can help. Work on the bread. Line up the baskets on the staging table and make sure the loaves all look nice. Facing forward and sticking up out of the top of the basket."

"Got it." He went right to work, doing as she'd asked. "It's amazing that you're going to sell through all of these baked goods. Faith really has a massive operation, doesn't she?"

Willow was carting over boxes of baked goods like cookies and scones and began arranging them on the display shelves. "She's successful. Very astute of you to notice."

"I'm not the smartest guy in the world. Somebody wrote a song about it. At least I vaguely remember hearing about it." He caught a glimpse of her smiling. Small victories. He was at least breaking down her recent icy exterior, a quality he was a bit ashamed to know he'd brought out in her. "Bread's finished. What else can I do?" He stepped closer, watching her work.

"I'm good. Faith just got here."

Sure enough, Faith was approaching with her dark curly hair and the silver streak. Panic set in. He didn't relish the thought of a conversation with her. She was always gushing with fondness for his dad. "Okay. See ya."

"Thanks. For helping." Her words seemed to require a great deal of effort. She looked up at him, and her paleness struck him again.

"Are you feeling okay?"

"All I did was say thank you."

He stepped even closer. "No. I mean are you actually feeling okay? You don't look great."

"Gee, thanks."

"I didn't mean it like that."

"I think my allergies are getting to me. I'm fine."

Faith was fast approaching. "Okay. Good." He made his escape, then pretended to rearrange his veggies while watching Faith and Willow chat.

Customers soon started arriving, including a man he recognized from last week who sidled up to his table. "My wife and I really enjoyed your cucumbers last week. I'd like to get some more," the man said as he looked over the rest of Reid's offerings. "And a pint of tomatoes."

Reid realized that he wouldn't have this repeat customer without Willow's help. He really did deserve a disparaging song about him. "That'll be twelve dollars," Reid said.

The man happily handed over exact change. "I'm sure I'll see you next week."

Reid thought about asking the man his name or simply introducing himself, but didn't want to be overly friendly and scare him away. "Great. Thank you."

Another customer arrived soon after, then another and

another. Reid stayed busy over the next hour, unable to ignore exactly how much of his business was people returning from last week. He was not only running out of inventory, he owed Willow a serious apology. Across the aisle, she was super busy, just as she had been last week. So much so that Faith had stayed to help. But now that there was a bit of a lull in the flow of customers, and to Reid's disappointment, Faith was making her way over to him. He braced himself.

"Hey. Reid. How's the market going?"

"Good." He avoided eye contact, then turned back to his truck to get the one remaining box of herbs.

"I'm glad. You've certainly seemed busy. I looked over a few times while Willow and I were working together and you've had a lot of customers considering it's only your second week."

"I think I owe that to Willow. She sent a lot of people my way." *And I got pissed off at her for it.*

"Sounds like Willow."

"Yep."

She nodded slowly. "I really wish your dad could be here to see you. He loved coming to the market. He always stopped by to say hello when I was running the Flour Girl stand."

Reid stuffed his hands into his pockets. "Yeah. It would've been cool for him to be here."

"So..." she started, making him more nervous. "Part of the reason I came over was to ask you about the garden we're putting in at the high school. I could still use your help."

"Do you need more money?"

She inched closer to this table. "What I really want is your help. Your actual help." She made a point of peering up into his face and holding too much eye contact. "We want to teach young people about the food they eat and how rewarding it can be to grow it themselves. You have a talent for gardening and I think the students would like learning from you."

So Willow was right. Faith had wanted more than the money. Unfortunately, money was an easy thing. "What kind of help do you need?"

"It's an after-school activity for now. And obviously school is out of session at the moment, but we could really use your help building the beds this summer so they're ready when students return. Then you could help them plant a fall garden and show them how to transition to warm-season in the spring. It would be a few hours a week after school."

It didn't sound like a massive commitment, but Reid wasn't about to fold himself into Old Ashby life. He might never be ready for that. "Can I think about it?"

"Sure. Let me know." Faith knocked a knuckle on Reid's table. "I should get back to helping Willow. I don't think she's feeling well today."

"I asked her about that, but she told me it was just allergies."

She glanced across the aisle at Willow. "Looks to me like more than that."

Reid had to agree. "I'll check on her later." *If she'll let me.*

"Is there anything I can do for you, Reid?" Faith asked.

He was struck by the question. "Actually, I'd love it if you could ask Willow about her music. Some day. Doesn't have to be now."

"She's never said anything to me about music."

"I found out she's been playing for most of her life. Guitar and piano. She writes songs and performs. She said she gave it up before she came here. But she's been playing the piano in my house over the last week and I have to say, she should rethink her decision. She's super talented. Her voice is incredible."

"Maybe you should tell her that yourself."

"I'm not sure she'd listen to me."

"Why? Surely you two know each other pretty well now. You're roommates and all."

He shrugged, not willing to go into detail. "She's shy about it. I think it might take more than my opinion to convince her."

Willow couldn't help but be obsessively curious about Reid and Faith talking. What could they possibly have to speak about? Reid didn't like talking to anyone, especially not people in town. And why did they keep looking over at her? Her Spidey-sense said something was up, but she'd had more than a few paranoid thoughts over the course of the last week. What else could she do while writing a song about Reid and having him simultaneously ignore her? Clearly he thought she and her song sucked. Which was annoying because Willow was pretty sure it sucked, too. She'd only kept working on it so that she could passive-aggressively tell Reid that he couldn't keep acting the way he was and expect her to be nice in return. Yes, she needed people to like her, but her upbeat nature didn't come from a faucet. There wasn't an endless supply.

Finally, Faith left Reid's stand and made her way back to
Flour Girl. Willow was condensing the last few loaves of bread
while there was a break in the customers.

"Everything good?" Faith asked, stepping behind the table.

"Yep. You should head home or back to the shop. I've
got it under control."

"Are you sure? You really don't look well."

Reid kept saying that, too. She was feeling under the
weather, but she chalked it up to an entire week of simmer-
ing resentment. "I'm a little tired. You know, run-down. But
it's fine. One or two good customers and this stuff will all be
gone and I can pack up."

Faith looked at her phone. "Isaac just texted me. It sounds
like he's pretty slammed at the shop. And someone called
about a last-minute birthday cake. I should head over there."

"Yes. Go. I'm good. We're so close to selling out, anyway."

Faith grabbed her bag from under the table and looped
it over her head, slinging it across her body. "By the way, I
talked to Reid."

"I saw." Willow did her best to not seem too interested.

"I asked for his help with this garden project at the high
school. We could really use his expertise. He said he'd think
about it."

Willow took great satisfaction in knowing that she'd been
right about what Faith had wanted. At least she wasn't off-
base about everything. "Do you want me to see if I can bad-
ger him into doing it?"

"Are you two not getting along?"

Willow and Faith very rarely talked about Reid, although

Faith did ask about him. "Not exactly. I think he's still mad about the cottage. But the repairs are coming along and I'll be able to move back in soon. Then maybe it'll get a little better."

Faith twisted her lips into a funny expression. "Huh."

"What?"

"He said I should ask you about your music. He said he thinks you're very talented and that you shouldn't give up on your dream."

Willow was going to strangle Reid as soon as she had the chance. Now he was playing mind games. "He doesn't have a clue about failure. Dreams are a lot less appealing when you're burned out from falling flat on your face."

"I'd love to hear you play. Reid said your voice is incredible."

"He did not."

"He did."

Willow's cheeks felt like they were on fire. Or maybe she was getting a fever. She shook her head and glanced over at Reid, who was packing up veggies for a customer. "I'm not sure he's the world's foremost music critic."

"You should do open mic night at the brewpub in town. Station Eight. They get a great turnout and it's lots of fun. I could talk to the owner. Make sure you get a good spot."

Dammit, Reid. The can of worms that he'd opened up was *not* good. "That's sweet, but no thanks. I'm taking a break from music. Clearing my head. Figuring out what I want."

Faith nodded slowly, seeming unconvinced. "Okay. Sure. Of course, I'd still like to hear you play and sing."

"Why?"

"Because I like it when nice people share their talents."

"I'll think about it." That was a bit of a lie.

Faith arched her eyebrows. "You sound like Reid. He's thinking about it, too. Sometimes you just have to jump in headfirst and figure out the rest later."

Willow really did not want to disagree with Faith. She liked her too much. But Willow's relationship with music wasn't a matter of jumping in. She'd jumped. She'd waded. She'd treaded water in circles for a long-ass time. "I should go help this customer," she said, thankful for the woman who'd shown up at the stand.

"I'll see you later. Get some rest on your days off, okay?"

"I will." Willow shuffled over to the waiting customer. "What can I help you with today?"

"I'll take the rest of your lemon poppy-seed scones. And the rest of your muffins. Looks like I'm buying you out, huh?"

"Yep. Just three loaves of seven-grain bread left."

"I'll take one of those if it'll help."

"Great." Willow bagged up the woman's items, then processed her credit card. As soon as she walked away, Willow's bubbling rage was returning again. How dare Reid tell Faith about her music? She marched over to his stand, confronting him with her fiercest stare. He looked back at her, eyes growing wide and almost frightened. *Good. Be afraid. Be very afraid.*

"What the hell, Reid?" she asked as she ducked behind his table. "You told Faith about my music? Is this your way of trolling me? Not cool."

"You look like hell, Willow. Seriously."

"Stop trying to avoid the topic. It won't work. I'm pissed at you."

"So you're telling me it's a day ending in *y*. And I'm not avoiding anything. I legitimately think you're sick."

She crossed her arms. "I'm not." Although she might be. She did feel flush. And hot. But that was probably all Reid's fault. Everything was his fault.

"Come here." He beckoned her with a curl of his finger.

"What? Why? Are you going to murder me?"

He grasped her shoulder and stepped into her personal space. They were nearly toe-to-toe. Her pulse started hammering. Then he placed the back of his hand against her forehead. "You're hot, Willow."

She felt dizzy. So dizzy. *No. You're hot.* "Stop trying to change the subject."

He looked down, chin to his chest. His gaze connected with hers. It felt like stepping into one of those dreams you can't shake for days, the kind where you do bizarre things and act like a fool. "You're the most ridiculous human being I have ever met." Even when he insulted her, he couldn't completely break the spell.

"Right back at ya." Willow sniffled. Her nose tickled. She scrunched up her face to make the feeling go away because she didn't want to stop peering into Reid's soul. Maybe it could help her figure him out. But no. A sneeze was coming. There was no stopping it. Her head jerked. Violently. *Ka-choo!* Reid jumped back. It happened again. *Ka-choo!* Then again. *Ka-choo!* And again. *Ka-choo!* What in the hell was going on? She felt like she was expelling demons through her nose.

"That's it. You're going home." Reid wrapped his arm around her shoulder, sucking her back into his alternate reality. He might not like it when she touched him, but damn, she liked having him touch her. His warmth did something to her. Things were fluttering inside of her. Butterflies? Pigeons? Great horny owls? Or were those called great *horned* owls?

He started walking her to his truck. "Come on, sicko."

"Don't call me that. And what about my stand?"

"Give me the keys to the Flour Girl van. I'll pack up what little you have left over, and you can text Faith and tell her to come get it."

"But...but...but..." Willow sputtered as he opened the rusty old truck door for her.

"But what? Get in. You're sick. And quite possibly delirious."

"I'm not. And what about your stuff? You have veggies left over."

"The market director takes them to the community food bank. It won't go to waste."

"Then just leave the last of my stuff, too. The bakery is closed tomorrow. It's what Faith would want." She dug into her pocket and pulled out the key to the Flour Girl van, handing it over. Suddenly she didn't have the energy to fight with him anymore.

"I'll be right back. Don't go anywhere." He rolled down the window, then closed her door.

Willow could've sworn he smiled. Maybe she *was* delirious. Maybe he was going to murder her. She sat back in the seat, unable to muster the strength to think about it any-more. It seemed like only a minute passed before he hopped into the truck and started it up. The engine rumbled to life. Willow's insides rumbled, too.

Reid pulled out of his parking spot. "Let's get you home."

Eight

Let's get you home. The words stuck with Willow. They played in a loop in her head, uttered in a gentle voice Reid had almost never used with her. She curled into a ball and rolled over in bed, tugging the quilt up to her chin. She couldn't get warm. But she also felt like she was on fire. And she couldn't get comfortable, either.

Let's get you home. This wasn't home. Not even close. Aside from time spent at the bakery, she'd been mostly miserable since she'd arrived in Old Ashby. And yet she felt something shifting in this strange new world of hers. She wasn't sure what it was. Maybe it was the virus or whatever she'd happened to catch. If so, it'd eventually work its way through her body and be gone, and she'd be back to feeling the old way. Like she was existing. And not much else.

"Willow?" Reid's voice came from somewhere beyond her door, which she'd turned her back to.

"Whatever you want, Reid, it will have to wait. I'm busy dying right now."

"I told you so." He cracked the door and it squeaked on the hinges. "I was right. You're sick."

She wanted to flip him off like she had that morning, but she didn't have the strength. "Hooray. You win the grand prize for being right, which is nothing except the fact that I'm going to have to argue with you later."

"How about the energy to eat?"

The idea of food wasn't particularly appealing, but Reid had never offered her a single thing to eat and he'd flat-out refused to cook for her. "Eat what, exactly?"

"I made soup. Chicken noodle."

Despite her considerable lack of energy, Willow forced herself to turn over. He was standing right there, holding a tray with a bowl that had wisps of steam rising from it. "I don't know."

"It's homemade. I even made the noodles."

She narrowed her sights on him, not believing what he'd just said. "You did what?"

"Homemade noodles are better. And easy to make." He lifted the tray higher. "Come on. You'll feel better if you eat. Go ahead. Sit up."

Willow pushed against the mattress with both hands to maneuver into a sitting position, but it took too much effort. She collapsed against the headboard in defeat.

"Hold on. Your pillows are all messed up," Reid said. He set the tray on the nightstand, then perched on the edge of her bed. "Sit forward. Let me fix it."

"I can't. It's too hard. You go ahead. Leave me behind. Save yourself."

A quiet laugh escaped his lips. "You can be so melodramatic." He cupped her shoulders and gently tugged them forward. "Just sit up for a second. Lean against me if it's too hard."

"You'll catch whatever this crud is."

"I won't. I don't get sick."

"Of course you don't. You're a robot, aren't you? You're a cyborg." Willow did as he'd asked, sitting up and taking him up on his offer by leaning into him. She settled the side of her head against the hard shelf of his shoulder. His chest pressed against the side of her neck. His arms bracketed her shoulders as he reached behind her to tug the pillows into place. This was practically a hug. An embrace. And it did something to her. It made her insides turn soft and gooey. She closed her eyes and tried to inhale his smell through her stuffy nose. Even at death's door, it was so nice to be close to him. She was pretty sure she hated him, but she could be convinced otherwise.

He eased her back against the fluffy pillows. "Better?"

"Better," she lied. In truth, she felt worse. She wanted to be where they'd been two seconds ago, in a hug that wasn't real.

He picked up the tray and set it on her lap. There was not only a big bowl of soup, there were saltine crackers, not a chef's gourmet touch but the quintessential sick person food. He was good at everything. Even this. Because of course he was. "I do think you'll feel better if you eat something."

"Thank you. I can't believe you did this for me."

He shrugged and crossed his leg, still sitting on the edge of her bed. "My mom always took such amazing care of me when I was a kid. I will always remember that about her. It almost made it fun to be sick."

"My mom was the same. I know exactly what you mean." Willow grinned and tears stung her eyes. Her mind was swirling with memories and the melancholy that always seemed to come with them. She loved her family and she'd turned out to be nothing but a disappointment. "But you hate me. So this doesn't totally add up."

He picked at a spot on his jeans. "I don't hate you, Willow. I'm just someone who's not easy to get along with. I'm not like you. I like my solitude. I like quiet."

Willow looked down at her soup and picked up the spoon. "I hate those things."

"I rest my case."

Willow blew on the soup and took a sip of the broth, which was rich and perfectly seasoned. She groaned with pleasure. "So good." She took an actual bite, scooping up tender chicken and the most luscious noodles she'd ever tasted. "Scratch that. It's the best soup I've ever had. Ever."

Reid got up from the bed. "Good. I'm glad you like it. I'll get out of your hair, but eat the whole bowl if you can. They've done studies. Chicken soup does actually make you better."

"Wait."

Reid stopped at the doorway. "What?"

"Thank you."

He turned back to her. "You're welcome."

"I thought you didn't cook for people anymore."

"I don't."

"Then what changed? I mean aside from me getting sick? Because we both know you could've easily opened up a can and called it a day."

"I don't have it in me to serve you soup from a can, okay?" He leaned against the doorframe. "Plus…" He squinted and pinched the bridge of his nose.

"Plus what?"

"Hearing you play music all week did something to me."

"Did it make you feel bad about yourself? Because that wasn't totally my aim. I mean, it was a little bit of my aim, but mostly I was just trying to be honest."

"It's not about the lyrics. I deserved that. Well, some of it." He drew in a deep breath and quietly blew it out. "I guess that being around another creative person made me want to create."

Willow felt the most profound glimmer of happiness overcome her. "Really? That's amazing. Maybe that was all you needed to reconnect with your love for cooking."

He held up both hands. "Don't get ahead of yourself. It's soup. And I don't need to reconnect with anything." He stepped back into the room and walked over to the window, lowering the shade. It was dark outside now.

"Why did you tell Faith that I play music?" She took another spoonful of soup.

"Because I didn't want to be the only person in this town who knows about it. And I thought she could get you to play more."

"She wants me to do open mic night at Station Eight."

"You should do it. You're talented, Willow. Truly talented."

"Some people don't agree."

"Of course. Not everyone is going to like what you do. But I do. Hopefully that counts for something."

She looked up at him. He was now standing at the end of the bed, looking scruffy and a bit like his torso was too long and exactly like the guy who should be voted most likely to make her do something irrational. He smiled, ever so slightly, but it was like looking at the sun, albeit on a cloudy day. "I'm not performing any time soon but thank you for saying that. That means a lot to me," she said.

"As the subject of your ire, I'm glad."

"Nice use of your vocabulary words. Maybe I can work that into my lyrics." At first glance, it wasn't a bad idea until she realized that the first rhymes for *ire* that popped into her head were *fire* or *desire* and, well, that put the whole idea on the fast track to disaster.

He laughed quietly. "I have no doubt that you will."

"Will you stay while I eat? It's nice to not be alone."

His eyes darted to the door and she wondered if part of him was desperate for escape. Her only comfort was that she knew he would simply tell her that he didn't want to stay. He wouldn't save her feelings. "Sure."

He pulled the small side chair from the corner of the room and dragged it next to her bed. This was so much better than even a few hours ago. And she was so happy for it. "What should we talk about?"

"I don't know. You pick. You're the patient."

She saw her chance and she had to take it. "Perfect. Tell me why you left the restaurant in Boston."

Reid should've known better than to leave the subject of their conversation to Willow. He *did* know better. But if he didn't want Willow to write an entire album about him, maybe he should stop putting up so many walls. "I burned out. I couldn't do it anymore."

"Tell me about the burnout." Willow popped half of a saltine into her mouth, then returned to her soup, happily slurping.

He couldn't lie—the sight of her enjoying his food made him feel like he was floating. He was sure he'd successfully hidden it, but he'd been nervous about cooking for her. He'd been on edge watching her try the soup. That was always the most painful part for a chef—witnessing the moment when someone puts your creation in their mouth and there's no way to hide from their reaction. You simply had to endure it, good or bad. It was so much of the reason he'd always tried to stay in the kitchen. "You sound like a therapist."

"I got burned out by music. I want to know if it's the same." She took another bite, then licked the back of the spoon.

He cleared his throat and crossed his legs, attempting to gather his thoughts. It wasn't easy when Willow was going around licking things. Thoughts of her tongue were fighting to intrude. "Here's the thing about the restaurant industry. When you go to culinary school, it's drilled into your head that things have to be perfect. Every time. Again and again. Forever. If you go into fine dining, your food doesn't have to just be perfect, it has to be exceptional. And innovative. And exciting. An experience. Unforgettable." He paused and took a breath. It wasn't his former career that he hated talking about so much as it was having to remember everything. "I was obsessed. It was all I thought about. Day and night. I had no chill. I never took time off or went on trips. I just wanted to get better and better. I wanted everything to be perfect. I had no friends. No time for personal relationships."

"Which is how you end up with expired condoms."

Reid shook his head in dismay, but he still had to laugh. He was a ridiculously private person and here he was, not only spilling his guts to Willow—she'd found the real tea by digging around in his bathroom. "Uh. Yeah. You can definitely blame the condom situation on my former career."

"How long did you do all of that?"

He drew in a deep breath through his nose. "I'm thirty-five now. I was chef de cuisine at the restaurant in Boston for seven years, but I had that same position at two other restaurants before that. And I was a sous chef and station chef before that. Mostly in Boston, but I did move to Chicago for a while. It takes time to work your way up. So, I don't know. Twelve years? Thirteen?"

"No time off in between jobs?"

"No way. At first, I was hustling. Always trying to get something better. Once I got the last job, I was pretty sure I'd made it."

"From everything I read, I'd say that you did. You won so many awards."

His shoulders drew tight and he rolled his head to the side, trying to loosen the tension. One moment they were having a mostly light conversation, and the next she was suddenly steering them into the deep center of his regrets. "Awards are meaningless."

"Don't say that. You should be proud of yourself. Don't try to blow off your hard work."

Those accolades had once meant everything. Now they were sitting in a box in the attic. He'd never even shown them to his dad. There was never the right moment after Reid came home. Plus, the minute his dad confessed that he was sick, Reid's accomplishments became laughably pointless. "Awards aren't always about the work. So much of it is right place at the right time. Dumb luck."

"No, Reid. Stop. I'm serious about this." Willow shook her head and slid the tray onto the bedside table. The soup was gone. She'd eaten every last drop. "Obviously, I've never eaten some of the fancy-ass food you used to make, but that bowl of chicken noodle soup was better than anything I've ever had at a nice restaurant. That soup had a soul. I could taste the love that went into it. For real. That's not luck. That's talent. Don't you dare try to say that's nothing."

He cursed himself. That bowl of soup had done something to Willow. Several minutes ago, she was struggling to sit up in bed. Now she had so much fire that it was even harder than usual to tear his eyes away from her. "You want to talk about treating talent like it's nothing? Five seconds into hearing you sing, I knew that it was a crime that you decided to give up music. Because of what? Because you got booed off a stage?"

"My burnout and yours are not the same."

"Then enlighten me."

"You got burned out by *all* this success." She dramatically swooped her soupspoon in the air. "So much success that you didn't know what to do with it."

He got up from the chair and dragged it back to the corner. He was restless for an exit from this subject. "Don't make it sound like it was sunshine and rainbows. It wasn't. It ruined my life, okay?"

"On the other hand, I was burned out by failure. So it's not the same. At least you got to reach the top of the mountain. Stand up there. Look around a little. Meanwhile, I ran around the base of the mountain, trying to find a way up and failing."

"You know what they say about getting to the top of the mountain."

"What? That's it's awesome?"

"All there is to look at is lightning." He reached for the tray, but Willow stopped him with her hand around his wrist.

Her skin was impossibly soft. She peered up at him with eyes that were vulnerable and plaintive. He wanted nothing more than to kiss her. Even though she was sick. Then finally they could stop talking and maybe—just maybe—they could explore a different dynamic. "Lightning is exciting."

"It isn't. It happens, then it's gone in a flash, and there's nothing left."

"I don't believe you really feel like that. Don't you have amazing memories?"

He broke free of her grasp, but he couldn't bring himself to break free from her gaze. The way she looked at him made his heart jump up into his throat. He wasn't entirely dead inside. Something was inside him, fighting to get out. Willow made that part of him want to survive. But why did she have to have this power over him? "It ruined my life, okay? I ran myself into the ground. It was so bad that I nearly died in a car accident." He swallowed hard, deciding it was better if he just came out with it. She could stop digging for his secrets, and that would be a massive relief.

"Your scar. Near your hairline. Is that what that's from?"

He instinctively rubbed the spot. "You noticed that?"

"I did."

"The accident was my wake-up call. I didn't have enough sense to admit that I was burned out. And I was so exhausted one night that I fell asleep at the wheel and wrapped my car around a tree. Eleven days in the hospital. I had to tell myself the truth. I hated my job. So I came back here to recuperate and reconnect with my dad. And that was when I found out he was sick."

"He didn't tell you before that?"

"No. He didn't tell me because he didn't want to tear me away from the thing he thought I loved more than anything."

A single tear rolled down Willow's perfect cheek. "Your career."

"Exactly. I stayed away for years because of a fucking job." He heard his own voice break in two, but he had to keep going. Just get it out. Move on. "I blew off holidays and birthdays because I was chasing something not worth catching. I always told myself that there would be more time. Another time. Well, there wasn't. He died six weeks after I got here."

She clasped her hand over her mouth, her eyes wide and watery. "I'm so sorry."

"Thanks."

"Can I give you a hug?"

He wanted it more than anything. But he did not want hers or anyone else's pity. "No. I'm fine. You need your rest. I should go." He reached for the tray again.

"I think you'll feel better. I think I'll feel better, too."

"You're sick, Willow."

"Which is why I could use the hug just as much as you can. And you said it yourself. You never get sick."

He blew out a breath born of exhaustion. How long could he possibly keep fighting her? She kept pushing harder and harder to get close to him. He didn't have the strength to ward her off forever. And there was a tiny part of him that didn't want to stay away anymore. "Fine."

He sat on the edge of the bed and held out his arms, but he wasn't prepared for what it would feel like when she sank against his chest and wrapped him up in the warmest embrace he'd ever experienced. He closed his eyes and returned the hug, letting go of the distance between them, inch by inch, and coiling her up in his arms. She somehow felt smaller than he'd imagined, maybe because her personality and life force always made her seem so *substantial*. He rubbed her shoulder with his thumb. Back and forth. Back and forth. His heart returned to his throat. Thumping. Pulsing. Pushing. Something was stirring inside him, moving in on him like a tide. He longed to lie back, bring Willow with him, and see where they could take each other. Away from here. Or perhaps nowhere at all. Maybe he was exactly where he needed to be. Maybe the real question was where Willow belonged.

"I should go. You need your rest." He patted her shoulder then pushed her away, picked up the tray, and headed for the door.

"You aren't mad again, are you?"

Her words stopped him in his tracks. "I'm not mad."

"Do you want to do something? We could watch a movie. Or play cards. Or we can keep talking. We'll just keep it fun and light?"

That was an invitation he hadn't seen coming. He wanted to say yes more than anything, but he'd broken more than enough of his own rules that night—cooking for her. Hugging her. Telling her the things he liked to keep buried. "Maybe some other time. Now get some sleep."

Nine

Holy hell. So there was a real person under Reid's stubborn, frustrating-as-fuck facade. He and Willow had made progress on Saturday night. Toward what, she had no clue, but it felt positive and constructive. He actually said something of substance. He showed her the tiniest sliver of vulnerability. Yay.

Then, on Sunday, things started sliding backward. Reid still brought her everything someone with a nasty-ass cold needed, including soup—the chicken noodle for lunch, but with a life-altering grilled cheese on Flour Girl sourdough. Despite feeling like crap, Willow wanted to make out with that sandwich. She wanted to defile it. And she sort of did since Reid had declined to stay and talk to her while she ate, mumbling something about keeping things moving with the repairs to the cottage. Because of course. Despite whatever blip of connection they'd shared, he ultimately wanted her out of the house.

He served a different soup for dinner that night—creamy

roasted tomato and basil, along with a reprise of the grilled cheese. It happily filled her belly, but the rest of her felt empty. Reid was being distant again. Would she ever figure him out? If so, it was going to take more than two months to get to the bottom of things. It might take a lifetime to decipher Reid.

By late Monday morning, she was thankfully feeling mostly like her old self. Her energy had returned, and she couldn't take another minute in that room, so she tossed on a sweatshirt and a pair of cutoffs to venture back into the world. She stepped out into the hall and listened for signs of life. As was normal for this house, there were none. "Reid?" she called as she started down the stairs.

"In the kitchen," he answered.

Considering his standoffishness yesterday, Willow had some reason to give him space. But she wasn't a quitter, and the old vibe between them was something she wasn't willing to flatly accept. They could be friends if he'd simply give into it. "Good morning," she said as she wandered into the kitchen.

"It's nearly noon, so I'm not sure it qualifies as morning." Reid had his back to her, standing at the kitchen sink with the water running. He was wearing jeans and a gray T-shirt—the most boring of clothing choices, and yet his straight shoulders filled it out in a way that made her especially pissed that he couldn't always be nicer to her.

"It's eleven thirty-seven. Still a.m." Willow stepped closer and leaned against the counter with her hip.

"Somebody's feeling better." In the sink, he was washing off some garden pruners. The water rolled over his knuckles. His fingers. His hands—good God, his hands. Why had she never noticed them like this before? They were generous and rough. But somehow nimble.

"Way better. Must've been the soup." She gestured with a nod. "Just finish working outside?"

"About to start. I got up early and worked on the cottage this morning." He shut off the water and grabbed a rag to wipe the tools clean.

Of course he had. Getting her out of the house was a big priority. "I know you probably don't want my help, but can I tag along? I need to go outside. I need sunshine and fresh air to complete my recovery. I'm basically a plant with more complicated emotions."

He peered down into the sink and shook his head, but he was smiling. "I'll take your help. Come on. Let's go."

"Really?"

"I have never heard anyone get so excited by the prospect of working in the garden."

I'll take any invitation you want to give me. "I've made my plant nerdery abundantly clear."

Willow slipped into her sneakers, which she'd left at the front door, then trailed behind Reid as they walked outside and back behind the house to the gardening shed. He walked up the rickety wood ramp, then opened the creaking door. He disappeared inside and Willow followed. It was dark and a little musty, but oddly romantic. Maybe that was just being so close to Reid while he was in a not-terrible mood. "Whoa. There's a ton of stuff in here."

"There is. I probably need to clean it out at some point.

Most of this belonged to my parents, but some of it belonged to the original gardener, I guess. That was sort of before my time."

"Do you mean the original owner?"

He shook his head as he took down a handheld soil cultivator from the peg wall. "No. I mean the gardener. The woman who owned this property was pretty wealthy. Never married. She had full-time staff. That included my mom, who was her housekeeper. She let my mom and dad move into the guesthouse right after they were married. It's where they brought me home from the hospital."

Now Willow felt even worse about the flood. "Oh, God. No wonder you were so upset the day the washing machine overflowed. I'm so sorry."

He looked at her with his piercing eyes. "Don't be sorry. I found other issues after I opened up that floor, so it's for the best. I was feeling really sentimental about it at first, but now I can fix the problems that were hidden before. It means the cottage will live a longer life."

Willow felt a glimmer of relief. "Are you sure?"

"Yes." He pulled down a shovel from the wall. "Anyway, the owner died when I was six years old and she left the entire property to my mom. My mom was her nurse at the end, taking care of her, feeding her. Inheriting the house was her reward, I suppose. My parents and I moved into the main house after she passed away. Of course, we couldn't afford to have a full-time gardener. Or any gardener, to be honest. I think that was hard for my parents.

Having to let people go. They knew exactly how hard everyone was working."

"Was your dad working as a chef already?"

"He was cooking at the diner in town. It's not there anymore, but it used to be across the street from Hines Hardware. But then Oak and Ivy opened and he applied for a job there, sort of on a lark. He was entirely self-taught and didn't have much experience doing anything other than flipping pancakes and burgers. He got the job and that was the last place he ever worked." Reid looked around the shed. "I think that's all we need for right now."

"Okay. Sure." Willow shuffled outside, then waited for Reid to close up. "It sounds like your parents were both amazing people. That's nice."

"They were. I was really close to them. While they were alive." His voice wobbled.

The sound broke Willow's heart more than a little bit. She reached out and touched his arm. "I think you're still close to them. Living on this property. Taking care of it. You must feel their presence at least some of the time."

"Sometimes. Maybe."

"The people we love don't ever really leave us."

Reid looked at her, seeming skeptical. "Except that they do. When someone is gone, they're gone."

"But our memories don't go away. Neither does our love for them. It's still there. It's still inside you."

"And that's part of the problem." He shrugged it off, but it was like his pain was in plain sight. Sitting right there on the surface. And he was ignoring it.

A tear leaked from Willow's eye. "Do you want to talk about that?"

"Not really." Tools in hand, he walked past her, out into the garden.

Willow stumbled along behind him. "I'm here if you change your mind. I'm a good listener."

"You know what, Willow?" He turned and confronted her. "You never tell me anything about you."

"That's not true. I do talk about myself. You don't reciprocate. This is my way of evening things up a bit."

"I still feel like I know nothing." He turned back and resumed his trip into the garden.

"What do you want to know?"

"How did you and Bailey meet?"

Willow really wanted to stay on their previous subject, but she also had to respect Reid's boundaries. She couldn't force him to face his feelings. "We met in college. We were randomly matched as roommates. Like seriously random. When I first met her, I thought we would never get along."

"Why? You get along with everyone." Reid came to a stop at one of the beds of cucumbers and dropped his tools on the ground.

Willow didn't wait for an invitation, but went right to work, removing the tired, dying leaves from the bottom of the vines. "We were just so different. I was walking around barefoot with long blond hair and my acoustic guitar, and Bailey had her short dark hair and wore a black leather jacket everywhere. Plus, there were the obvious differences in our financial situations."

"What do you mean?"

"She showed up at school with a complete set of Louis Vuitton luggage."

"Really? She seems to live pretty humbly here." Reid pitched in, performing the same garden tasks as Willow. It was nice to work alongside him.

"She does now. But her dad is super wealthy. He does real estate development. But he's also an asshole, so she's cut herself off from any involvement with him. Including the money."

"That's not easy to turn your back on."

"It's not. But Bailey is pretty stubborn. And I think the longer she was away from home, the more she realized that her upbringing had been pretty toxic. That made it easier to walk away."

"Okay, well, you're basically just telling me about Bailey now. For someone who seems so willing to share, you're seriously skirting the topic of talking about yourself."

"There's not much to know. I grew up in Ohio, went to college in the same town I grew up in, then decided to move to New York to pursue music."

"Why not LA or Nashville?"

Willow shrugged. "Because I like to make things harder for myself? Honestly, I just always really loved New York. I got to go once for a school trip in high school and I was hooked from the very first minute. Then Bailey and I went another time while we were in college and I knew I wanted to live there. I just love it so much. I can't imagine living anywhere else."

★ ★ ★

It was nice to hear Willow talk about herself because she always wanted to talk about him. He hated being the focus of anyone's attention, like on Saturday night, when he brought her the chicken soup and she managed to drag out so many of his secrets. She'd unburdened him, probably more than she realized, but that left him conflicted. He was so attracted to her it hurt. But there was no safe way to get closer to Willow. She was going to leave. She'd said it herself. She couldn't imagine living anywhere other than New York. The place that was the polar opposite of Old Ashby. And once she did leave, he'd return to the life he'd had before her, except he knew he would feel even more empty.

After an hour or so of weeding, watering, and tidying things up in the garden, the sun overhead was so strong that Willow took off her sweatshirt. He hadn't counted on that. She was wearing a white tank top with skinny straps and Reid had to force himself to not stare while coming up with a plan to get her to put on more clothes. "Maybe we should we go inside, cool down, and have some lunch?"

"Are you offering to cook again?"

He could hardly believe this had become a regular thing, but there he was. "I am."

She clapped furiously fast. "It's my lucky day."

"Don't make a big deal about it, okay?"

"Too late."

Willow grabbed her sweatshirt. Reid led the way back inside and they both kicked off their shoes, then went into the kitchen. "What do you want?"

Willow shrugged, then began to wash her hands at the sink. "I don't know. You choose. Everything you've made for me so far has been amazing."

He didn't want to go with anything too elaborate. He'd already more than broken the promise to himself of not cooking for her. "How about a BLT? On more of the Flour Girl sourdough?"

"That sounds perfect."

"Great." He felt good about this—a simple meal meant simply to nourish them. It definitely was not about impressing. Or seducing. After washing his own hands, he went straight to work, pulling out a large sheet pan to cook the bacon in the oven.

"What can I do?" Willow asked.

"Slice a tomato or two? Grab the big ones. They're over there in the basket by the window."

"I'm on it."

Reid fetched the rest of the supplies—the bacon, a head of romaine lettuce, also from the garden, and a jar of mayo. He brought them to the counter, next to where Willow was working. He busied himself with laying out strips of bacon on the sheet pan, then slipping it into a cold oven so it would render and crisp up properly. He jacked up the heat, then set a timer.

"Done," Willow announced. "How long will the bacon take?"

"Fifteen minutes."

"Cool. Do you mind if I go into the other room for a minute? Something's been tooling around in my head."

"Yeah. Of course."

She traipsed out of the room and he tried not to think too hard about why she was so enticing in a tank top and shorts, barefoot, with her hair up in a ponytail. He tried not to think about how easily they got along when he wasn't putting up walls.

Moments later, he heard the piano. He became very still and looked out the kitchen window at the view of the garden while he listened carefully. Whatever she was playing was different than the song about how much she hated him. It was slower, a little aching. And Reid wondered about this power Willow had over him. Her music captured him in a way nothing else did.

He walked up to the kitchen doorway to hear better, but it wasn't close enough, so he padded through the foyer, being painfully careful to not make a single noise. She was singing now, mostly just sounds. Was this a new song? What had sparked the idea? As a creative person, he was fascinated by sparks. What made Willow feel compelled to create? With cooking, it was most often the ingredients. That was such a huge part of what made him love the garden. But music? That was a whole other level. He couldn't begin to comprehend the brilliance of a mind that could pull music out of thin air—a beautiful arrangement of notes, set to a tempo, then layered with poetry. He was so in awe of her artistry.

He stepped to the living room entry and leaned against the wood frame. She played for another minute, then stopped, dropped her hands into her lap, and looked up at the ceiling. Her right hand returned to the keyboard and she played around with a few keys, her gaze still directed straight up. Then she stopped again.

"Something new?" Reid asked.

Willow whipped around, eyes wide and cheeks flushed with pink. "Just an idea. It was in my head when I woke up this morning."

He ambled up to her and the piano. "Is that how it works? The music comes to you?"

She turned toward him and slid her bare leg up onto the piano bench. Her skin looked so silky and smooth. "Usually. There's almost always something percolating in my head. A few notes. Something. But sometimes I get hit by more."

"Do you write it down?"

"Depends on what it is. Sometimes I make a voice memo on my phone. I just sing into it. But once something comes to me, it's hard to do anything other than write."

"How do you get anything done?"

"It can be hard. I can't control it." She nodded and the warmest, softest smile spread across her lips. "I have to tell you, there's something about this house that's making music come to me. There's a hum to it. Or something."

How was it possible for her to pick up on that? His awareness of the spirit of this house was all wedged in memories. Things he'd lived, like birthdays and Christmases and summer days. But she'd never met his dad. She'd never known his mom. "That's amazing." *You're amazing*. The words were sitting right there on his lips and he wondered why he couldn't simply come out with it.

"Really? You weren't convinced when we talked about it in the shed."

He shook his head, transfixed by her. "I guess it's just that I'm fascinated by the way your creativity works." *Say something nice to her. You're thinking it.* "But you're a fascinating person."

She closed up the piano and rose from the bench. "I think the word you're looking for is *peculiar.*"

"Nope. You're fascinating. And amazing. Even if you drive me up a wall sometimes."

"Careful. That's the nicest thing you've said to me." She lightly gripped his forearm and placed the back of her hand against his forehead. "Are you sure you never get sick? Because I think you might be now."

He shook his head again. It was an attempt to loosen her pull on him. But the tug was still there. Right in the center of his chest. His mind churned with thoughts about how he'd never met anyone like her, all while his body was processing the effects of her hand on his arm and the impossible pink of her lips. "I'm perfectly healthy."

"I noticed."

He swallowed, or at least attempted to. "You *noticed*?"

Her icy blue eyes blazed with heat and intensity. She tightened her grip on his arm. "How you're a perfect human specimen? How you look like a god without your shirt on? Yes. I noticed, Reid. I have eyes. It would be impossible to ignore."

Heat flooded his cheeks. "You're pretty damn perfect yourself."

Willow opened her mouth to speak, but no sound came

out. Her eyes scanned his face, sweeping back and forth. "I can't take this anymore."

"Take what?"

"This." She popped up onto her toes, gripped his other arm, and leaned into him.

Oh, shit. Oh shit oh shit oh shit. Reid's brain switched into hyperdrive, but some unreasonably calm part of him took over and told him to drop his head. Willow countered by raising her mouth to his. Their lips drew closer to each other, inch by inch, breath by breath. The instant they touched, he threaded both of his hands into her silky hair, cupped the side of her face, and wiped the rest of the world from his brain. The only thing left or worth worrying about was that kiss. Forget creativity and talent—Willow's mouth on his was pure inspiration. He tilted his head to the side, waiting for her to part her lips. A millisecond later, she did, and his tongue found hers, then hers circled his, and it was like letting wild horses out of a corral, or something like that. If Reid had any brain at all, he would've come up with a more poetic metaphor. Willow squeezed his arms and arched her back, pressing her stomach against his. He reached down and grabbed her ass, both hands filled with her fleshy deliciousness while his fingers dug into the velvety skin of her upper thighs.

Willow dropped to the floor in a sudden rush, pulling him down with her. Then she pushed his shoulders with both hands, and he didn't put up the slightest resistance. She had him flat on the living room rug. She straddled his hips, settled her weight on him, and dug her fingers into his hair, totally in charge. She lowered her head and kissed him with reckless abandon, mouth open and wet and so fucking hot. She rolled her hips against his crotch. His cock flooded with warmth and blood. He wanted her. And she wanted him, too. It felt so good. So perfectly good.

But then it felt bad. This was happening fast. Too fast. And it would only be a matter of seconds before clothes would start coming off. *Shit.* He already had his hands up the back of her top. When did that happen? Her skin was so soft. Too soft. This was too much. He'd sworn he wouldn't get close to Willow. Or let her get close to him. *Well, fuck.* Nakedness was about one minute away and then they'd *really* be close.

He didn't see a way out. And the weakest parts of him didn't want him to come up with an exit strategy. His dick was hella excited by his prospects at the moment. His dick did not care about cooking lunch. It cared about whatever Willow was hiding under her tank top and inside her shorts. But his dick was definitely the most shortsighted part of his body. It was time for his brain to step in.

He pulled his lips from hers and turned his head to the side. "Willow. I'm sorry. This is… It's not a good idea. It will just make things messy between us."

"Messy? Things are already messy." She eased back, seeming super confused, then sat completely still.

She's not wrong. There was no sensible explanation for what Reid was doing. Other than there was something lurking inside him that had some harebrained idea that staying away from Willow might keep him from turning his life into even more of a shit show. He shifted his hips and rolled just enough to one side to send Willow a message. She lifted her leg then slumped to the floor, pushing her hair back from her face, flustered.

He scrambled to his feet and took several steps back away from her. He was treating her like she was a bundle of dynamite, but the truth was that he was the one who might explode. All of that passion he felt when he cooked…it extended to other things when he was inspired, and Willow was the walking, talking embodiment of inspiration. He tried not to stare at her, but it was impossible. She was so goddamn beautiful, eyes wide and lips red and raw from kissing him.

"Well?" Willow pled. "I can't figure you out. Seriously. One minute you like me. The next minute you don't."

"It's not that."

She got up to her feet. "Well, I'm just going to come out with it, okay? I think you're hot as shit and I've wanted to kiss you pretty much from the moment we met. And it obviously crossed your mind or you wouldn't have kissed me back. So what is your deal? I don't care what the answer is. Just tell me the truth. It will make both of our lives a whole lot easier."

The timer in the kitchen began to beep. "The bacon."

"Fuck the bacon. Tell me what you're thinking. For once. Just be fucking honest. Don't worry about my feelings. Just tell me what you're thinking."

"I shouldn't have kissed you back." He turned and started for the kitchen.

"Are you still going to make me a sandwich?" Her voice was close enough to tell him she was following him.

He couldn't believe what a mess this had become. He should've stayed away from Willow when she was at the piano. He should've forced himself to ignore everything she was. "Yes. I'll leave it for you on the kitchen counter."

"You aren't going to eat with me?"

"No. I need to go work on the cottage."

Ten

Willow woke to the alarm on her phone. She didn't bother with the snooze, but she did allow herself a moment to slump back against the pillows, sigh dramatically in the darkness, then say the thing that needed to be said: "What the fuck." She'd uttered those words more than she liked to admit since she'd come to Old Ashby, but they were different now. It was no longer a question. It was a declarative statement. Everything with Reid had gone sideways. All because of a kiss.

She threw back the covers and went to the small bureau in her room, tugging out a pair of jeans and one of her Flour Girl T-shirts. The kiss wasn't the problem, even if she was still trying to wrap her head around it. One minute she'd been sitting at the piano and the next thing she knew, she was straddling Reid on the living room floor with his very noticeable hard-on rubbing between her legs. It was all a blur. A hot and messy shock to the system. Then he'd rolled out from under her and did what he always did—got the hell away from her. Either she was a terrible kisser, which didn't seem plausible since she'd received zero complaints in the past, or he truly didn't like her. Which also didn't seem right. They were getting along now. For entire minutes at a time. Leading her back to where she'd started: "What the fuck."

She got her T-shirt over her head when she realized that remarkably, the kiss wasn't her biggest problem. It was that her car was still at the bakery. Reid had driven her home from the farmer's market on Saturday, and he was going to have to give her a ride to work. She was not only going to have to wake him up, she would have to endure the seven millionth grumpy and awkward interaction with him. At least she was getting good at it.

She finished getting dressed, grabbed her bag, and tiptoed out into the hall. The house was dark and eerily quiet this time of day. Reid was surely dead asleep. As she stood at his door with her hand poised to knock, her brain inconveniently delivered an imagined image of his chaotic hair across the pillow, his bare chest peeking out from the covers. He was probably impossibly sexy when he was sleeping. It was hard to be a curmudgeon when you were unconscious.

She knocked softly on the door. "Reid? Are you asleep?"

"What?" he asked. "Willow? What time is it? Are you okay?"

She grinned and leaned against the doorframe. "I'm sorry, but my car is still at the bakery. Can you give me a ride to work?"

With a thud, his feet apparently hit the floor. "Yeah. Of course. I need a minute to get dressed."

"Don't wear anything too fancy. It's a casual affair."

"Ha ha."

She thought she'd been at least amusing, but apparently not. She ducked into the bathroom, swept her hair up into a ponytail, and brushed her teeth. A few moments later, she heard Reid's door open and he shuffled to the bathroom.

"Can I pee?" He squinted adorably into the light. Damn him and his cuteness.

"I don't know. Can you?"

His shoulders drooped in defeat. "Willow. Come on. I'm half awake."

"Sorry. Yes. Bathroom is all yours." She squeezed past him and their bodies brushed, stomach-to-stomach. It was the most insignificant interaction, but it still made heat rise in her face. Even though he didn't want that for them. Apparently. Resigned to her fate, she went downstairs and waited.

Reid clumsily came down the stairs and snatched his keys from the hook. "Come on."

"Wait. Aren't you going to wear shoes?"

"Flip-flops are shoes." He held the front door for her. At least chivalry wasn't dead.

"Is that safe?" She descended the stairs with Reid in her wake.

"I wear flip-flops all the time when I'm driving." He started around to the side of the house that was hidden from the cottage, where there was a ramshackle wood garage that leaned a bit to one side. It was the home of his dad's old truck.

"I was always told to never wear flip-flops and drive."

"I did it on Saturday and you made it home just fine." He opened his door and Willow did the same, climbing inside.

"I was sick as a dog."

He blew out a frustrated breath and turned to her. "I'm sorry you don't approve of my footwear. You still need a ride to work, so this is happening."

He turned the ignition and the truck sputtered to life. He slung his arm over the back of the seat and turned toward her to back out of the garage. She tried to ignore how inexplicably hot it was. Of course there were other details to look past, like the way he smelled like sleep and his deodorant and how that made her wistful for what might have happened yesterday afternoon if he hadn't put an abrupt stop to the kiss— him pulling off her top and throwing it aside, then taking off the rest of her clothes. Making her even hotter for him…

"You're fidgeting a lot. Are you okay?" he asked as he pulled onto the main road up to town.

Was she that transparent? Or could he read minds? *Of course I'm fidgeting. I want to fuck you so bad that it makes my chest burn. It's impossible to sit still. I keep imagining you touching me and me touching you and I'm in a constant state of torment.* "Sorry. I'll try to stop."

"You're apologizing again."

It was so like her to be drawn to a guy who was indifferent or acted like an asshole half of the time. Why couldn't she ever learn?

Reid turned onto Rosemary Street and a minute later, he was pulling up in front of Flour Girl. Inside, the lights were on. Willow reached for the door handle, but she had to say something. Clear the air. Find a way to make herself slightly less miserable. She turned to him. "I know you don't want me to apologize, but I'm sorry I kissed you. Or if I made things weird by kissing you."

He looked straight ahead, shoulders bouncing slightly from the rumble of the truck engine. "No need to apologize. Let's just forget it happened."

"But I hate this." She waved her hand back and forth between them. "It makes me sad. And mad. I like it when we're nice to each other."

He grumbled and closed his eyes. "I like it when we're not fighting, too. I vote that we focus on that. That's enough."

There were a million things she wanted to say, points she wanted to bring up about how there was no good reason for them to not always be kind to each other, or kiss, or fuck for that matter. But she needed to get to work and she needed to stop trying so damn hard with Reid. She opened the car door. "Got it. Thanks for the ride." She hopped out before he could respond, slammed the door, then stormed across the sidewalk and into Flour Girl. "Hey Faith. I'm here," she called, stalking into the kitchen.

Faith looked up from her work. "I wasn't sure you were going to make it. Are you feeling better?"

"Physically, yes." *Mentally, no.*

"Good. I'm glad. You can start on the banana chocolate chip muffins."

"Sure." Willow grabbed an apron and looped it over her head, then wrapped the tie around her waist. She pulled out the laminated recipe card from Faith's file and wheeled a bin of flour over to the worktable. As she weighed out the dry ingredients and combined them in a large mixing bowl, she thankfully felt the boil of her blood lower to a simmer. At least *something* was going right.

"Still feeling a little under the weather? You seem quiet." Faith slid several baking trays of cookies into the oven.

"Do I?" Willow began combining her wet ingredients.

"You're usually super chatty. Especially first thing."

"I'm just trying to focus."

"Oh. Okay." Faith set the magnetic timer that they kept on the front of the oven. "Have you thought any more about doing open mic night at Station Eight?"

Willow kept working on the batter. "I don't think it's a good idea."

A look of surprise crossed Faith's face. "Why?"

"Because it will open a big can of worms."

Faith pressed a hip into the worktable and crossed her arms. "I don't know Reid that well, but he doesn't seem like the kind of person who would gush about anything. And he was gushing about you."

That part still confounded Willow. And he'd been so complimentary yesterday afternoon. But then he'd pushed her away. "Playing in someone's living room is different than performing for a crowd."

"Do you have stage fright?"

Willow managed a small smile. "Actually, no. I rarely get nervous when I play."

"Then what is it?"

"If the audience doesn't like me, I can't take the rejection. Not anymore." She'd come to Old Ashby still feeling raw from what happened that night at the Hi-Life. Little had she known she'd have to endure even more rejection, albeit of a different kind.

"That's part of the creative process, isn't it? You put your work out in the world and sometimes people like it, and sometimes they don't. Those miso and black pepper biscuits I came up with certainly aren't for everyone."

"I loved them."

Faith shrugged. "And some people thought they were gross. It doesn't mean I won't keep trying."

"But you have a hugely successful business. And you were trying something new. It's not quite the same."

"The most important word in that sentence is *trying*."

Willow began scooping batter into muffin tins. "I've spent my whole life trying. Chasing a dream that left me running in circles. I feel like everyone around me has just been humoring me. I'd really just like to do something that can make everyone proud."

"What about you? What makes you proud?"

Willow shrugged. "I'm proud that I'm getting better at baking."

"You know I have two grown-up kids, right?"

Willow felt bad, but she'd never asked Faith much about her private life. "I didn't know that. Were you married?"

"Sixteen years. It ended in divorce."

"I'm sorry."

"I'm not. I got two amazing kids out of it. Angie lives in Philadelphia. She's a social media marketing manager. Bryce is up in Maine. He's an oyster farmer."

"I'm sure they're awesome. I mean, they have you for a mom."

Faith smiled and blushed. "You're sweet. And they *are* awesome. But it doesn't matter what they do. I will always be proud of them. I will always admire them as people."

"My family isn't really like that. My parents worship my brother, Gabe. He has all of these big achievements. I want to accomplish something, too."

"Courage and bravery are accomplishments, Willow."

Willow drew in a deep breath through her nose, unconvinced. "I still don't want to do open mic night."

"That's your choice. But I'd like to hear you sing before you leave us at the end of your two months here."

The end of your two months… That still felt like a finish line she might never reach.

"Oh. By the way," Faith continued. "I'd also like you to start making the macarons."

"Seriously?" Willow could hardly believe it. Macarons took so much precision. Mixing the cookie batter was considered an art. "Do you think I'm ready to do that?"

Faith didn't even look at Willow. "I do."

"Huh. Okay."

Willow popped the muffins into the oven, doing her best to take Faith's advice to heart. It wasn't as easy as Faith made it sound. It simply wasn't. She knew that one thing for a fact.

By the time Willow was on her way back to the house, she was more mentally exhausted than anything. All that thinking had taken it out of her. She was just pulling into

Reid's driveway when her phone rang. It was exciting to see her brother's name on the caller ID. She put the car in Park and killed the engine. "Gabe, hi. I'm so glad you called. How are you?"

"I'm great. Fantastic, actually. But the important question is how are you?"

Willow couldn't escape the undercurrent of his question—he wanted to know if she'd recovered from the incident at the Hi-Life. "I'm good. I'm actually in Connecticut for most of the summer."

A few moments of silence played out on the other end of the line and Willow instantly felt like shit. He was mad she hadn't filled him in on any of this. "Yeah. I know. I can't believe you didn't tell me."

"I was going to. I swear. I guess I just for—"

"Willow. Stop. It's fine. I'm just giving you crap."

Willow opened her car door for some air and looked out at the garden. Reid was hard at work, not wearing a shirt, as per usual. The late-afternoon sun beamed through the canopy of trees, casting golden light onto him like he was a statue, or at the very least a creature from another planet. The latter would explain a whole hell of a lot. "How did you find out I'm here?"

"I went to the city to surprise you. That's when I discovered Bailey was living in your apartment."

Willow was now even more confused. Bailey hadn't told her this. Then again, they hadn't talked. At all. Willow still hadn't shared what had happened with the guest cottage, or the fact that she was Reid's temporary roommate. She'd texted Bailey multiple times, hoping they could find a time to catch up on the phone, but Bailey was always too busy. "Where did you stay? You always crash with me when you come to the city."

"It was fine. Bailey didn't care."

"She let you *stay* with her?"

Reid's head popped up from the other side of his tomatoes and he looked right at her. Apparently her voice had carried. Willow grabbed her bag, climbed out of the car, and slammed the door.

"Are you mad?" Gabe asked.

"Well, yeah. Sorta."

"Why? It was no big deal," Gabe said.

She couldn't decide what bugged her most about this. That no one had told her what was going on, or that Bailey had decided Gabe was okay to stay at the apartment, but not Willow. "I'm just surprised, okay?" She walked around to the front of the house and sat on the bottom step.

"Which is why I'm calling you. Plus, I had to check on my baby sister. How's Connecticut?"

If ever there was a loaded question, that was it. "Good. I got a job at a bakery."

"I heard."

Willow shook her head. If he knew everything, why did he even call? "Gabe, I just got home and I need to take a shower. I stink from work."

"Okay. You'll have to get me up to date on the new job at some point. I hope you have time to write music."

"I do." It wasn't a complete lie. "Love you."

"Love you, too."

Willow ended the call and looked at Reid. He was still weeding. She could go talk to him, but she was no longer going to be the person trying to build a bridge. It had become a humiliating pursuit, and she'd had more than enough of that.

Reid spent the majority of most days mentally torturing himself, but today had been a whole new level of hell. The bulk of his time, he was in the garden, unable to think about a single thing other than the kiss with Willow. The memory was in more than his head—it had worked its way into his bones. It had become part of him, and now he would have to deal with the repercussions. He had to give her some sort of explanation for his reaction, even when he'd have a hell of a time putting it into words. All he knew was there was a war going on inside him—one side wanted him to act only out of an abundance of caution, and the other side wanted him to scream *fuck it* and kiss Willow again. And again. And again.

For the moment, Willow was sitting on the front steps, her phone in her hand after just having had a heated conversation with someone. He didn't want to be nosy about it, but he also hated the idea of her being upset, and by the look on her face, she was exactly that. She got up and stuffed her phone into her bag, then started up the stairs.

He had to do something. Say *something*. "Hey, Willow," he called. *Good. That's a start.*

She came to a stop, then turned around slowly. "What?"

Now what, asshole? He strode between the garden beds

until he was only a few paces from the bottom of the stairs. His heart was thumping hard against the base of his throat. *Be nice. Do something nice.* "Can I make you dinner tonight?"

She planted one hand firmly on her hip. "Depends. Are we going to eat together? Because I'm tired of eating your food by myself. It's delicious and everything, but I hate eating alone."

He was amazed that his presence was the thing she'd requested. She had every reason to accept his offer but otherwise keep her distance. Especially since yesterday. "Whatever you want."

"Does this mean we're back to being nice to each other? I just want to make sure I know what I'm walking into."

He took another step closer. "Willow, I'm sorry. About yesterday. I should've said that in the truck this morning, but I'm one of those people who needs a good half hour to wake up before I'm able to form coherent sentences."

"I'm going to need a little more explanation than that."

He nodded slowly. Why was she so good at this while he was so bad? "Right. Of course. I can do that. Over dinner. After a glass of wine. Or two."

Willow laughed quietly. "Okay. Sure. What time? I could use a nap before then, and I definitely need to take a shower."

Reid swallowed hard. He was in need of a shower, too. This was probably not the time to mention their mutual need. Or think about it, for that matter. "Six thirty? Does that work?"

"As long as you're planning on wearing a shirt."

He suddenly became keenly aware of his state of undress. "Obviously, I will wear a shirt."

"Very little is obvious anymore, Reid. Almost nothing." With that, she resumed her trip up the stairs and into the house.

Despite the sour tone of her departure, Reid felt a glimmer of optimism that at the very least, he and Willow could keep things friendly between them. He wasn't going to waste his momentum. He immediately sprang into action, returning to the garden and harvesting vegetables for the meal. He'd always been a cook that let the ingredients be his guide and now was no different. Even so, he had to tell himself to keep things in check. This should be a simple meal, however much he enjoyed having her appreciate his food. He had an apology to make. That was it.

He went to work in the kitchen. His plan was to make a summer vegetable risotto with an obscene amount of Parmesan and Romano cheese, plus lots of lemon. He prepped everything, then went upstairs to get cleaned up. Out on the landing, he heard Willow's musical snore and knew it was safe to use the shower. He stepped into the bathroom, the humidity hanging heavy in the air. She'd just been in there. Without her clothes. In the shower. Under the warm water. He closed his eyes for strength, but that left him to contend with the sweet smell of her shampoo. Willow was everywhere. She could not be ignored.

He stepped under the spray and the hot water rolled over his bare shoulders, loosening his muscles and trickling down his chest and legs. The memory of the kiss hummed in his body—Willow in his arms. Her impossibly soft lips on his. Her tongue. Her luscious curves. It was all too much to think about. Blood rushed down through his belly and up from his thighs. His cock grew hard and heavy. There was no avoiding this. Eyes clamped shut, he gripped his rock-hard shaft, rubbing his thumb back and forth over the swollen tip. That one touch was enough to make him rocket into space, but he held on tight and took long strokes. Willow swirled in his head, just like the steam in the shower. He imagined her touching him, exactly like he wanted to be touched. His chin dropped to his chest. A deep, primal groan left his lips. He spread his feet wider, his thighs tensed. His dick somehow got even harder.

He wanted to take this slow. He wanted to savor the fantasy. But time was of the essence. He had a meal to prepare and he wanted it to be perfect. Even if another physical thing never happened between Willow and him, he had to make a good apology. The memory of Willow returned. He felt her straddling him, rocking her body weight against his dick. His balls drew tight against his body. So taut it made it hard to breathe. The pressure built. Fast. Like lightning. His spine stiffened, bracing for release. His neck felt like it might snap. And then a rush—a freaking tidal wave of electricity—stormed through his body. In hard pulses, each one carrying a little more relief. He shuddered with the final release. He could breathe again. His muscles calmed the fuck down.

Was it pure satisfaction? No. It was a respite. It took off the edge. Just enough so his brain could participate in the evening. He turned and rinsed off his body, washing away the evidence, then shutting off the water and stepping out of the shower. He swiped at the foggy mirror, combed his fingers through his hair, and looked at himself. He was going to get his act together. He wasn't sure what that looked like anymore, but he knew one thing—he couldn't allow Willow to suffer because he was struggling with his life.

In his room, Reid dug out the nicest pair of jeans in his closet and a not-too-horribly rumpled light blue button-down shirt. He despised all shirts with a collar, but he wanted to make an effort, and rolling the sleeves up to his elbows made him feel a little less constrained.

A half hour or so later, dinner was well underway.

"That smells *so* good," Willow said from behind him.

Reid turned and was floored. There was Willow, walking toward him, barefoot in a black-and-white checkered sundress, hair wavy and a little messy. Her face was radiant and rested. He took a deep and silent breath to center himself. He also took a moment to congratulate himself for having had the foresight to jerk off in the shower. If he hadn't, he'd be sunk at this moment. "You look incredible."

"Thanks. All of my other clothes are dirty or smell like cookies."

Reid laughed. "The dress is nice. It's very pretty."

Willow wandered closer to the stove and leaned against the counter. "What are you making?"

Reid returned to stirring the contents of the pot. "Risotto. I have to stand here and stir or it won't turn out right."

"Is it almost done? I'm starving."

"It's going to need at least another twenty minutes. I picked a bunch of cherry tomatoes if you want a snack. In the colander. I haven't had one yet, but the last ones were super sweet."

Willow stepped to the kitchen sink, took one, and popped it into her mouth. She moaned softly. He decided then and there that he should do everything he could do to encourage that sound from Willow whenever possible. "Oh, my God. They're like candy. You have to try one," she said.

"Can't stop stirring."

She grabbed a handful. "Open your mouth."

"Willow. I can't leave the stove. And you're all the way over there."

"Just catch it."

"I'm not into sports."

She stuck out her tongue, her eyes flashing with mischief. "Humor me."

"Fine." He did as she asked, feeling like a complete fool with his mouth open wide while he continued to stir the risotto with one hand.

"One. Two. Three." Willow took aim and tossed the tomato. Reid jerked his head to one side, only to have it miss his mouth by an inch and hit his cheek. The tomato fell to the floor. "Dammit. One more try."

"That's a perfectly good tomato. Can't you just get a little closer?"

She took a single step then stopped. "Are you going to tell me what happened yesterday?"

Dammit. It was just like Willow to bring this up now. He ladled some chicken stock into the risotto and stirred, then looked up at her. "I was hoping to do that over dinner."

"I was hoping to do it now so dinner doesn't get ruined."

He didn't want to argue the point. She had every reason to want to do things her way. "You surprised me when you kissed me. But I wanted to kiss you back. That was all real. But I didn't bargain on things getting as heated as they did."

She took two more steps until she was right next to him. "What did you think was going to happen? That you were going to cup my face and run your hands through my hair and I was going to shrug it off? There's been serious tension between us. From the beginning. At some point, it was either going to turn into kissing or more arguing. We both know that."

Willow truly was like no one else he'd ever met. She just said whatever had been left unsaid. "Yes. I suppose you're right."

"And you had to know that we couldn't share some innocent peck on the lips, then just go back to being roommates."

He sighed. "You're right. You're absolutely right. I shouldn't have participated with such enthusiasm if I wasn't prepared for there to be more. I don't know what I was thinking. I was sucked in by your music. I've never been around anyone who can create the way you can. It's intoxicating."

Willow crossed her arms over her chest and shook her head at him. "That's nice, but only if you mean it."

"I mean it. It's the truth. Everything I said to you yesterday was the truth, too. But I'm not always in the best headspace, okay? We've been around each other enough that I'm sure you've picked up on it."

She nodded. "I have." She popped a tomato into her mouth.

"So, yes. I wanted to kiss you back yesterday. More than anything. But then we started and my brain kicked in and I started to think about how I'm kind of a disaster right now and you're leaving at the end of July. It didn't seem right."

She sighed and shook her head. "What am I going to do with you?"

"I don't know how to answer that."

"Surely you're familiar with the concept of a summer fling."

"I thought that only happened in movies about horny teenagers."

"Oh, no. Flings are available to all horny people. Even horny thirtysomethings." Willow grinned, then bounced both eyebrows at him flirtatiously.

He laughed. "You want to know what you should do with me? *I* don't know what to do with you."

"Maybe take a tomato from me." She stepped up to him and held up her offering, plump and red and shiny between her fingers. It felt like more than temptation. It was like she was holding a lit match and the floor was covered in cotton fluff soaked in gasoline.

He wanted more than the tomato. He wanted another sign that she wanted him the way he wanted her. He opened his mouth like before and she didn't hesitate, even though she moved in slow motion, slipping it between his lips then resting her thumb on his lower lip. He closed his mouth, planting a nearly imperceptible kiss on the pad of her thumb. He pulled the tomato into his mouth with his tongue. It was sweet and juicy and slightly tart, everything he suspected Willow would be. He dared to make eye contact, getting lost in the mysterious depths of her magical blue eyes. This was more than want now. It was need. And he was done with making mistakes.

"You forgot to keep stirring," she said.

"Oh. Shit." So much for not making mistakes. Reid had completely stopped stirring. He was just standing there with a spoon in his hand, the taste of tomato in his mouth, and a semi in his pants. He looked down at the pan. The rice had completely dried out and was sticking to the pan. He scooped another ladle of stock and dumped it in. The pan sizzled. He stirred, but it was a clumpy disaster now. "Fuck. I need to start over." He flipped off the burner.

"Maybe *we* need to start over."

He froze. Was she saying what he hoped she was saying? After the thumb on his lip, he was thinking she might be. He turned and looked her straight in the eye, wishing he had the courage to tell her how her mere presence made him weak. How he thought about her at night. How he thought about her in the garden and in the cottage and while he was brushing his teeth.

"I'm willing to try if you are," he replied, reaching for her hand and grasping only a few fingers.

"Just a fling, right?"

"Right." *Whatever that means.* He wasn't sure he was capable of committing to it, but he'd sure as hell try. He leaned closer and placed the lightest kiss against her temple, inhaling her sweet scent like it was a drug. She shuddered. Actually shuddered. Like she was having an orgasm. Like he'd just managed to drive her to her peak with one tiny touch.

If only she knew the things he could do to her if he was actually trying.

Eleven

The moment when things shifted for Reid was crystal clear to Willow. It was when he decisively pinned her against the kitchen counter and kissed her so hard—so *possessively*—that she got dizzy. This was different than yesterday. It was like he'd been waiting for years to kiss her like that. That was the instant that she knew, down to her bones, that he wanted this, too. He wasn't going to change his mind. This was actually happening. It was exhilarating, but it was a little sobering, too. He was so serious about everything, especially the things he really set his mind to. There was reason to doubt that Reid was capable of a fling.

For now, he was focused on the front of Willow's dress, his fingers fumbling with the buttons while he pressed his forehead against hers. He managed the first few, then pulled one of the straps down her shoulder. She hadn't bothered with a bra when she'd dressed, which was a brilliant move on her part as it gave him ready access to her breast. He lowered his head and drew her nipple into his mouth. Willow's eyes clamped shut as her skin flushed with heat and her nipple became hard as a rock. It sent a sizzle straight to her clit, so powerful that she bucked against his thigh.

"You like that, don't you?" He kissed her neck, his stubble scratching at her tender skin. He teased her nipple with his fingertip, rubbing so lightly it was almost like he wasn't there. But he *was* there. Oh, yes, he was.

"Fuck yes." Willow undid one more of her own buttons, leaving her dress open to her waist, letting her other strap fall from her shoulder.

Reid took the hint and cupped both of her breasts from the underside, licking one nipple then the other, flicking hard against the tight and sensitive skin with his tongue. Willow couldn't stop staring at how hot it was, this beautiful man she'd thought she'd never get to be naked with, and now he was working her tits so masterfully that she was already close to coming. She hitched her leg up over his hip, pulling him closer even when there wasn't a freaking millimeter between them. She felt exactly how hard he was, even through his jeans and a few folds of her dress and her panties. She needed to be naked with him. Now.

"Can we…" She struggled to form words. His mouth and tongue on her body made it hard to breathe.

He dropped to his knees, pulling her dress down to the floor, leaving her standing there in the kitchen in only her panties. As kind and careful and hesitant as he could be, this was a whole new side of Reid. He was in control. And she fucking loved it. "Can we what?" He gripped her hips, digging his fingertips into the fleshiest part of her ass, kissing his way across her lower belly, right along the lacy top edge of her cheeky underwear.

She already knew how wet she was for him. She already knew that she was going to need him to fuck her more than once. In more than one way. "I was going to ask…"

He curled his fingers into the waistband, then dragged her panties down her hips, past her knees, and left them down around her ankles. She stepped out of one leg and he grabbed her thigh, lifting it up and resting it on his shoulder. *Oh shit.*

With his index finger he drew a line down her center, starting at her belly button, then straight down until he found her clit. Willow shuddered at his touch as he rubbed the tight bundle of nerves in tiny circles. It felt so good it was hard to keep her eyes open, but she also couldn't look away. It was way too hot to see the dark hunger in his eyes.

He slipped a finger inside her, then another. "You are so fucking wet for me, aren't you?" He thrust with his hand, his other fingers balled into a fist, so she felt the full force of each pass when it met her body.

"Um. Spoiler alert. I want you."

He laughed, then his eyes closed halfway and he used his other hand to spread her wide. He zeroed right in on her clit, sucking and licking in circles. Sucking and licking. He kept fucking her with his hand, curling his fingers into her most sensitive spot and pressing hard. He wasn't gentle with her at all—it was like he was punishing her pussy with all of his pent-up frustration and she was so there for all of it. She liked dark Reid. She couldn't wait to get his clothes off and her hands around his cock and unleash some of her own frustration.

For now, the edge of the kitchen counter was digging into her ass and she was barreling toward her peak. She closed her eyes and dropped her head to one side, then dipped her finger into her mouth, swooped her wet tongue around it, then used it to touch her nipple. She teased herself, just like he had. Reid groaned and she opened her eyes, pinning her chin to her chest and looking down at him. Their gazes connected and it was so raw and intimate and familiar, it was like they'd hit fast-forward on whatever it was that was there between them.

Willow felt the approach of the orgasm like it was a hunter stalking her. It buzzed in her body—it pinged its way back and forth from her clit to her nipples. As talented as he was with his hand and his mouth, she still wanted his cock inside her. The need was so bad she ached. But that desperation bubbling away in her belly made the tension build even more quickly. The pleasure was there. Right there. For the taking. And she suddenly gave way, dropping her head back and gasping. Reid slowed his thrusts and the swirl of his tongue, but he didn't stop completely. He simply matched her breaths with an expert touch, until finally he pulled back his mouth and hand.

"What were you trying to ask me?" He sat back on his haunches, seeming nothing less than incredibly proud of himself.

Willow could hardly think straight. It was certainly difficult to stand, so she didn't bother, dropping to her knees on the kitchen floor. She combed her fingers into his hair and kissed him. His whole mouth was wet. He had *not* been shy about going down on her. And she wasn't going to be coy about any of this, either. Her fingers scrambled through the buttons on his shirt and she smoothed her hands over the hard contours of his bare shoulders as she tugged the sleeves down his arms. Every bit of need she had for him was making her impatient. Restless. "Can we go upstairs?"

He wrestled the rest of his shirt off. "Too many hard surfaces in here?"

"Yes. But I also need you to fuck me and the only condoms I know of are upstairs in my room."

"Right."

She stood and took his hand. For a moment, he was still on his knees, their fingers twined and him looking up at her with so much lust and desire it was like he wanted to consume her. "Come on," she begged.

He grinned. "You don't have to ask me twice."

Willow *needed* him to fuck her. She'd said the words, which was how Reid knew that he'd done well for himself down in the kitchen. And now that she was holding his hand and leading him up the stairs, a sense of inevitability washed over him. He'd fought the idea of Willow from the moment she arrived, and he'd been so sure that if they ever crossed this line, it would be a huge mistake. But this felt right. Or maybe he was just so mesmerized by watching her ass as she walked up the stairs that his dick was making rationalizations.

"Now, *this* is better," she said as she walked backward into her room, pulling him along. When she reached the bed, she slipped her fingers into the waistband of his jeans and tugged him even closer.

He sucked in a sharp breath knowing how close she was to touching him. They both looked down, his forehead pressed against the top of her head as she unlatched the button and drew down the zipper. The anticipation was killing him. Absolutely murdering him. But there was something so good about the pain of waiting...

And then she finally did it. She pushed his jeans to the floor and slipped her hand into the front of his boxer briefs. The whole world fell away as she molded her palm around his cock and curled her fingertips under his balls. He dropped his head back and a deep groan erupted from the base of his throat. Her touch was pure fire.

"You're perfect," she said as she stroked his cock from base to tip. Her voice was soft and husky and there wasn't a better noise in the entire world. She was happy. He could hear it. But she wanted more.

"No. You are." He had to kiss her, so he lifted his head and claimed her mouth. She was so fucking sweet and hot it was hard to understand how someone could be two amazing opposite things at once.

"Fuck me, Reid," she said into his ear, taking a not-so-gentle nip of his lobe. "Seriously. Fuck me."

He needed no further instruction. "Condom?"

Willow scrambled for the small dresser in the corner, where her bag was sitting. Reid tossed back the covers on her bed then sprawled out, watching her unzip a small bag and remove the foil packet. His eyes raked over her body, feeling simultaneously like he'd already committed every one of her curves to memory and that he had so much to learn. Her breasts were so gorgeous and he couldn't wait to have them in his hands again. He couldn't wait to suck on her nipples and make her squirm. He couldn't wait to be inside of her. His cock needed every inch of slick heat his hand had enjoyed down in the kitchen.

Willow kneeled on the mattress and Reid propped himself up on both elbows, not entirely prepared for the pleasure of her fingers on his cock as she rolled on the condom. He loved watching her. He couldn't get enough of her watching him. He reached for her, needing her softness against him, hard.

Willow straddled his waist and leaned down, pressing her chest against his and kissing him, her mouth open and wet, until his mind went blank. She dug her fingers into his hair and he cupped her ass with his hands. Her back was arched, body weight pressed against his shaft, teasing him, making him want her more. There was nothing that mattered more than the two of them. The rest of the world, with its expectations and limitations and rules, could go fuck itself.

Willow reached down between his legs and took his cock in her hand. She guided him inside her and…he needed a minute. Or two. She sank down onto his body and he was wrapped up in the most sublime warmth and closeness he'd ever felt. Why exactly had he stopped that kiss yesterday? He could have had all of this then.

But maybe this was the way things were supposed to be.

They began moving together, falling into sync with no effort at all, like they'd fucked thousands of times. This was not like first time sex, even when it was raw and unrehearsed and every split second brought a new experience. It was like they'd already figured each other out and now it was down to striving for what was going to make the other happiest.

Willow leaned down again and kissed him, her lips somehow sweeter than before. Reid almost felt guilty for the taste. It made him feel too lucky. Willow ground her center against him harder. She knew how to make herself feel good and there was nothing hotter than that. Her breaths came faster. Uneven. And untethered. She clamped her knees even harder against his hips. Reid did his best to stay focused. He was not going to be the guy who reached his destination first. Willow would come first. He was determined.

She kissed him, rubbing her lips across his, fitful and restless. She was close. He could feel it. He sensed it in the way she couldn't close her mouth. He thrust even harder, fighting off his release as her body steadily pulled him closer and made it that much harder to keep the tension at bay. Then she let go, burying her face in the crook of his neck. Reid gave way mere seconds later, his cock pulsing inside her while she tugged on him, over and over again. He couldn't see. Words were impossible. He only felt warmth. And contentment. And relief.

He held on to her tight, his arms wrapped around her waist. Willow collapsed on top of him and she tried to roll to his side, but he wanted one more minute of the two of them as they were right then and there. So little in his life had felt right over the last several years. He was desperate to hold on to that sliver of perfection for as long as possible. He pulled her tighter against his chest, his eyes closed and his hands roving over the landscape of her back. He hoped like hell this wasn't a onetime thing. He could spend the next month doing that and it wouldn't be enough.

"That was incredible," he said, wishing he could be clever about it, but his brain's capacity was severely minimized.

"It was. It really, really was," Willow muttered softly. Then her stomach chimed in, growling loudly. She pushed herself up with both hands planted in the center of his chest and bugged her eyes. "I know what you're thinking. Where did Willow learn such sexy pillow talk?"

He laughed, then realized his failing. "Shit. I didn't feed you. We have to fix that, now."

Willow slid to his side, and Reid hopped out of bed, strode into the bathroom so he could toss the condom and wash his hands. Back inside her room, Willow was sprawled out on the mattress, her arm casually draped across her stomach. That song about a woman's body being a wonderland worked its way into his head. He wasn't sure how he felt about John Mayer, but Reid understood the inspiration behind those lyrics. "Come on. Let's go eat something."

"Now, hear me out. What if I want to stay in bed forever? I know you're a big fan of arguing with me, but do you have a good comeback for that?"

He smiled and planted a knee on the bed, reaching out his hand. "You haven't eaten and I promised to feed you. That's not something I take lightly. Come on."

"So you like arguing as much as you like fucking. Interesting." She groaned then climbed off the bed. "My clothes are in the kitchen. Guess I have to make this trip in the nude."

"Or you could throw on something else."

"I don't know if you see how often your logic doesn't serve you." She stepped past him to her dresser.

He grabbed his boxers, then swatted her on the ass as she bent over and unsubtly wiggled her hips. "I'll meet you downstairs."

Reid went down to the kitchen and first picked Willow's dress and panties, along with his shirt, up from the floor, then folded them neatly and placed them on the far edge of the counter near the doorway. He hated seeing his abandoned risotto sitting on the stovetop, but in a lot of ways, it was better that nothing had gone the way he had planned. He scraped out the pan into the trash, then slipped it into the sink and filled it with hot soapy water.

"Better?" Willow appeared, wearing the baggy pajama pants and tank top he found mysteriously alluring.

"I liked you the other way better, but I'd also like to eat without a boner." He went to the fridge and began rummaging through the drawer. "Do you just want a snack? Cheese and crackers?"

Willow walked up behind him and placed her hand on his shoulder, leaving him with the question of whether he could make it through their mini meal without a hard-on. "Yum. Yes. I should have some cheddar in there."

He gathered some of the cheeses he'd bought at the tiny gourmet market in town, along with a container of grapes, and the half bottle of white wine he'd used to start the risotto. "We are not eating that Day-Glo orange stuff you bought. It tastes like rubber."

"You had some?"

He brought his findings to the counter and retrieved a box of crackers from the overhead cabinet. "I didn't need to have any. I already know."

Willow spotted the wine bottle and grabbed two glasses, then filled them. "You are such a snob."

"It's one of the perils of my former career." He arranged everything nicely on a cutting board, then added a few cheese knives.

Willow peered down at his handiwork as she handed him his glass of wine. "Very nicely done, sir. Let me guess. I believe this is triangle cheese." She pointed at one of the blocks. "Then we have round cheese, and finally, white cheese."

He laughed. "Those are Manchego, smoked Gouda, and Irish cheddar. But I appreciate your willingness to embrace your gourmet side."

"I mostly have a willingness to eat." Willow cut a big hunk of the cheddar, plopped it on top of a cracker, then popped it into her mouth. "Oh, man," she said when she'd mostly finished chewing. "That is way better than the orange stuff."

"Told you." He dove into the cheese and crackers, doing his best to match Willow's enthusiasm, then took a sip of his wine.

"Can I ask you a question?" Willow cupped the wineglass in her hand.

"Of course."

"Why did you hate me so much when I got here?"

"I didn't hate you."

"You didn't like me, either."

"I'm someone who likes to stay on a path. I was on a certain path and you interrupted that. A whole bunch of times, I might add."

"Hmm." She didn't seem overly convinced.

"My turn to ask you a question."

She rolled her eyes. "Oh, boy. Here we go."

"I just want to know if your dream of making it in music was about your creative pursuit or if it was about chasing fame."

She sighed and pressed her lips together tightly. "Are you going to tell me I'm superficial if I say that it was both?"

He shook his head. "No. Absolutely not. You're incredibly talented. I think you have a lot of reasons to expect that you could become famous." The idea was foreign to Reid. He'd always wanted to excel while staying under the radar. But he wasn't Willow. She had star quality. He'd seen it the first day they met.

"It's all so random. One lucky break and your whole life changes. Not everyone gets that break."

He leaned a little closer. "Of course. But that means you could be one performance away from getting what you want."

She squeezed his hand. "Where did you come from, Reid Harrel? I can't decide if you're my nemesis or my guardian angel."

"Maybe I'm both."

"Maybe I need more time to figure you out."

Time. They didn't have much. That was the way a summer fling was supposed to work, apparently. "Now, where were we?" he asked, nestling his face in her neck.

Willow took his hand and guided it between her legs. "Here? Were we here?"

He laughed quietly against her soft and sweet-smelling skin. "I don't know if that's where we were, but it's definitely where I want to be."

Twelve

Willow woke up in Reid's room, in his much larger bed, because as he'd put it last night, there's way more room for sleeping, but there's also more space for me to fuck you. Had things taken a turn for the better? Oh, hell yes, they had.

Funnily enough, waking up next to Reid wasn't even the most surreal part of Willow's morning—it was that she managed to do it at 4:28, a mere two minutes before the alarm on her phone, which was somewhere downstairs, was set to go off. She hated the fact that she had to get up. What she really wanted was to press her naked body against Reid's and convince him to continue the fun of last night. Unfortunately, two minutes was not going to be nearly enough time with Reid. Sexy times would have to wait until later.

She grabbed a T-shirt, then hurried down to the kitchen and grabbed her now buzzing phone and silenced the alarm. There'd been very little actual sleeping last night, so she started a pot of coffee, then finished cleaning up the kitchen from the ill-fated risotto attempt. On her way back upstairs, she realized that she'd woken up with something new in her head. It was the tiniest of ideas—just a few notes. With no time to sit at the piano and work it out, she decided to let it tumble around in her brain while she got dressed.

Ready for work, she hesitated out on the landing. The door to Reid's room was still cracked. She'd earned the right to sleep in his bed with him, but had she earned the privilege of waking him up and kissing him goodbye? She didn't regret labeling their hookup as a summer fling, but were sprinkles of more romantic behavior acceptable to him? She might as well try. Reid would sure as hell tell her if she was wrong.

She perched on the edge of his bed, right next to his beautiful sleeping self. He was lying on his side, one hand tucked under the pillow, lit only by the very faint blue light of his alarm clock. Willow really wished it wasn't so dark outside before 5:00 a.m. She would've given anything to watch him. She smoothed her hand over his bare shoulder. That touch alone was enough to make parts of her tingle. "Hey," she whispered. "I have to go to work."

He stirred and rolled to his back, then reached for her hand. "Oh, damn. I forgot about that." He rubbed her fingers with his thumb. Even in the darkness, she admired his smooth chest, loving the fact that she could touch it now. "Can I make a second attempt at dinner tonight?"

She grinned so wide her cheeks hurt. "Absolutely. Yes."

"I won't mess up again. I already feel bad enough that we didn't have an actual meal last night. I have to redeem myself."

"Sounds perfect."

He propped himself up on his elbow and tugged her closer, kissing her softly. "I'll see you when you get home."

Electricity fluttered in her chest. "Yes, you will."

Willow knew it was kind of a cliché, but she felt like she floated through the hall, down the stairs, and through the yard to her car. It was more than the afterglow of sex. Having Reid's attention and affection made her feel like she had won the lottery. Old Ashby was no longer looking that bad. In fact, it was looking damn sunny.

"You're awfully chipper today," Faith said a few minutes after Willow's arrival at the bakery. "It's probably the perfect time for you to start with macarons."

"Yeah. Sure." Willow felt like she could conquer the entire world right now. Certainly colorful French meringue cookies sandwiched with buttercream or dulce de leche or lemon curd had nothing on her. "I've watched you do it dozens of times now."

"You know where the recipe is."

Willow went to fetch the card and began reading the instructions carefully.

"Since you're in such a good mood, can I pester you about one more thing? Open mic night?"

Willow might be feeling optimistic about life, but it did *not* extend to performing music. Sure, Reid had given her a little pep talk about it last night, but it was going to take more than that. "I'm just not sure it's a great idea."

"I know. I know. But hear me out. I ran into my friend Ted last night. He owns Station Eight." Faith set aside what she was working on and approached Willow. "We've been talking about turning a few of the open mic nights into a benefit for the garden at the high school. It'd just be a low-key thing where we ask for donations."

"Okay…" Willow had that feeling. Like she was about to get roped into something.

"He suggested doing the first one on the Thursday before July Fourth, and I said yes. But he wants me to recruit some good performers. So this is me doing exactly that."

"You haven't even heard me sing."

"Don't need to. Reid said you were incredibly talented. That's all I need to know."

Willow sighed. The pressure was creeping in. "Can I ask why this means so much to you? Is it just because your sister works at the school?" She got out a tray of eggs and began cracking and separating the yolks from the whites. Faith didn't answer right away, which made Willow look up from her task. Faith had one hand on the worktable like she needed help to remain standing. "Are you okay?" Willow grabbed a kitchen towel to wipe her hands and walked over to her.

Faith waved Willow off, but she couldn't hide the tears running down her face. "Yep. Yep. I'm fine."

"No. You're not. What's going on?"

Faith closed her eyes and pinched the bridge of her nose, then wiped her cheeks with the back of her hands. "I… I…"

Willow reached out to cup Faith's elbow. "Just take a breath. I'm here."

"You have to promise me you won't tell Reid."

Willow was completely caught off guard. "Whatever it is, I don't know that I can do that."

"What if I told you it was a dying man's wish?"

Willow's heart seized up in her chest. "Reid's dad?"

"Yes." Faith nodded. "The garden was his idea. It came to him when he met my sister and she talked about how the schools had cut programs like wood shop and home ec. He hated that because he knew that some kids really need to learn practical skills. For some of them, those skills lead to a career. And I think he missed his son, so he liked the idea of being able to be around young people and be a positive influence."

Now it was Willow's turn to get teary. She wished she'd had a chance to meet Reid's dad. She wished he wasn't gone. Graham's absence had left an unimaginable void in the lives of two people she cared about very much. "I'll do the open mic night. Whatever you need. And I'll talk to Reid about volunteering for the garden."

Faith reached for Willow's arm. "Just promise me you won't tell him about his dad's involvement."

"Why? I don't understand why his dad wouldn't want him to know."

"It's not that Graham didn't want Reid to know. He figured that it would come out eventually. It's that he didn't want him to feel obligated to help. He never wanted his son to do anything more than exactly what his heart told him to do."

Now Willow had even more regret that she'd never met Graham. She also felt as though she had a deeper understanding of why Reid was such a complicated person. "Okay. I won't tell him that part."

"Well, thank you. For both things." Faith drew in a breath so deep that her shoulders rose up around her ears. "Now let's not talk about it anymore, okay? We have a fuckload of baking to get done today."

"Got it. I've got macarons to master."

Hours later, Willow had batches of three different macaron flavors ready to go out for a catering order. They'd been tricky at first, but she quickly got the knack of it.

"These look fabulous. Truly. I'm beyond impressed." Faith popped one of the cookies into her mouth. "They taste great. Nice and crisp on the outside, chewy on the inside. Excellent job."

Willow's heart swelled with pride. It felt so good to not only be good at something, but to get *better* at it. "I'm starting to think I might not be half bad at baking."

Faith slid her a look of admonishment. "Don't word it like that. You have talent. I know it. In fact, I think I need to just teach you everything. Take the training wheels all the way off."

"But I'm only here for six more weeks."

"So you take those skills and use them elsewhere. Or maybe you'll decide that Old Ashby isn't so bad."

That certainly gave Willow a lot to think about. "Thanks for the vote of confidence."

"Any time."

"Can I take a few macarons home?"

"Absolutely. Of course."

"Package for you, Faith," Isaac said as he walked into the back room toting a box that was nearly as tall and skinny as him.

Faith rubbed her hands together. "Oh, good. That's the new Flour Girl banner for the farmer's market. I can't wait to see how it turned out."

However much Willow was dying to get home and see Reid, she also wanted to see what was in the box. Isaac put it up on one end of the worktable and Faith sliced through the tape with scissors. They quickly unrolled the banner. It was super eye-catching with a pale aqua background, and the Flour Girl logo in black and white.

"I like it," Isaac said. "Way bigger and brighter. And not so tired looking."

"It's gorgeous. Can't wait to put it up this Saturday," Willow said.

"Thanks. It might take two people. This is a lot larger than the old one," Faith said.

"I can get Reid to help me with it."

"I thought you said he was salty," Isaac said.

Willow hoped she wasn't the color of a tomato right then. It felt like her face was on fire. "We're getting along a lot better now." She wasn't about to offer more.

The chime on the bakery door rang. "I'd better get out there," Isaac said.

"Let's roll this back up and toss it in my office until we need it," Faith said.

Willow helped Faith roll it back up. "Was it expensive to have this made?"

"Not too bad. Just under two hundred dollars. It's worth the investment."

"Did it take long?"

Faith shook her head. "A little more than a week? You upload the design online, and it's shipped a few days later. Why?"

Willow shrugged. "I told Reid that he needs to come up with a name for his stand and maybe get some signage. I think it'll help with his business."

"The world loves a good brand. I'm happy to give you the ordering info."

"Can you text it to me?"

"Sure."

Willow hopped into her car and drove a little too fast, just to get to Reid as soon as possible. On the way, she busied herself with ideas for Reid's veggie stand at the market. The idea she'd had that first day they were there together popped into her head. *Hot Guy Farm*. She giggled to herself as she pulled into the driveway. And then she saw Reid's truck, and she got a different idea that made way more sense.

Reid was prepping vegetables for that night's risotto when he heard Willow's car door close outside. His pulse immediately picked up in anticipation of seeing her. Touching her. Kissing her. He stood a little straighter and cleared his throat, reminding himself that what they were doing was supposed to be fun…and nothing more.

"Hello?" Willow called from the front hall.

"In the kitchen." He tucked his veggies into the fridge, then went to wash his hands at the sink.

"There you are." Willow walked up behind him and placed her hand on his back, then smoothed it in circles as he rolled his soapy hands in the warm water. He loved her touch, but he was still trying to figure out the rules of the fling. This seemed awfully affectionate. And their goodbye that morning had felt the same. "Busy?" she asked.

"Just finishing up some prep for dinner." Reid shut off the water, then grabbed a kitchen towel and faced her while he dried his hands.

Willow leaned into him ever so slightly, peered up into his face, looking beautiful. "I missed you today."

Apparently his tolerance for sweet words from Willow was zero, because that was as much as he could take. He threaded his hands into her hair and lifted her mouth to his, claiming it with a rawness that surprised even him. "I thought about you today. Every minute you were gone." As soon as the words came out of his mouth, he was pretty sure they were a violation of the rules of flings, but he didn't give a damn. He couldn't put the genie back in the bottle. He kissed Willow's neck and unbuttoned her shorts with one hand while he pushed her T-shirt up with the other.

Willow was keeping pace, pulling his T-shirt up over his head then flinging it across the room while she stomped her way out of her shorts. "Every minute? Seriously?" She went to work on his jeans, quickly sending them to the floor, then doing the same to his boxers.

Reid had some catching up to do. He dispatched her T-shirt, then her bra and panties. "Seriously." He snaked his hands around her waist and pulled her close, kissing her deeply.

"What did you think about me?" she asked, reaching down and taking his cock in her hand.

Reid suddenly had to clear his throat. It felt way too good. "You don't want to know everything that goes through my head."

"But I do. I do want to know. I want any glimpse I can get into that handsome head of yours." She stroked him harder, making it difficult to think. It was a bit like she was holding his dick hostage, waiting for more information.

Well, two could play at that game. He burrowed his face in her neck, knowing her weakness for that. "I thought about every way I could fuck you," he whispered into her ear. "I thought about fucking you hard and fucking you slow. I thought about bending you over the bathroom vanity and taking you from behind. I thought about sitting on the living room sofa and having you ride my cock. I thought about it all, Willow."

Willow swayed on her feet like it was hard for her to stand up. "Let's do that," she croaked. "Let's do all of it."

He had to laugh, albeit quietly and gently. He loved her enthusiasm. "Come on. One at a time." He took her hand and started for the living room. He stopped in the foyer and reached into the bag on the table, which was from that morning's trip to the drugstore.

"You bought condoms?" she asked.

"I told you I was thinking about you." He struggled to open the box while Willow stood behind him and kissed his back. The anticipation was already killing him.

"That's a pretty big box."

He pulled out one of the packets. "We have a pretty big list."

Willow grabbed the condom from his hand, then flitted into the living room. He followed her, and it was like she knew the things he'd fantasized about. She got right down on her knees in front of the sofa, the place where he was about to perch. He settled in and spread his legs, then Willow kneeled before him, like a gift he felt damn lucky to receive. He reached down and cupped her breasts in his hands, rubbing her nipples with both thumbs. Their gazes connected, neither of them shy about anything, and it was impossibly hot. He loved that it was like this between them. No barriers.

She leaned forward and he moved one of his hands to the top of her head, gently rubbing her scalp while he took his cock in his hand. She planted both hands on his upper thighs and lowered her head, taking the tip into her luscious mouth. It was hot and wet. It was everything he'd ever wanted. He let go of himself and massaged her head, fingers roaming through her silky hair while she took more and more of him into her mouth. She gripped him hard on the way down to the base, then so soft on the way up that he was riding nothing more than her lower lip. All the while, she huffed hot breath against his dick, sending him way too close to coming. When she began to rub his balls with her thumbs, he couldn't take much more. This was like express mail with delivery by 8:00 a.m.—arriving much earlier than he wanted.

"Willow. You know I want to fuck your mouth, right? But more than anything, I want to be buried inside your pussy. Right now."

She looked up at him with her baby blue eyes, lids partly closed, gorgeous lips still riding his cock. She was going to be the death of him. He just knew it. She seemed to sense how close he was, though, and slowly loosened her hold on him. She grabbed the condom from the couch and ripped open the packet, then once again sent him barreling for the peak by rolling it on.

Much like the first time they'd had sex, she straddled his hips. He wanted to know exactly what was waiting for him, so he slipped his hand between her legs and explored her slick heat, being careful to plant his thumb right on her clit. Willow straightened, thrusting her stomach toward his chest. "Yes. That. Do that." She rode his hand, rolling her hips and pelvis and already short of breath. "Oh, shit. Reid. I'm going to…" She gasped. "I'm going to come…"

He quickly moved his hand and guided his cock inside of her. Willow came just as he was all the way in and she rode out the orgasm, arching her back and fucking him so hard that he could hardly see straight. His orgasm slammed right into him like a freight train with hundreds of cars behind it. Colors flashed in his mind. Pleasure rolled through his body. And all he could think was that being honest with Willow had been the best idea ever. He'd told her what he wanted and it turned her on.

She collapsed against him, sweaty, and wrapped her arms around his neck. He reached down and cupped her ass. He could stay inside of her forever. That's how good it was. "That was the best greeting I have ever gotten from anyone, ever," he said.

She laughed quietly, then kissed him. "Uh, yeah. I'm not sure I've ever come that fast. Knowing you bought the condoms was so hot. It's nice to know you were thinking about me."

"Of course I was. How could I not?"

Willow eased back and looked at him expectantly. "I hate to ask this, but what time do we eat? I'm starving."

"I was thinking seven if that's okay. If you're hungry now, I'm happy to make you a sandwich."

Her eyes flickered with electricity. "That would be amazing."

"I'm on it."

Willow got up from his lap and they walked into the foyer. Reid ducked into the tiny downstairs powder room and disposed of the condom, then joined Willow in the kitchen. She was wearing his T-shirt, sitting on the counter near the cook top, swinging her legs.

"Hey. That's my shirt," he said, grabbing his boxers from the floor.

"Strategic choice on my part. Now I get to watch you cook while my eyes linger on your bare chest."

He grinned and went to the fridge and pulled out a container filled with peppers he'd grown in the garden. He'd roasted them a few days ago and packed them in olive oil with fresh herbs. He also grabbed several different cheeses from the drawer.

"Fancy grilled cheese?" he asked, his arms full.

"God, yes. Sandwiches are your love language."

He pulled out the cast iron pan and placed it on the stove, then lit the burner. "*If* I have a love language, then maybe?"

"Everybody has a love language."

Reid spread butter on the bread, then began constructing Willow's sandwich. "Then what's yours?"

She shrugged. "Helping people?"

"You do like to do that, don't you?"

"So much so that I want to convince you to help someone because I'm helping them, too."

He gauged the heat in the pan by holding his hand above the cooking surface, but it wasn't quite ready. "I don't know what that means, but I'm not sure I like the sound of it."

"Faith asked me to do open mic night at Station Eight, but this time it's as part of a benefit for the garden at the high school. I said yes."

Willow regularly surprised him, but he was taken aback by this. "I didn't think my speech last night would make such a quick impact."

"I take everything you say to heart. Well, the nice stuff at least." Willow hopped down from the counter and went to get a glass of water. "Now here's where I tell you that I think we should *both* help. You should take Faith up on her offer."

Reid was sure the pan was ready by now, so he placed the sandwich in it, which made a sizzle. "She needs to let it go. I know I said I'd think about it, but it doesn't appeal to me at all. I have more than enough garden of my own to worry about."

"Maybe you could tell her that you'll do it on a trial basis? If you don't like it, you can quit."

Reid pressed his lips together tightly. He didn't want to say something unkind to Willow. She wasn't the one who was pressuring him, it was Faith. "Why do you even care? You're going to be gone by the time they get the garden built anyway."

Willow stepped up to him at the kitchen counter. "That's true. I will be gone then. But I'm still going to care about what happens to you. And Faith."

Reid grabbed a spatula and pushed the sandwich around in the pan, then flipped it over. "I'll be fine. Don't worry about me. And Faith will find somebody to help her. I wonder if she's even asked anyone else or if she's just focused on me because she's seen my garden."

"I think she really wants you to do it."

"But why me?" He glanced at Willow, who was watching him intently. He loved being closer to her, but he didn't enjoy feeling scrutinized and questioned.

"Maybe you should be asking her that question."

Reid scooped the sandwich out of the pan and placed it on a wood cutting board, then pulled out a chef's knife and sliced it in half. The melted cheese oozed perfectly. Maybe sandwiches *were* his love language. He transferred it to a plate, then he slid it across the counter closer to Willow. "Here. Eat."

"Thank you." She took a bite and her face lit up. She arched her eyebrows and comically blinked about a dozen times while she chewed. "Whoa." She grabbed a paper towel and wiped her mouth.

"Good?"

"This is the most baller grilled cheese I have ever had." She took another bite, then licked her lips. Good God, he loved watching her enjoy his food. "Which is saying a lot because the other ones you made for me completely slayed."

"Good. I'm glad." He moved the pan to the back of the stove so it could cool off, but the truth was that he needed to cool off, too. He didn't like feeling like he was being cornered.

"Look. I don't want you to be grumpy about the Faith thing."

"I'm not grumpy." Maybe if he said it out loud, he could manifest it. Will it into existence.

"I know you by now. You're grumpy. Which is sad, because we just had sex."

"Which is why we should change the subject."

"No. We should change the subject because you told me you don't want to do it, and I need to respect that." She took her now empty plate to the kitchen sink.

"But are you going to use that as an excuse to not play open mic night?"

She shook her head. "I'm not. I told Faith I'd do it and I keep my promises."

Precisely the reason he didn't go around making promises. "Okay, then." He hoped like hell that was going to be the end of this topic.

"So, there's one more thing. I have an idea."

"Like a song?"

"It's funny that you should say that because I did have a song idea this morning, but that's not what I'm talking about. It's your stand at the market. It needs some work. You need a banner. But that means you'd need a name…"

Naming a business and having a banner made—it all seemed so intentional and forward-looking. Reid just wasn't in that headspace. He wanted the here-and-now. "Willow, I'm fine. My stand is doing fine. It's really not necessary." He leaned closer and kissed the top of her head. "But I love that you care about it at all."

"Of course I care. And if you aren't going to take it on, will you let me do it? For you?"

He knew there was zero point in arguing, and if he did, he'd only delay what he really wanted right now, which was to go upstairs and get naked with Willow. "Sure. Go for it."

"But we need to decide on a name. I have an idea or two on that front, too…"

"As long as it doesn't include anything embarrassing, just do it. Surprise me." He took her hand and started leading her out of the kitchen.

"Now, when you say embarrassing, is Hot Guy Farm a 'no'?"

He smiled and pulled her closer in the foyer. "That definitely falls into the category of embarrassing."

"But it's truth in advertising. You're hot. You sell vegetables."

"Willow, you're the one who's hot." He reached down and squeezed her ass. "And you're all mine as soon as we get upstairs."

Thirteen

The sun had just barely come up when Reid walked into the house from bundling his veggies for the market and heard Willow at the piano. He took a beat and stood in the foyer listening. He'd always loved having music in the house, but Willow's music, performed by her? That was next-level, and not just because he suspected that some of what she was writing might be inspired by everything between them.

It had been a week and a half since he and Willow had first had sex and it had been the most blissful stretch of time in his life since he'd been a kid. But was a fling supposed to change a person's life? It seemed like the answer to that question should be no. A fling was fleeting, and he'd known from the beginning that Willow was a temporary fixture in his world. She wouldn't be in Old Ashby forever, and that meant that however good he was feeling, it wouldn't last. The days were flying by, like time was trying to hurtle them toward her departure. That was the part he couldn't stand to think about—the end.

He went into the kitchen to grab a cup of coffee and noticed that the carafe was still full. He'd put on the pot before he went outside, assuming Willow would want a cup, but she'd apparently been too inspired by her song to bother with caffeine. He poured them each a cup, then joined Willow in the living room, clearing his throat to announce his arrival. "Hey. You didn't get your coffee." He placed her mug on top of the piano.

Hands still on the keys, she stopped playing and looked up at him. He loved the softness of her eyes, the way that they were warm and open to everything. Full of optimism. "I smelled it. I remembered thinking that you were a god for getting up early and making it. But then I got distracted by the piano." She scooted across the bench. "Thank you. Come. Sit."

He really needed to get dressed, but he'd be late for the market one hundred times before he'd give up on the opportunity for this. As much as she kept insisting that she really was leaving music behind, something in her wouldn't let her do that. He sat next to her and she returned to the song, which was light and bright and sweet. It apparently didn't have lyrics yet, so she hummed along.

"This is new?" he asked.

She nodded, looking down at her hands as she played the tune over again. "Yep. It's not close to being done, but I like the start."

"It's beautiful. If you finish it in time, will you play it at Station Eight? Or will you play one of your older songs?"

"I kind of just want to play something new, if I can get it ready. Ever since the night I bombed, the thought of playing my older music makes me queasy."

Reid understood that deeply. If he thought about the specific dishes he'd been preparing night after night while he descended into his burnout, he felt like he never wanted to eat again. It was part of the reason why he now only prepared the simplest of meals. "I can imagine."

"We should get going. I cannot *wait* to hang your banner today." She closed the piano and grabbed her mug, then started for the stairs.

Reid didn't care what the banner looked like or said, he simply enjoyed her enthusiasm. "Then I'm excited, too."

"No, you're not. I know you by now. You're worried, or at most, you're ambivalent."

He followed her upstairs. "But I *am* excited. This is me, excited."

She turned to him on the landing. "Whoa. Dude. Slow your roll. You're mowing me over with your enthusiasm."

He laughed. "Sorry. I'll warn you next time."

They went their separate ways. Even though Willow was sleeping in his bed every night, her clothes were still in his mom's sewing room. It was a good thing, too, because he got sidetracked whenever he saw her naked. They met up in the bathroom after getting dressed, standing side-by-side and brushing their teeth, flirting with sly glances and comical bouncing eyebrows. It was fun and a little hot, but more than anything, it was effortless. He wasn't about to label what it felt like; he only knew that he couldn't imagine that moment with anyone else.

Soon after, they were out the door, and Reid drove them to Flour Girl, Willow clutching the long cardboard tube containing the banner the whole way. "Do you want help loading up the van?" he asked.

"I'd love that."

"You can just leave the banner with me if you want," he said as they hopped out of the truck.

"No way. You'll peek and ruin the surprise." Willow headed for the back door and Reid followed.

"You seriously think I'm that guy?"

"Yes. That is exactly what I think."

He trailed Willow into the bakery. Faith popped her head up from behind one of the ovens along the right-hand side of the room. "Oh. Hey. Good morning, you two. Reid, what brings you here?" The hopeful lilt at the end of her question was unmistakable.

"Just helping Willow load up the van for the market," he answered.

"Oh. Okay. This oven is acting up again, so I'm afraid you'll only have about half your normal amount of cookies, Willow." Faith stepped out from behind the oven and wiped her hands on her pants.

"Is it still doing that thing where the temperature won't stay consistent?" Willow asked.

"Actually, it's worse now. I can't get it to do anything. As soon as I turn it on, the LED readout flickers and doesn't display any actual numbers."

Reid hesitated. Even though he'd never been a pastry chef, he knew a lot about oven malfunctions from his many restaurant jobs. He didn't want to get involved with Faith—that would only open him up to questions about the garden project. Then again, he'd been in Faith's place, overworked and struggling with equipment. "Sounds like the temperature sensor. Do you have a maintenance plan with your lease for the oven?"

Faith cocked her head to one side and narrowed her eyes. "Actually, no. I bought this secondhand from a bakery in Chester that was going out of business."

Reid sighed, then walked over to the oven. "May I?"

"Be my guest," Faith said with a wave of her hand.

He reached behind the unit and unplugged the cord, then waited a few seconds and plugged it back in. He switched on the power, then cranked the temperature dial. Sure enough, the display flashed and flickered. "It's definitely the temperature sensor. Do you have a reliable repair person?"

"I don't. Our last guy retired and I haven't found anyone new. It's hard to get someone to come out here. I don't know if you've noticed, but we're not exactly a bustling metropolis." Faith folded her arms across her chest and leaned against the worktable.

"So now what?" Willow asked. "We use that oven all the time."

"I can't afford a new one, that's for sure," Faith said. "And I don't really have time to hunt down a used one."

"I can probably fix it. I've done it before. It's not overly complicated. The only cost would be the part." Reid unplugged the oven.

"You'd do that for me?" Faith asked. "I can pay you for your time."

"That's not necessary. I'm happy to do it." He reached into his pocket and pulled out his phone, then snapped a photo of the model number. "You've been so nice to Willow."

"Willow makes it easy to be nice," Faith said.

Truer words might never have been spoken. "I'll source the part, then I'll coordinate the repair with Willow."

Faith reached out and touched Reid's arm. "Thank you. I appreciate it. So much."

Reid managed a smile. Hopefully this would put an end to the discussion of the garden. "You're welcome."

"We should get going," Willow said.

"Sounds good." Faith wandered to the back of the workroom.

Willow grabbed two plastic bakery crates from a stack near the back door. Reid took several as well, then followed Willow outside. About fifteen minutes later, they were finished loading up the van.

"I'm a little surprised you offered to help Faith," Willow said as she closed the back doors.

"Why? Because I didn't want to help with the garden?"

"Yes. I still don't understand why you don't want to do it."

He shrugged. "The thought of making any sort of commitment right now makes me sick to my stomach."

"But you committed to fixing the oven."

"That's nothing. An hour, tops."

"What about the market? That's a commitment."

"That's my own thing. And necessary. I can only eat so many of my crops and I can use the money."

"You committed yourself to fixing the cottage."

"Also different. That's mine. And it's got an end date."

"Oh yeah?" She gently tugged on his shirt. "When's that, exactly? As near as I can tell, you haven't worked on the cottage in at least a week."

She wasn't wrong. Reid hadn't touched the repairs. He hadn't wanted to. He wanted to be with Willow, full stop. But now that he was confronted with the question, was he putting pressure on her? He'd been the one who suggested she sleep in his room. Maybe he was keeping her too close. Maybe she didn't want that. "I should get back to it. I'm sure you'd like to have your own space. I'm sorry. I guess I don't really know the rules of a fling."

A look of puzzlement crossed Willow's face. "I think the only real rule is to not fall in love."

"Sure. No big worries about that." Reid cleared his throat. "But you're right. I need to get back to the repairs. I know that."

"It's okay that you've been slacking. We've been having fun. A lot of fun." She smiled that smile—the one where her entire face lit up.

He put his hand on her hip and pulled her closer. "In my defense, somebody I know keeps distracting me."

She closed her eyes halfway and raised her chin like she was daring him to kiss her. He'd take that bet any day. The kiss was soft and fleeting, but it still managed to smooth all his ragged edges. "We should get going," Willow had the sense to say.

"Yes. I'll see you there." Reid hopped into his truck and

led the way, with the Flour Girl van close behind him. They split off from each other when they pulled into the market so he could back in one side of the concourse and she on the other. He started unloading his truck, just as Willow did the same. As soon as he was done, he headed over to help her. He knew the Flour Girl routine by now, so it didn't take long for them to finish.

Willow glanced at the time on her phone. "We have ten minutes until they open the market. Let's put up your banner."

"No time like the present."

Willow grabbed the box and skittered across the concourse with Reid at her side. She set it on the table where he kept his extra inventory, then slowly slid the banner from its cardboard home. "I can't even believe how nervous I am. Do you like the color?" She showed him a few inches of one corner.

"Yeah. Sure. Green. Makes sense. Makes you think of vegetables and things that grow."

She shook her head in dismay. "It's not just any green. It's the same green as your truck. Or pretty close, at least."

Dammit. She'd put a lot of thought into this and he was totally blowing it. "Of course. It's perfect."

She handed him one end and they stepped away from each other to unfurl the banner. When he saw it, he nearly started crying. In the center was a line drawing of a pickup that looked exactly like his dad's truck. Above it, in a tall and stately font, read: Harrel & Son. Beneath the truck, it read: Quality produce, Old Ashby, CT.

"Well? Do you like it?" Willow asked.

He found it hard to breathe or swallow, let alone form

words. It was the strangest sensation, but he felt his dad's presence. Sadness and happiness battled inside him, but he wasn't about to fall apart. He wouldn't ruin this perfect moment with Willow. "I love it. I absolutely love it."

"You do? I'm so glad. I thought it was the perfect name."

"It is." He grasped her shoulder and planted a kiss on top of her head. "It's absolutely perfect." *You're perfect.*

"Come on. Let's hang it up." Willow opened up a small plastic bag with some metal S-hooks and handed him one. She took her end of the banner, fished a hook through the grommet at her corner, and hung it up. Reid did the same with his end, then they both stood back to admire her handiwork. He wrapped his arm around her shoulders and sighed.

Willow pointed at the banner. "I was thinking that if you ever, you know, get married or have a kid, then they can work with you in the garden and then *they* can be the son in Harrel and Son. Or it could say Harrel and Daughter. You might need to change the sign down the road."

Down the road. Married. A kid. These were things Reid never would've thought about for himself before. But then Willow showed up on his doorstep and pried open his eyes. And his entire world. "Thank you, Willow. I love it more than you'll ever know."

Every time Willow looked up from the Flour Girl stand and saw Reid selling his veggies with the Harrel & Son banner as a backdrop, her heart swelled a little more. She'd managed to make him happy—a task she'd once thought was impossible. Even better, she'd made him happy with her clothes on. Not that she didn't enjoy making him happy with her clothes off… She did. She fucking loved that.

"That'll be eleven fifty," she said to a tall, spindly man who'd opted for the final loaf of Flour Girl bread and a few assorted scones.

He handed over his card. "I guess I need to get here earlier for cookies, huh?"

Willow completed the transaction with the handheld card reader. "We were understocked today. We rarely sell out this early. I'm so sorry."

"No worries. I'll see you next week." The man beelined it to Reid. Willow didn't even need to do referrals anymore. Harrel & Son was plenty busy.

She started to gather empty bread baskets when her phone rang. She fished it out of her back pocket and saw her brother's name on the caller ID, then nestled the device between her ear and shoulder. "Hey, Gabe. What's up?"

"I can't believe you didn't tell me."

"Tell you what?" She slid several baskets into the back of the van.

"You quit music? Completely? How is that even possible?"

Oh, boy. Willow opened the second door on the van and sat on the floor of the vehicle with her legs over the side. "Bailey told you, didn't she?" She didn't really have to ask the question, but she wanted confirmation.

"Yes, but that's not important."

Willow was more than a little annoyed. "I thought she was super busy. I don't even know how you two had time to talk about this."

"Well, we did. What the hell, Willow? How could you just throw everything away?"

Willow fought a tornado of competing emotions—betrayal from Bailey, frustration with Gabe, and a bit of sadness over what might have been. "You were there that night at Hi-Life. You know how bad it was. And you, more than anyone, know how hard I've worked. You went to every single school talent show. You drove me to the music store for guitar strings. You listened to the tapes I made in my bedroom. All of that for nothing. I can't spend my whole life getting my hopes up, only to be disappointed. I can't do it anymore." She had to suck in a deep breath. Yes, her response had been a lot, but there was a whole lot still built up inside of her over this.

"You're right. I was there." His voice was suddenly calm. "Which is why it's so upsetting to have to hear this from Bailey. Will, I'm your brother. I love you. I care about you. Why wouldn't you talk to me before you made such a big decision?"

It would've been so easy to come up with an excuse, but Willow didn't have the fortitude. "Because I knew that this is how you would react. I needed to do this for myself. Give myself some space to do something different."

"Quitting is not something you do for yourself. I would argue that it's the opposite."

"I have every right to prioritize my mental health."

"But what are you going to do? Be a waitress forever?"

"Hey!" Willow snapped. "Judgmental much? There's nothing wrong with any of the jobs I've had. I love working at the bakery. It's fun and rewarding. My skill set is getting stronger every day. The owner says I have a real knack for it."

"Anybody can learn how to bake bread, Willow. Not everyone can sing. Not everyone can write a song or hold an audience's attention."

"Baking is an art, too."

"I still don't think you should quit music."

She scooted back and leaned against the side of the van. Why was everyone around her so insistent that she march forward with music? She was desperate to end this conversation or at the very least this line of questioning. She just needed to put Gabe off for a bit. "I haven't quit completely. I've been writing some since I got here. And I'm doing an open mic night at a little brewpub in town next week."

Gabe blew out a sigh of relief. "Good. I'm so happy to hear that. Because I got you another gig at Hi-Life."

Willow could *not* believe what he was saying. "Shut up. You did not."

"I did."

"How? And why do you think it's okay to book me a gig without even asking? I'm in Connecticut right now. You know that."

"And you have access to a car. I know that, too. I have a colleague who's a silent investor in the club. He helped me get you in."

Anger and frustration bound her shoulders tight. She'd spent *years* trying to get a spot at Hi-Life. Making phone calls. Sending emails. Showing up and begging to talk to someone who could put her on a bill as a supporting act. And

it took Gabe one minute to do the same? How was she supposed to compete with that? "I never asked you to do this."

"It's next Saturday."

"What? Gabe. No. Absolutely not. I'm here for the summer. I can't come back to the city. Plus, Bailey said she doesn't
want me there."

"I already talked to her and she's fine with it. She agrees
that this is more important."

Willow felt like half of her life had tilted off its axis. Just
when she was getting happy in Old Ashby, Gabe was pulling her back to the city. "What if I say no?"

"You can't. I already said you'd do it. And I already made
plans to be there. Plus, you haven't heard the best part. You're
opening for Sierra Smith."

"You are so full of shit." She clamped her hand over her
mouth, hoping like hell no one at the market had heard that.
She wasn't a prude about profanity, but she was represent-
ing Flour Girl, especially sitting in the back of Faith's van.

"That's probably true, but in this case, I'm not."

Willow's heart was thumping in her chest like a rabbit
running away from an attack dog. Sierra was one of Willow's biggest modern-day idols. She loved everything about
her—her music, her voice, her vibe. She was next-level. In
truth, she was everything Willow had hoped to be. "If you're
lying, I will never speak to you again."

"It's the truth, Will. I swear to God."

Willow pulled both of her legs up and rested her chin on
one knee. "Wow."

"I know."

"What if I tank? Flopping in front of Sierra Smith's fans will be the final nail in the coffin." As terrifying as that was, at least she'd have her answer about whether stopping her pursuit of a music career had been the right decision.

"You won't, Will. I won't let that happen."

"Like you stopped it with your face last time?"

"That was different. I don't think that was the right crowd for you last time. Sierra's music is a much better fit with yours. I think you'll do amazing. Maybe this is what you needed. A little boost in confidence to help you get back on track."

Willow didn't know what to feel. She was confused and conflicted. She didn't want to leave Old Ashby, no matter how ludicrous that would have sounded a few weeks ago. More than anything, she didn't want to leave Reid. Things were good between them. Actually, they were great. A little better every day. But it was foolish for her to pin any importance on what they were doing. It was supposed to be a fling. No getting attached. No falling in love. Just that morning, Reid had said he needed to get back to the repairs on the cottage, which would mean only one thing—the question of whether she should return to living on the other end of his property. "I don't know, Gabe. I have responsibilities here. I can't just walk away from those things."

"It's one night. I'm sure you can charm whoever you need to charm and get away."

Of course, Willow knew that it was likely true that no one would actually care if she went away. Faith could get Isaac and Ella to run the Flour Girl market stand next week or maybe Faith could do it herself. Willow already had Sunday off from work. In some ways, the timing was perfect. "I have to give you an answer now, don't I?"

"Well, yeah. It's a week away. But you also don't need to give me an answer because I won't take a no."

"Fine. I'll do it."

"You'd better get practicing. Because this is happening."

Willow felt a little sick. The pressure was already getting to her. "Okay."

"Thanks, Gabe. You're the best big brother ever," Gabe said in a high voice that Willow could only assume was supposed to sound like her. "I can't believe you did this for me. Thank you for believing in my talent and fighting for me."

Willow blew out a lengthy exhale. "Thank you for believing in me. It means a lot."

"Of course. Anything for you. I think it'd be good if you got here Saturday morning. Don't want to risk a flat tire or hitting traffic. I'll get Bailey to take the day off from writing. The three of us can hang out. It'll be fun."

"Okay. Will do."

"Love you, Willow."

"I love you, too." Willow ended the call and scooted toward the van doors, letting her legs dangle off the edge. She was in a bit of a daze and seeing Reid across the concourse was making it worse. She didn't want to leave him. Not even for a night. Something about it didn't sit right with her. Beyond wondering how in the hell that had happened, she had one larger question staring her down—what was it going to feel like when she had to leave for real?

★ ★ ★

Reid's truck rumbled along on the way back to the house after the market. He was in an unusually good mood. He was *humming*. Under normal circumstances, this would be more than welcome. But with her big news looming overhead, it was a bit irritating. "Are you okay?" Willow asked.

"What? Yes. Today was great. I owe that to you."

"You do?"

He glanced over at her and smiled. It was a sight that took her breath away every time. "Yes. The banner really meant a lot to me. The thought you put into it. And the way you found to honor my dad without it being too much. It was perfect."

"Good. I'm glad you liked it."

"Can I tell you something a little weird?"

"Please. I love anything weird."

"When we hung up the banner. It was almost like my dad was there. I felt his presence. Just for a second. That's never happened before."

Willow reached across and squeezed his shoulder. "That's amazing." Her voice cracked. Why was she getting upset? Everything about that moment was perfect on the surface. It was the conversation with her brother that was making things feel off-kilter.

"You're being unusually quiet." Reid pulled into the driveway and parked right outside the garage. "What's up?" He killed the engine, then pulled the keys out of the ignition.

Willow usually had no problem saying most of what she was thinking to Reid. But she didn't know what to think about her conversation with Gabe. "I got a call from my brother. After I sold out of everything. He booked me a show. A big one. In New York. Next Saturday."

"Oh, my God, Willow. That's amazing. Tell me all about it."

Just hearing Reid's enthusiasm made Willow feel even more unsteady. "It's the same club as last time." She drew in a deep breath and looked out the window. It wasn't that she saw flashes of that night at the Hi-Life—it was that the humiliation was still living inside her. "I don't know what the hell I'm doing. I said yes because it's my brother and I can't really say no to him, but if I listen to my gut, this feels like a mistake."

Reid placed his hand on her shoulder. "That's fear talking. I don't think it's a mistake. I've heard you play. I've heard you sing and I've heard your songs. You should take any and every chance you get to put your music out in the world. You just haven't had your moment yet."

Willow blanketed his hand with hers and squeezed. She just wanted a little certainty in her life. She wanted something to be settled. "And that might not be my moment, either."

"But it might."

"Will you come? To New York with me? It's only one night."

"Oh, man. Willow, I'd love to do that, but don't you think this is something you need to do on your own? Plus, it's next Saturday, right? I can't miss a market day. The first summer is a probation period. If I'm not there, I lose my spot."

Willow knew she shouldn't be so disappointed. So she put on a brave face. "You're right. I just need to suck it up and do it. On my own. I'll be fine."

Reid unbuckled his seat belt and wrapped her up in a hug. If it was certainty she was looking for, his arms around her were a good start. "You'll do great. You'll be amazing. And I'll make up for my absence by screaming my lungs out at Station Eight next week."

"I have a really hard time imagining that."

He placed the softest, sexiest kiss on her lips. "I will show up for you. I definitely will."

Fourteen

Five days had gone by way too fast. *Way* too fast. That was what long days at the bakery, hours of guitar and piano playing, and getting naked with Reid every spare minute had done to Willow's sense of time. It was gone.

"Nervous?" Reid asked Willow as he drove them into town for open mic night.

Willow wasn't sure why she'd ever told Faith that she didn't get nervous. She did sometimes. It wasn't debilitating, but it was there, baked in to her insecurities. "A little. I don't know anyone here other than you and Faith. And Ella and Isaac."

"See? That's practically a crowd."

"I suppose."

"And you know Carlos from the hardware store. And approximately one hundred people from the farmer's market."

Willow laughed. It really helped to relieve the pressure. "I don't know that any of those other people will be there, but thanks. My point is that nobody has any reason to like me. That's the most nerve-racking part."

"Isn't that part of the deal when you're trying to make it in music? You have to hope strangers will like you?"

"Except I'm not trying to make it in music anymore."

"Then the pressure's off. This is for fun. Nothing else."

Willow remained unconvinced. "I guess the stakes are pretty low tonight. If I flop, I flop. It's two songs in a town where I don't actually live."

Reid stared straight ahead as he drove. "You won't flop. You're going to be spectacular."

He turned right onto Rosemary Street and they drove past the procession of places that were now familiar. This little town had grown on her, but tonight might change that. It could be the scene of another failure. Another marker in the history of her journey to nowhere. Station Eight was ahead on the left. A sizable group of people were milling about in front, which only upped Willow's anxiety. Faith had told her that very few people attended these nights.

"I mean it," Reid continued. "Everyone will fall in love with you. I don't see how they couldn't."

Of course, no one would *actually* fall in love with her. Including him. That was the deal. "You're saying that because you're hoping to get lucky later."

"Not true." He laughed. "I mean, I *am* hoping to get lucky later. But that's not what's motivating this."

"Then what is? You've been endlessly encouraging, and tonight is officially outside your comfort zone. You don't like to hang out in town. I don't totally understand why you're going out of your way to be supportive."

Reid pulled into one of the few open parking spaces on the street and killed the engine. "I do it because I care about you." He turned to her, his eyes open and earnest. "You're my friend, Willow. Probably my best friend."

Willow didn't know what to say. Bailey had been her best friend for as long as she could remember, and she still technically held that title, but she had *not* been there for Willow lately. Reid had. "You're my friend, too. I appreciate your friendship so much."

"You're going to kill it tonight." He leaned closer and kissed her. "Then we'll have a celebratory beer, go home, and I will ravage you as you deserve."

"Oh yeah?" Willow smiled, their lips still close. "Got anything special planned?"

"I can't tell you that. It'll just distract you from your gig. You need to focus."

"Dammit. Okay."

They climbed out of the truck and walked across the street, Willow toting her guitar. The old brick building that housed the brewpub had tall black-framed windows and a heavy wood door with a copper sign that read Station Eight. Inside, it was noisy and busy, with high-top tables ringing the room and lower ones in the center, in front of a small stage. A dark wood bar ran the length of the space on the left and at the very back, by the bathrooms, sat a pool table. A crowd of thirty or forty people had already gathered.

Willow already felt nervous, then she spotted Isaac, waving to them frantically from a table near the front. Faith and Ella were with him, and there were two empty chairs. "Looks like Isaac saved us some seats," Willow said.

Reid grasped her arm. "Can't we sit by ourselves?"

Willow was prepared to do anything to enable a cordial relationship between Reid and Faith. "You knew tonight was a benefit for the garden project and you still came. If Faith asks you about volunteering again, just listen to her. Then decide for yourself, okay?"

He grumbled under his breath. "I hoped that volunteering to fix her oven would be enough to get her to back off."

"Is that why you did it? Or was it because she's helped me?"

He peered down at her, his eyes full of uncertainty. "It was because she's helped you."

"Which is exactly why we should sit with her."

"Okay."

Willow wound her way through the crowd to the table. Ella, Isaac, and Faith all stood to greet them. Introductions were made, and it was only a little awkward when Reid and Faith said hello. Reid found a spot for Willow's guitar, then took a seat next to Isaac. Willow sat between Faith and him.

"Thanks for doing this," Faith muttered to Willow.

"No problem." Willow smiled.

Faith glanced at Reid, then directed her sights back to Willow. "Is there something I don't know about?" she whispered. "Something…you know…romantic?"

Willow's face went hot and dry. "A little. Nothing serious."

Faith cocked an eyebrow and clucked her tongue. "Interesting."

"Why? Why is that interesting?"

Faith shrugged, just as a man with graying long hair was walking up to the microphone at center stage. "I don't mean anything by it. I think it's cute."

The man straightened the mic stand. "Hello, everyone. I'm Ted. I'm the owner here at Station Eight. Welcome to our open mic night. We do these every Thursday, but for the next few months, the first Thursday of the month will also be a benefit for a garden project at the high school. It'll be a chance for students to learn the benefits of growing their own food, and will provide fresh produce for the school. We'll pass the hat a few times tonight. Please contribute what you can. For now, let's go ahead and invite up our first performer, Julie Adams."

The crowd clapped and Willow sat back in her chair, happy she was going last. They watched as a long and steady stream of performers took the stage. There was a poetry reading and a comedy sketch and like Willow would, a few people got up and played guitar and sang. Some people seemed nervous and some did not. A few people were very polished, but most seemed like they were just doing it for fun. Willow had to admire that. She loved the thought of not having an agenda. Maybe that had been part of her problem. She'd always had an agenda, even at a young age. She'd always wanted fame, or what she thought of as "real" success.

"Believe it or not, it's time for our last performer of the night," Ted said from the stage. "We're going to pass the hat one more time to take donations for the garden project.

Until then, please give a warm round of applause to welcome Willow Moore."

Just hearing her own name was enough to strike Willow with an instant case of regret. Reid, Faith, Isaac, and Ella erupted in applause, which was so shocking that Willow felt even more unsettled. Why was she doing this? Why had she agreed to get up on a stage again? This was a bad choice. She shouldn't have let people talk her into things like this. Faith put two fingers in her mouth and unleashed an ear-splitting whistle, and Ella hooted and hollered.

"Good luck," Reid said, standing up and kissing her on the cheek.

Willow grabbed her guitar, which was leaning against the wall. One step onto that stage and it was like she was stepping *out* of her body. Her cheek spasmed. Her fingers went numb. *Focus on the music.* She knew how to do that. She looped the guitar strap over her head and tapped the mic with the tip of her finger, then took a deep breath. *Come on. You can do this.* "Hi there. I'm Willow Moore. And I have two songs to sing for you tonight."

"Yeah!" Reid shouted from somewhere out in the dark.

Willow's face flushed with heat, but she took so much comfort from his presence. He believed in her, even when she didn't. She pulled a guitar pick out of her pocket and strummed the strings. A connection was made. She closed her eyes and took a deep breath. Then she did what came naturally.

Despite Reid's willingness to make a fool of himself when Willow arrived onstage, now that she was playing, he was frozen. Transfixed. It was the most bizarre confluence of feelings as she sang with an otherworldly voice and strummed the guitar she'd once refused to play for him. He was proud that she'd written these songs in his house, but strangely envious of her talent. It was part of her in a way that his talents never would be.

He also couldn't deny how beautiful she was under those lights. The day he'd met her, it'd been so hard to look away. He knew now why that was. She had a star quality—an undeniable magnetism—even if she didn't see it in herself. And for the second or third time, he felt a gush of gratitude that the washing machine had overflowed.

He nearly knocked over his chair when she finished her two songs, desperate to get to his feet, clapping furiously and giving her the standing ovation she so richly deserved. Faith, Ella, and Isaac were only a heartbeat behind him. The crowd seemed nothing short of adoring. Willow even took a bow.

Reid drew her into his arms the instant she was within reach, and cradled the back of her head to speak right into her ear. "You were so amazing." His voice cracked. His chest swelled. The thing he'd feared was rising up in him. He felt something for Willow. Something more than friendship. And that wasn't part of the arrangement they'd made.

Willow peered up at him, eyes wide and a bit watery. "Thank you for being here for me. Thank you for encouraging me."

He tugged her closer again and kissed the top of her head. "Don't thank me. It's only the natural reaction to how freaking talented you are."

"Alright, Reid, let me get in there," Faith said, trying to pry Willow from his arms.

Reid bristled but dutifully stepped aside, letting Faith, Ella, and eventually Isaac have their chance. Was Willow's life like this wherever she went? Did she naturally accumulate a family? That was so far from what Reid cultivated, it was hard to understand why she liked him at all.

Just then, the owner walked up and spoke to Faith. A moment later, Faith reached for Willow.

"Willow. I want you to meet my friend Ted," Faith said above the din of the crowd.

Ted held out his hand. "Nice to meet you, Willow. I've been hearing so much about you, but words didn't do you justice."

Willow's cheeks flushed with a radiant shade of pink. "That's sweet. Thank you."

"Faith tells me you've been a huge help at the bakery. Any chance you plan to stay in Old Ashby? I'd love to talk to you about a residency here. Two nights a month? A sixty-minute set? I'd pay you two hundred a night, plus a percentage of the bar. If you start drawing a crowd, and I think you will, you could make a decent chunk of change."

Willow's eyes went wide with surprise. "Oh. Uh. Wow. That's so nice of you, but I'm only here until the end of the month."

Disappointment smacked Reid in the face, but just as quickly, he was pissed at himself. He'd known all along that Willow was only there until the end of July. It still didn't hurt any less to hear her get an incredible offer and turn it down. He had to step away from the conversation. He couldn't listen to Ted, and Faith, and Willow talk about how she wasn't sticking around. He needed a minute.

He walked through the club and pushed open the door into the warm night air, only to run right into Isaac. "Hey," Reid said, then wandered his way to the curb.

"Hey, Reid." Isaac stepped beside him and scrubbed the back of his head with his hand. "Can I ask you a question?"

"Sure."

"Can I pick your brain sometime about farming? Or I guess I mean gardening on a bigger scale. Like you do."

Reid wondered if Faith had gotten to Isaac and this was all going to lead back to the project at the school. He dropped to a crouching position, feeling spent. "Sure. You can stop by my stand at the market on Saturday if you want. We can talk then."

"Cool." Isaac stooped down next to Reid, then did the sensible thing and sat on the curb. Reid followed suit. "I'm not into the idea of college. At least not now. But my parents want me to figure out some sort of path forward. I want to do something with my hands. Farming or work at the bakery full-time. But I'm not too sure about the bakery. I like being outside."

"As someone who spent way too much time in kitchens, I hear you. Me too."

"So, you're going to run the program at the school, right? I'm going to be a senior this year. I'd love to learn from you. Willow says your garden is amazing."

Just as Reid had expected. "I'm not running the program.

But if you want to come by and see the garden sometime, that's no problem."

"Oh. Huh." Isaac seemed stumped by Reid's answer.

"Whatever Faith may have said to you, it wasn't true."

"I just figured that since the garden was your dad's idea, you'd want to be involved."

Reid felt dizzy. Like the whole shitty world had tilted off its axis. "Wait. What?"

"It was his idea, right?"

Willow's voice came from behind them. Reid turned to see her walking out of Station Eight with Ella and Faith. He scrambled to his feet, his hands in balls. He wasn't about to hit anyone, but he needed to hold his anger somewhere. "Out of the hundred times you asked me to volunteer for the garden project, you couldn't tell me that it was my dad's idea?" he asked Faith.

Willow reached for his arm. "Reid. Take a deep breath."

"Willow. No. I need an answer from her." The desperation in his voice was unsettling, but losing his dad was hitting him in a whole new way right now. Faith had purposely kept a part of his father from him.

Faith stepped up to Reid. "We need to talk."

"I'm so sorry," Isaac pled. "I thought you knew."

Faith shook her head. "It's okay, Isaac. Reid and I just need to talk." Her voice was entirely too calm and even.

"I don't need a conversation," Reid said. "What I want is an explanation. You talking and telling me everything. I don't want to have to ask any questions."

Faith looked up and down the street. "Can we go somewhere quiet?"

"No. Just tell me so Willow and I can go home." He had to force his own voice from his throat. Inside, he was crumbling. Sinking. Disappearing.

Faith walked to the curb where Reid and Isaac had been sitting. Reid wished he was holding Willow's hand as he followed Faith, but he didn't want her to feel like she had to be his security blanket.

"The garden was your dad's idea." Faith peered up at him. "He came up with it when he met my sister. He was such a generous person. He wanted to help. And he loved to garden. It was only natural."

"I don't need you to tell me who my dad was." Reid felt so fucking protective of his dad's memory right then, like he wanted to gather it up in his arms, hold it to his chest and selfishly keep it for himself, forever. He swiped a tear from his face.

"Of course you don't." Faith drew in a deep breath. "When you came back home before he died, he told me that he liked the idea of you working on the project. I thought he should ask you, but he had so much guilt over not telling you about his illness. Plus, he never wanted you to do it out of some sense of obligation to him or his memory. He only wanted you to do it if you were drawn to it."

Reid felt absolutely sick to his stomach. He'd never be as good as his dad. If he was, he would've said yes to the garden project, simply on the merit of the idea. Rather than fighting it the whole damn way. "Okay. Thanks." His voice wobbled for what felt like the hundredth time. He was tired. He couldn't think anymore. "Willow, I need to go. If you want to come with me. I mean, I'm sure someone else could give you a ride." He started for the car, feeling untethered from everything, especially his dad and Willow.

"There's one more thing," Faith blurted.

Reid turned to her, silently willing her to come out with it.

"Your dad and I were in love. We had a relationship for three years."

Willow gasped, then clutched Reid's arm. He was reeling. What the fuck? He blanketed Willow's hand with his. That one touch felt like a lifeline. It was the only thing that kept him standing.

Tears streamed down Faith's face "I loved your dad so much. He was such a good man. I would love it if you and I could be closer, but I understand if that's too much."

Finally, words funneled down from his brain to his lips. "I don't understand. He never said anything about you to me."

She nodded with her lips pressed tightly together. "I know. I think he didn't want to tread on your mom's memory. He always talked about how much she meant to you."

"So…those times that you came by the house? After I got back?" Reid struggled to keep up with the memories running through his head. "When you were bringing him bread? Was that you two saying goodbye?"

She laughed quietly, but the tears were still steadily streaming down her cheeks. "Your dad and I agreed we wouldn't say goodbye. Goodbye is the hardest part."

Reid couldn't help but think about what Willow had said weeks ago, about never saying goodbye to the people we love. Maybe that had been Reid's mistake. He'd spent too much time atoning for his past choices by trying to find the right way to say goodbye. He should've focused on *I love you*.

"Reid? Are you okay?" Willow whispered, squeezing his hand.

No. I'm not. "I need…time. I need to get home."

"I'm here for you. Any time you want to talk," Faith said. "I'm sorry it came out like this. Willow, I'm sorry it happened right after your performance. You were amazing."

Shit. Faith was right. This had ruined Willow's night. "I need to go," he muttered to Willow, trying to hide his face from her. "Do you want to come with me? Maybe you should stay and hang out and revel in your amazing performance."

"I'm not leaving your side."

Of course he knew that was a temporary statement, but he'd take it for now. He'd take whatever Willow had to give him before she was gone. "Great."

As soon as they were in the truck, Reid started the engine, then pulled out of his space and tore off down Rosemary Street. The truck rumbled along, making too much noise as it always did. Reid's mind was a tumult of sad realizations about his dad. He allowed himself the false thinking that everything would've been fine if his dad hadn't gotten sick. In fact, so much would've been perfect. But that wasn't the life that was meant for him. He wasn't sure what he was meant for.

Reid pulled into the driveway, then backed up to the

garage and killed the engine. He and Willow were plunged into summer darkness, which was always a little lighter than other seasons, especially with the glow of fireflies as they bobbed and weaved through the garden. Just like when he used to chase them as a kid... "I'm sorry about all of that drama with Faith," he said. "It's not fair. You were incredible tonight. I hate that anything overshadowed your performance. And they offered you that residency. How cool is that? I know you can't take it because you're leaving, but that's still kick-ass. I'm so proud of you."

Willow unbuckled her seat belt and scooted closer. "Reid. Stop. You don't need to apologize for anything. I'm okay. I don't give a fuck about me right now."

He laughed quietly. It was always her tendency to put others first. "Then it's my job to give a fuck about you."

Willow rolled down her window, then took his hand and leaned her head against his shoulder. The night air lazed over them. The sound of crickets became the background music. And it occurred to him then that he loved her. In every way he could possibly think of loving someone. Maybe he'd needed to feel weak in order to admit it to himself. Of course, it didn't matter. He'd broken the rules by falling in love. It hadn't even taken him very long. Typical overachiever. He could never do anything halfway.

Fifteen

Willow woke on Friday morning feeling totally off-kilter, and the fact that Reid wasn't in bed with her only made it worse. He'd gotten up early to work in the garden after sleeping like a log last night, curled up around her. Willow had taken her chance to sleep in on a weekday other than Monday, since the bakery was closed for the Fourth of July. Plus, she'd wanted to give him space. Last night had been a *lot*. And she knew that the garden was where he went when he needed to think.

Willow, for her part, was doing nothing but thinking. Her show in New York tomorrow was looming overhead. She was dreading that, and not because it meant that she had to play live, although she wasn't necessarily looking forward to that part of it. It was because leaving was all under the guise of chasing something that held no more allure now than it had a month ago.

She tossed back the covers and checked her phone. She

had multiple text messages from Isaac and Faith. They both said remarkably similar things—that they felt terrible. That they were sorry about what'd happened. Willow assured them both that neither were at fault—it was circumstance that had caused it all. Faith asked for Reid's cell number. Willow provided it, but asked that she give him a day or two before she reached out. He needed time to decompress. And Willow, well, she needed time to make a confession.

She tossed on a T-shirt and a pair of shorts, then made her way downstairs, calling for Reid, but no answer came. She grabbed her sunglasses and put on her sneakers, then headed outside, but there was no sign of him in the garden, either. This was worrying. She then heard the buzz of the circular saw coming from the cottage. Mystery solved.

"Reid?" she called when she stepped through the open back door and into the kitchen. She hadn't been in the cottage in weeks and was surprised to see that he'd made some serious progress. The kitchen floor was completely finished, in a modern day version of the retro black-and-white checkerboard.

"In here," he answered.

She stepped to the hall. The hardwood floors were fully patched now. Reid was standing at the end, close to the living room, spreading drywall compound with a wide putty knife. "Wow. You've been busy."

"Yeah. I got a lot done on Tuesday and Wednesday. After you pointed out that day at Flour Girl that I hadn't been working on the repairs."

"I wasn't trying to put pressure on you."

"I know. It needed to get done."

She walked up to him, trying hard to gauge his mood. On the surface, he looked like normal Reid—ridiculously hot in a pair of jeans, handsome as hell, and pretty far inside his head. "How are you doing?"

He glanced at her and managed part of a smile. "Honestly? I'm still not sure. That was a lot of revelations for one night."

"Right? I hear you."

"Faith and my dad? I did *not* see that coming, although now it makes sense why she kept pestering me."

Yeah. Willow hadn't picked up on that either, which was incredibly disappointing. She was usually quite good at sensing what people were hiding. "I need to tell you something, and I will completely understand if you're angry at me about it. But I knew about the connection between your dad and the garden. I didn't know right away, but Faith did tell me the day I agreed to do open mic night. She asked me not to tell you. She said those were your dad's wishes."

He blew out a breath and bent down to scrape the drywall mud from the putty knife, then he closed up the plastic bucket and wiped his hands on a rag he'd tucked into his back pocket. "I'm not mad, Willow. I sort of guessed that you knew. You didn't seem surprised last night until Faith said that she and my dad were in love."

"Okay. Good." That was of some relief. "Does it make sense to you that your dad didn't want you to know?"

A grin crossed his lips that seemed both melancholy and nostalgic. "Honestly? It makes perfect sense. My dad always wanted me to do exactly what made me happy. He never,

ever tried to steer me toward anything. He just showed me the world and let me pick where I wanted to go."

A tear rolled down Willow's cheek, thinking about Reid's dad and what a generous soul he seemed to have been. "That's such a lovely way to be."

Reid shook his head and looked down at the floor. "Now I'm just stuck in this weird place where all I want is to talk to him. I want it so bad I can feel it. He should be here right now. He was a good person. People loved him. I loved him." His voice was trembling, but when he looked up at her, he was nothing if not resolute. "I'm pissed that he didn't get to meet you. And you didn't get to meet him."

More tears came. Willow nearly flattened herself against him, wrapping him up in a hug and pressing the side of her face to his chest. "I'm so sorry for everything that's happened to you. I'm so sorry that everything feels hard right now. I'm sorry if I made your life messy."

"Hey, hey, hey," he whispered. He lifted her chin, forcing her to look at him, then smoothed her hair back with his other hand. His normally troubled eyes were clearer today. "First off, my life was already messy before I met you. I'd just learned how to hide it. Plus, I will take messy and complicated any day of the week if it means I get to be with you."

She sniffled, regretting the way she probably looked right now. Pink and puffy, if she had to guess. "That's sweet. It's okay if you don't mean it. I still like hearing it."

"I'm being sincere, Willow. You mean that much to me." He leaned down and kissed her softly. Her only reaction was to bow into him. To melt in his presence. Then he slanted his head and took the kiss deeper, digging his fingers into the back of her neck. Willow rose up onto her tiptoes and held on to him tighter. She loved these moments when neither of them had to speak, when they could simply stop thinking about where one of them stopped and the other one started.

He reached down and cupped her ass, then lifted her up off the floor. Willow wrapped her legs around his waist, arms resting on his shoulders. Their tongues wound in an endless circle and Willow welcomed the dizziness…the way her mind swirled when he kissed her. The next thing she knew, he was walking into Bailey's bedroom and plopping Willow down on the bed. He whipped off his T-shirt in one seamless motion. A wave of warmth blanketed her as she looked him up and down. Struck by a sense of urgency, she took off her own shirt, then unhooked her bra.

He started to take off his jeans, but stopped. "Oh, fuck. A condom. I can go get it."

"No. Hold on." Willow raised her hips off the bed and reached into the pocket of her shorts, pulling out exactly what they needed.

"You brought a condom with you?"

"I was feeling optimistic when I got dressed?"

He laughed and pushed his pants to the floor, then got rid of his boxer briefs. He already had a hard-on that made Willow want to bite the heel of her hand. "I have never been happier for your optimism."

Wriggling her shorts and underwear off, she watched as he took in every little thing she did. She loved the way she felt when he looked at her like that, with fascination. Admiration. "Plus, you promised to ravage me last night, and as we both know, that didn't quite work out."

"Sorry I fell asleep. I think I'd had my fill of life."

"It's okay. We all need a break sometimes."

He took his cock in his hand and stroked himself several times, looking at Willow with his eyes half closed and dark with need. It was like he was deciding how he wanted her. Take her. And it was quite possibly the hottest thing she'd ever seen. She swished her hand across the quilt, feeling immeasurably lucky.

"I don't need a break right now." He took another long stroke. "I need to be inside you."

Willow's thighs were already quaking. She spread her legs for him. "Get over here."

"I want to see you touch yourself." He stepped to the edge of the bed, his knees meeting the mattress.

She groaned. How she loved it when he took charge. How she loved it when he got dirty. She placed her hand on her stomach and smoothed it down her lower belly, studying the look on his face as she slipped her hand between her legs and felt her own slick heat. He did not tear his sights from her. If anything, his gaze locked in harder. She gasped when she touched her clit, then rolled her fingertip over the tight bud in circles.

"Feel good?" He took another deep, long stroke, starting at the base then rolling his thumb over the tip.

"Not as good as it's going to feel when you fuck me." She rubbed a little harder. A little faster. The pressure was building. If he didn't hurry up, she was going to come without him.

He tore open the condom then rolled it on himself. "Take yourself to the edge."

The truth was that she was already there at the precipice. "No. You take me to the edge. Then push me over it."

A wry smile crossed his lips. "She bites back."

Willow shrugged. "I'm tired of waiting. I want you. I need you. More than you know."

Damn it felt good to have Willow say she wanted him. *Needed* him. Especially as he stood next to the bed with the most spectacular view of her sprawled out before him, waiting. Reid placed a knee on the mattress, then planted his hands near her shoulders. He lowered his head, but she raised hers to meet him. Either he was the magnet and she was the metal or it was the other way around but it didn't matter… that attraction was so strong it was part of the air in the room.

They fell into a kiss that felt like it had no end, with Willow's hands roving his back and her tongue running along his lower lip, driving him wild. Not that Reid's thinking was particularly steeped in logic at the moment, but he didn't see any reason for them to not stay like this forever. Especially in this tiny cottage, all alone…who was going to find them? Stop them? Forget the rest of the world. Willow was all he needed.

He reached between his legs and guided himself inside her. She pulled up her knees, encouraging him to go deep, and he did exactly that. Everything about being buried in her was a salve to his wounds. He'd needed this warmth and contentment and the pleasure more than he'd realized.

"Good?" He rolled his pelvis, doing his best to rock against her favorite spot with all the finesse he could muster.

"Better than good," she muttered into his neck, breathless. She was already fitful. Close to that edge. "You're perfect."

He knew that wasn't anywhere near true, but he drank it in like his life depended on it. He took his strokes faster. Harder. All the while peering down at Willow, soaking up her beauty with her eyes closed and mouth open. He felt like he had to start remembering every moment together. Every frame. Every millisecond. The pale color of her eyelids. The pout of her lips. The way he only saw goodness when he looked at her. Even if she came back from New York, and there were no guarantees with Willow, it would only be for a few weeks. And he could already feel how fast that time would fly.

"I'm so close," Willow muttered.

He'd known this. He'd been studying her breaths as they grew shorter and shorter. He redoubled his efforts, rolling his hips and warding off his own climax, even as the tension wrapped itself around his thighs and made it hard to think. Tighter. And tighter. Like something was going to break. And just like that, she called out and pulled him impossibly close with every part of her body that touched his. He settled his weight on her and gave in to the pleasure, waves and waves of it. Intense. Like fire. Then fading. Like light.

He collapsed at her side and neither of them spoke for minutes. Reid needed to catch his breath. To wrap his head around the fact that Willow was leaving tomorrow. "That was way more fun than repairing drywall."

"I should hope so."

"What do you want to do today? I don't have to keep working on the cottage. In fact, I was thinking that I should cook dinner for you. Then we can try to watch the fireworks. If it's clear enough, you can see them from the garden."

"That all sounds amazing." Willow rolled over onto her stomach and grabbed her T-shirt.

Reid took his cue and got up from the bed, then ducked into the tiny bathroom and got rid of the condom. By the time he walked back into the room, Willow was dressed. "Fair warning, but I'm not going to make you a sandwich tonight. I was thinking something a little more involved."

Willow adopted a concerned expression as he stepped into his boxers. "Don't go to any trouble. Or stress about it."

He pulled up his jeans and buttoned them. "I want to do it. You inspire me."

"Then we're even. You inspire me."

He grasped the back of her head and kissed her hair. "I love that about us."

They headed back to the house, hand in hand, and Reid once again made a point of trying to remember. This time, he wanted to hold on to the memory of what it felt like to touch Willow and have it be the most natural thing in the world. To welcome the sun on his face, breathe in the summer garden, and to know that not everything was terrible.

When they got inside the house, they went off in different directions—he to the kitchen and she to the living room to play piano and practice guitar.

Reid had actually gone to the market early that morning while Willow was still asleep, then he'd harvested everything else he needed from the garden. He planned to prepare an updated version of a dish he'd created at his last job. A month or two ago, this would have been a reckless act. His worst tendencies would have made him lean into obsession. How could it be better? How could it be the best? But Willow had taught him to take a breath. She'd taught him to be patient with himself.

"Okay. You've been cooking for like two hours," Willow said, turning up in the kitchen. "It smells crazy good in here. What are you cooking?"

Reid looked up at the clock. He'd nearly lost track of time. "Crispy chicken thighs with thyme and brown butter with basil scallion ricotta dumplings and charred asparagus. Then we're having a key lime tart for dessert."

Willow's eyes went wide with surprise. "You made all of that for me?"

He wiped his hand on a kitchen towel then slung it over his shoulder. "Of course I did. It's your last night here."

She cocked her head to one side. "It's not my actual last night. I'm coming back."

"Oh. Yeah. Sure."

Willow clutched his arm. "Hold on. Do you really think there's a chance I won't come back?"

He drew in a deep breath to buy him a few seconds to organize his thoughts. "I think there's a very good chance that this show will go amazingly. And let's face it, playing at that club in New York, opening for an artist that plays music similar to yours is a big opportunity. If it ends up being even just a glimmer of what you wanted, I want you to take it. If this opens a door, I want you to walk through it."

"But what does that mean? For us?" She sounded more distressed than he could've imagined possible.

"You need to do what's right for you. And whatever that is, I will support you."

"Even if that means staying in New York?"

He sighed. "Willow, come on. What's the difference? You leave now or you leave at the end of the month."

"All of my stuff is here."

"Stuff can be shipped."

"But I want to come back. To be with you."

His heart was breaking, and he had to wonder if this was a rehearsal of what it was going to be like at the end of July. How could it not be? Maybe it would be better if they only had to do this difficult thing once. "Can we be honest with each other right now?"

"Yes. Please."

"This isn't a fling. I don't think it ever was a fling."

Willow looked up at him sheepishly. "I really only sug- gested it so you would sleep with me."

He cracked a smile. He couldn't help it. "What am I going to do with you?" He pulled her into a tight embrace.

"Keep cooking for me? Ravaging me…"

But… There was a *but* lingering in the air. "That much I

can do. Otherwise, I vote that we don't make any promises to each other."

"None?"

"None. Not now."

She nodded, perhaps too easily convinced. "You're right. There's no sense in promising each other anything."

He wouldn't have put it quite so plainly, but he appreciated her directness. He reached down and pinched her ass. "Why don't you go get packed up for tomorrow? I have a lot of cooking to do."

"Okay. I might take a quick nap, too."

"Perfect."

Reid went back to work, replaying their conversation, hoping he'd said the right things. He wanted her more than anything, but he would not hold her back or hold her down. If they found their way to each other, dug up a way to make it work, then that would be a dream. But he knew very well that dreams didn't always have happy endings. He wasn't about to start deluding himself about that now.

A few hours later, Reid was putting the finishing touches on dinner, when Willow came downstairs wearing the sundress she'd been wearing the first time they'd had sex, right there in that kitchen. He already felt so haunted by memories in this house. Now he had an entirely new set of things to remember—some set with intention and some created simply by their meaning. But she'd brought so much happiness into his life. He refused to feel sad about that. At least not now.

"You look beautiful," he said, bending down and kissing her shoulder.

"Thank you. I'm starving."

"We're just about ready. The table is set and everything."

Willow peeked into the tiny dining room off the kitchen, a place where they'd never eaten, not once. "It is?"

"No. Not there. Out there." He waved her over to the window above the kitchen sink and pointed out into the garden where he'd set up a table and two chairs. "I thought we'd eat outside."

She squeezed his hand. "It's so beautiful. Thank you."

"No need to thank me. I wanted to do this for you." He tossed aside the kitchen towel that was draped over his shoulder. "I'm going to run upstairs and change real quick. Then we can eat."

"Sounds good. I'll be waiting."

Reid tore off up the stairs, darted into his room and put on a clean pair of jeans and a white collared shirt, which was about as close to getting dressed up as he got these days. When he arrived back downstairs, the front door was open and he spotted Willow walking out to the table with a bottle of wine and two glasses in her hands. *Smart woman.* "Go ahead and sit," he called to her. "I'll bring dinner to you."

"I'll pour the wine," she yelled back.

Reid rushed into the kitchen and plated their meal, reminding himself to not get too fancy about it. Not too buttoned-up. This was home-cooked food made with love. That was enough.

Plates in hand, he descended the steps and strolled into the garden. Willow looked at him, smiling while the breeze blew her hair from her face. Lit by the setting sun behind her, this was another snapshot to hold on to. One to keep. Forever. "For you, ma'am." He placed her plate in front of her.

She laughed. "Do *not* call me ma'am." She leaned down, breathing in the aromas while Reid took his seat. "Wow. This smells amazing."

"Thanks." Reid placed his napkin in his lap, then held out his wineglass. "To you, Willow. May you kick serious ass tomorrow night."

She shook her head. "To you, who has already kicked serious ass with this meal. Thank you."

He smiled and picked up his fork, but he waited for Willow to take the first bite. She closed her eyes and hummed while she chewed. "I think I should probably write a song about this."

"That good?"

"That good." She went in for another forkful.

Reid took a bite of his own, quite happy with the results of his work that day. Was the food perfect? No. Was it pretty damn good? Yes. And everything else about who he was with and where they were seemed exactly right. "All packed up for tomorrow?" he asked.

Worry crossed her face, something he hated to see. "Yep."

"Gas in the car?"

She laughed. "Yes. I'm good to go. All set."

Good to go. "Great."

"I guess I'll leave right before you head to the market."

This was really happening and Reid needed to accept that. Even when it made his stomach sour. "Sounds good."

Willow offered a smile and he returned it, then draped his arm across the table and offered his hand. She took it and gave his fingers a gentle squeeze. And any more discussion of tomorrow and beyond no longer seemed necessary.

"So we'll be able to see the fireworks from here?" Willow asked, looking off into the distance.

"Usually," he replied. "Of course, we don't have to watch them."

Willow regarded him with a quizzical look. "We're already bucking Fourth of July tradition by having a five-star meal in the garden rather than hot dogs in a backyard. Why would we skip the fireworks?"

Because I want to squeeze every good thing I can out of this time with you. "All I'm saying is that we can make our own."

Sixteen

Willow had never been good at goodbye, and that morning was no exception, although she managed to reach her goal of keeping it together in front of Reid while she grabbed a cup of coffee, tossed her bag in the car, and got in behind the wheel.

"I'll see you tomorrow," she said as she buckled in. She wished she had something more poetic or profound to say, but her brain was awash with too many thoughts and concerns. What if she failed? What if she didn't? What if she and Reid didn't work out? Or if they did…what would that even look like?

"No promises, okay?" Reid replied, leaning down to kiss her cheek.

"Right. No promises." Willow had never been fully on board with the idea, but it wasn't worth an argument. Being at odds was their old dynamic. She far preferred their new one.

So she brushed aside sentimentality, closed her door,

waved goodbye, and saved the tears for Connecticut Hwy 8. It wasn't just the goodbye that was making her cry, it was stress and uncertainty. But about twenty minutes in, she realized it was such a waste to bawl out all of this emotion when she could instead funnel it into something productive—the lyrics that weren't quite done.

By the time she got to Brooklyn, she not only had her new song, she'd rehearsed it at least ten times. She also had a stroke of good luck, finding a parking space, on the street, right in front of her apartment building. She pulled Bailey's VW into the spot as well as she could—parallel parking had never been her forte. She grabbed her guitar and overnight bag and walked up the sidewalk. Ahead, her familiar six-story building wasn't beautiful, but it had always been charming, with an art deco facade of sandy brown stone, marred by dark metal fire escapes zigzagging up the far ends. The center entrance was set back about thirty feet. The original listing had described it as a courtyard, but it was really just a few shade trees planted in a cutout in the pavement.

As she approached the door, her downstairs neighbor, Ola Onyeabar, along with her fluffy white dog, Miss Princess, stepped outside. Ola had come to the US from Nigeria with her mother, who was recruited as a doctor. Ola had a long career in textile design and had made enough money to retire last year at sixty. "Willow. I haven't seen you in a while."

Willow waved while Miss Princess sniffed her shoes. Willow had learned long ago that Ola, although very friendly, was not a hugger. "I've been in Connecticut. My friend Bailey is in my apartment."

"So that's why it's been so quiet. It's been good. Not so much music. I can hear the questions on *Jeopardy!*"

"I'm glad it's been good." *Note to self: be quieter when you move back in.* "I'll be back by the end of July."

"No rush. Take your time," Ola said as she meandered down the sidewalk.

Willow let herself into the building, then started up the stairs to the third floor. Every step closer to her apartment felt oddly significant, like she was creeping back into her own, old life. Sticking her key in the lock of 3B and stepping over the threshold into her apartment was surreal. She hadn't been gone that long, but it still felt like a lifetime. "Hello?" she called, her voice slightly echoing in the tiny space.

"You're here." Bailey peeked around the corner from the living room.

"About time," a familiar male voice said. All six feet and a bunch more inches of her brother Gabe appeared out of nowhere. Well, not *nowhere*. He'd been in the living room with Bailey. In gray pants and a black dress shirt, he looked like he was headed to a business meeting, but that was Gabe—always ready to seize an opportunity and look perfect doing it.

Willow gave Bailey a hug first but had questions for her brother. "Gabe? You're here already?" Willow did her best to hide her disappointment. She'd been hoping for some quality time with Bailey. Willow still hadn't told Bailey about Reid, not that she hadn't tried. She and Bailey simply hadn't connected in a while.

Gabe nodded, flashing his brilliant white smile and combing his fingers through his well-kept light brown hair, several shades darker than Willow's. "Got in a little while ago."

Bailey tucked a lock of her short brown bob behind her ear. She was wearing a dress—a flowery knee-length cotton thing that was entirely out of character. Bailey usually wore pants. And black. What were they teaching her in this screenwriting class? "Gabe and I were catching up. And waiting for you, of course."

Willow drifted into her brother's arms. There was a distinctly weird vibe between Gabe and Bailey, but maybe it was because Willow was feeling off-kilter. "It's nice to see you."

Gabe kissed the top of her head. "It's nice to see you, too."

Willow stood back, finding herself oddly short of conversation starters considering she was with the two people she loved most in the world. "How are my plants?"

"Good. The pink princess has a new leaf," Bailey replied.

"Ooh. I want to see." Willow set down her guitar and bustled into her living room. To the left was her comfortable blue sofa under the tall windows that provided the only natural light in the apartment. To her right was the sleeping loft with her desk, TV, and a bunch of overloaded bookshelves underneath. Willow went to the corner, where her pink princess philodendron sat on top of an old wood barstool she'd found out in the alley. "She looks so pretty," Willow said, admiring her plant and the new dark green leaf splashed with pink, but also noticing that the soil was overly dry. "She needs a drink." Willow slipped past Gabe and Bailey and into her sorry excuse for a kitchen, which was basically a sink, a two-burner stove, and twenty-four inches of laminate countertop. She found her watering can and gave the plant an even dousing.

"Will, come on." Gabe walked into the kitchen. "You want to take care of plants? Aren't you excited about tonight?"

Willow shrugged. "I am. I'm also trying not to think about it too hard. Otherwise, I might throw up."

"You're going to meet Sierra Smith." Gabe shook her shoulders. "She's been your idol for years."

"Am I too old for idols? It feels like I am."

Bailey joined them. "You're never too old to admire a talented person."

The talented people Willow admired most these days were Faith and Reid. Her connection with Reid, and their creativity, were especially near and dear. She loved that part of their relationship because it never felt like the respect and admiration that flowed back and forth between them came from any sense of obligation. They simply had a mutual understanding of what it took to pull something out of the deepest part of your soul and allow the rest of the world to consume it, knowing they might not understand or appreciate it.

"I guess." Willow sighed. Why wasn't she happier to be there? Five weeks ago, she would've been jumping up and down. Now she felt out of place. Maybe *she* was the problem and not the places. "What should we do for lunch?"

"I was thinking we'd go into the city since we have to be there later anyway," Gabe answered. "Maybe something swanky like Balthazar?"

Willow didn't want to put a damper on things, but expensive French food at a noisy restaurant sounded horrendous. It wasn't going to help her nerves. "I need some downtime before the show. Gabe, maybe you can get us some sandwiches from the deli on the corner?"

"Sure. Whatever you want," Gabe answered. "Bail, do you want to come with me?"

Bail? What's with the nickname? Willow had to intervene or she'd never have any time with her best friend. "I need a few minutes with Bailey. To catch up."

Bailey glanced at Gabe and smiled. "Probably a good idea."

"Of course. What does everyone want?" Gabe fished his phone out of his pocket, pulling up a blank page in his Notes app then handing it over. "Just write it down. I'll never remember."

Willow and Bailey added their orders, then Gabe left. The instant he closed the door, Willow blurted, "What is up with you and my brother?"

Bailey grimaced. "What does that mean?"

"You guys are friends now?"

"We've always been friends. Gabe and I have always gotten along. Is that a problem for you?"

When Bailey put it like that, Willow knew exactly how out there her line of questioning was. "I guess not."

Bailey started for the living room. "Come on. Let's sit."

Willow followed, returning her plant to its perch, then settling in on the opposite end of the couch. "I'm surprised you're wearing a dress."

Bailey's eyes became little slits as she narrowed her stare. "What? Why?"

"I've never seen you wear one. Well, maybe once. But it was definitely black."

Bailey looked down at herself. "This is mostly black."

"But there are little flowers on it."

"I haven't had time to do laundry. Plus, it's summer in New York. It's hot."

That *did* make sense. "Okay. Sorry."

"What is up with you?"

"I don't know." Willow truly did *not* know, which was beyond disconcerting. "It feels weird to be here. Something feels off and I don't know why. And I really wanted to talk to you, but Gabe was here, too."

"It's just the two of us now. What do you want to talk about?"

So much. Too much. "I flooded your cottage."

Bailey waved it off. "I did that once. Luckily, I caught it right away. It still took fifteen minutes to mop up the water."

Willow winced. "Yeah. This was a little worse than that..." She went on to describe the more biblical nature of her flood.

Bailey clamped her hand over her mouth. "Oh. Shit."

"Reid had to tear out a bunch of the floors. And some baseboards. And drywall."

"You've been living there with all of that going on?"

"No. I've been living in the main house. With Reid."

Bailey bugged her eyes. "How's that been? Is he being any nicer?"

Willow picked at her thumbnail. "He is. He definitely is..." She looked up and witnessed the moment when Bailey figured it all out.

"Oh, my God. You fucked my landlord."

Willow hated that Bailey had reduced it to something that sounded so meaningless. "We're *romantically* involved, thank you very much."

"You know, it's okay to just leave it in your pants every now and then."

"Hey. It's a lot more than that." All Willow could think about was the hundreds of times that it felt like more. Even before they started having sex—like the night that he took care of her when she was sick. "He and I connect. On a lot of things. We understand each other."

"I don't get this at all. You're the one who was so bothered by how standoffish he was."

"So much of that was about losing his dad. It devastated him. And he's still fighting his way back."

Bailey shook her head, still seeming in disbelief. "Wow. That is just...wow."

Just then, Willow heard the front door. "Lunch is here," Gabe called.

"We'll talk more later." Bailey jumped up from the couch.

"Okay. Cool," Willow replied, hoping that proved to be true. There was so much she was feeling right now and she needed a friend to help her through it.

For Reid, the mere act of getting his ass to the farmer's market felt like an achievement. He couldn't stop replaying the events of that morning with Willow, especially the moment when she blew him a kiss before she backed out of the driveway. The look on her face had absolutely killed him.

She was uncertain about herself and her future. He could relate—he felt the same way, but it was fine for him. He didn't want that for her. He wanted her to walk into that club tonight and slay. He wanted her to know it in her bones that she was meant for bigger things.

More than anything, he couldn't escape the fact that their goodbye hadn't felt like a small event. It'd felt weighty and consequential. Willow had gotten to him exactly as he'd feared she would. She'd lodged herself in the middle of his cold, hard heart, warmed it up and made it softer, and he was positive she wasn't coming out any time soon.

He climbed out of his truck and began unloading his veggies. Across the way, Faith and Isaac were busy setting up the Flour Girl stand. He waved at Faith when they made eye contact, then he went to hang up his banner. He unfurled it and slipped it onto the hooks at the back of his stand. *Harrel & Son*. Would he ever look at that and *not* tear up? Doubtful. Would he ever look at it and not think of Willow? No way. Wasn't going to happen.

With ten minutes to go until the market officially opened, Reid stood before his table, noticing that Faith was doing the same. They hadn't talked since Thursday night at Station Eight. He'd been too overwhelmed that night to tie up the most obvious loose string. But with a few spare minutes and Faith right there, it seemed like a good time.

"Hey, Faith," he said with a wave as he traversed the open concourse.

"Hey. How are you today?"

"It's weird that Willow isn't here."

"It's just one Saturday."

Reid hoped that was true. Then again, he didn't. He wanted more for her. He really did. "But maybe it's a good thing because it'll give us a chance to talk."

Faith stepped closer. "Yes. Absolutely. I'm so sorry about the other night. I never wanted it to come out like that."

"Please. Don't apologize. I can't fault you for doing everything my dad asked you to."

"Well, thank you. That's very kind of you to say."

"And if anyone needs to apologize, it's me. I wasn't very nice to you. I'm sorry I did that. I will definitely do better now that we understand each other a little more."

She smiled. "I'm hoping we can get to know each other better, Reid. I think it could be healing. For both of us."

Reid felt himself tearing up again. He loved the thought of having someone to talk to about his dad. To remember. That would mean so much. "Maybe we can have you over to the house for dinner." *We.* Why had he said that? "I mean, I'd like to have you over. I can't speak for Willow. She's got her own plans."

"What do you think it would take to get her to stay in Old Ashby?"

Reid drew in a deep breath. "You know, I'm not sure I know the answer to that, and even if I did, I'm not sure I'd want to convince her of anything. I want her to do whatever she wants."

Faith smiled wide. "That's very wise of you. And exactly like something your dad would say."

That comment buoyed him in a way he hadn't expected.

"Thank you. That's really nice. And speaking of letting people do what their hearts want, I'd like to commit to running the garden at the school. For you and your sister and the students." Tears gathered at the corners of his eyes. "And for my dad, of course."

Faith's face lit up and she bounded out from behind her stand, flinging her arms around Reid's shoulders. "Thank you so much. I'm so excited. Your dad would be so happy and proud right now." She held him tighter.

And Reid did the thing he'd never thought he would do—he hugged Faith just as tightly in return. "I'm excited for it, too. I really am." At least it gave him something to look forward to.

"I'm excited, too."

Reid and Faith stepped out of their embrace. "Oh. One more thing. I meant to catch Isaac before he left this morning. Can you give me his cell number? I wanted to talk to him about coming out to tour my garden."

"Absolutely. I know he'd love it."

"Oh. And I think that part for your oven should arrive next week. I'll give you a call to set up a time to fix it?"

"You know where to find me."

Just then, there was a commotion of people behind them. Sure enough, there were customers forming a line at Flour Girl. "I'll let you get to it," he said to her.

"Thanks," she replied. "Looks like you have customers waiting, too."

Indeed, there were a few people at his stand. Familiar faces, in fact, including his favorite customer, the man with the bushy beard. "Good morning," Reid said as he stepped behind his table. "What can I help you with today?"

The man smiled. "Cucumbers, of course. I'll take three. Yours are the best. Never bitter. And a pint of cherry tomatoes."

"Got it." Reid gathered his items. "I noticed your wife and kids aren't with you today."

"Good eye. Both kids got a cold at day camp. Lola and I are tag-teaming. She's wiping noses and I'm doing the shopping."

"Well, I hope to see them next week." Reid handed over a paper bag filled with vegetables. Then he held out his hand. "I'm Reid, by the way."

"Hi, Reid. I'm Ray. It's nice to put a name with the face."

"Yes. I feel the same way."

Seventeen

Reid was wiped out by the end of the market, but he really wanted to finish the repairs on the cottage before Willow returned to Old Ashby. *If she comes back*, he reminded himself for what felt like the hundredth time. They'd made no promises to each other. And he'd always made it clear that he would make the cottage whole again. Now was not the time to go back on his word.

An electronic chime sounded as he opened the door to Hines Hardware.

"Can I help you with anything today?" the man at the register asked.

Reid was on an extroverted roll. There was no reason to stop now. "Yes. Are you Carlos?"

A curious look crossed the man's face. "I am. Have we met before?"

Reid held out his hand. "Hi. I'm Reid. My friend Willow

told me your name. I was in here a few weeks ago. I ordered subfloor and drywall? I had a flood."

A look of recognition crossed his face. "Oh, right. I remember. How are the repairs going?"

"Good. I just need a few things so I can finish up. Need to get some paint mixed, some new switch plates, and a few other things."

"Well, come on. Let me help you get it all together."

Ten minutes later, Reid was back at the register with every necessary supply and Carlos was ringing him up. Reid regretted that it hadn't been his natural inclination to be friendly from the get-go. It certainly made for a quicker trip to the hardware store. "Thanks again for your help," he said.

"Any time, Reid," Carlos replied. "Any time."

Reid climbed into his truck and drove down Rosemary Street, through the canopy of trees and past the familiar businesses like Flour Girl and Station Eight. With his windows rolled down, it still felt hot and stuffy. Reid had never been a fan of July. It was too hot, too long, but now he could identify with July. He'd once been too much—too focused, too determined, too zeroed in on "winning," whatever that was supposed to mean. It had taken nearly dying to pull him out of it. The proverbial hitting of rock bottom. And then he came home and hit the *actual* bottom when he lost his dad. That made him stuck. And he'd been pretty sure that the lonely purgatory he'd carved out for himself in Old Ashby was everything he deserved.

But then a woman with pale blue eyes and a voice that was otherworldly turned June on its head. And then the real fireworks arrived and she did the same to July. She stirred up a chaotic whirlwind of arguments and stolen kisses, of plump, ripe tomatoes and the return of music to his family home. Willow was a torrent. A storm that marched right through the center of his life and stripped everything to its bare branches. If he'd been asked ahead of time if he was up for the challenge of her arrival, he would've said absolutely not. No fucking way. But it turned out that she was everything he'd needed. And he didn't want it to end.

He watched as people strolled down the sidewalk on either side—groups of teenagers, couples, and families. Some folks were riding bicycles, while others stopped to look in shop windows, or ducked into restaurants. This town was alive in ways Reid hadn't bothered to notice before. But he sure did see it now. And for the first time since he'd returned home, he felt lucky. Even when his future happiness was anything but guaranteed.

He pulled the truck up in front of the cottage and started unloading the final supplies. As he stepped inside the cottage, even with the aroma of drywall mud and new flooring lingering in the air, he realized that it still smelled the same as it had when he'd been little. No matter what happened, he'd always have this place and the main house to remember his mom and dad. To remember what it was like to feel like an essential part of a family.

He went straight to work, putting down a paint-splattered drop cloth to protect the floor. He'd seen his dad use this old piece of canvas dozens of times and the various colors told the history of their family. The original light blue from

Reid's bedroom and the celery green of the walls in the kitchen. The creamy tan of the living room and the white of the banister that led upstairs. He smoothed out the fabric as well as he could and once again, he felt close to his dad. Just like he had the day Willow had given him the banner. Except this time, it wasn't so fleeting. His dad's presence was all around him, comforting and peaceful.

He thought about what Willow had said about keeping loved ones in your heart. He was overcome with yet another intense wave of yearning to talk to his dad. *Just one more time.* And then something occurred to him as he opened the can of paint and poured it into the metal tray—there was nothing for him to lose. There was nothing for him to be embarrassed about. If anything, he'd learned that day that talking to people only opened doors. Reid needed a few more open doors in his life.

He pushed the roller into the paint, worked it back and forth to load it up, then straightened and started to give the living room walls the face-lift they needed with a fresh coat of creamy white. "So, Dad," he said out loud. "I know we haven't talked in a while, but I met this girl. Her name is Willow. And I think you would really, really like her."

With her guitar in hand and Bailey and Gabe tagging along, Willow got to the Hi-Life around six for sound check. There was already a long line outside—people wearing Sierra Smith T-shirts and eagerly waiting for the doors to open. As Willow walked past everyone and they all glanced at her, probably because she was toting a guitar, she wondered what it would be like to have people be so eager to see you that they'd wait for hours. Willow had devoted hundreds of hours of her life to dreaming up scenarios like that, but it still felt like it wasn't meant for her.

Inside the Hi-Life, the smell of stale beer made Willow's stomach lurch.

"You okay?" Bailey asked.

Memories of her last time there flooded her mind. The boos. The dead silence from the rest of the crowd. Then the laughing. "I need a sec to get myself together."

"Go do your thing. Gabe and I will be right here."

Willow took a deep breath, then walked over to the sound-board to talk to the club's sound man, whom she recognized. "Hi. You're George, right? I'm Willow Moore. I'm opening tonight. I actually played a gig here about two months ago?" Why was her voice wobbling? She wanted to be self-assured, but willing it into existence wasn't working.

"Sorry. Don't remember you. Lots of people play here." He peered down at the soundboard, adjusting knobs. "You're all set up there. Just you, right? No band?"

"Just me."

"Cool. The headliner finished checking a while ago. If you want to be my best friend, you'll do one song so I can go get dinner."

Willow forced a smile. This was the price of being no-body. "Sure. No problem."

"Go for it."

Willow walked around to the side of the stage, through a velvet curtain, then up a ramp and onto the stage, past Sierra's band's considerable setup, including a twenty-foot back-drop of Sierra's face. Willow opened her guitar case, looped the strap over her head, and stepped to the mic, which had clearly been set by someone way taller than her. "Ready?" she asked into the microphone.

George gave a thumbs-up.

Willow strummed her guitar once, checked her tuning as fast as humanly possible, then took a second to look out at the club. George was there. Bailey and Gabe. A bartender stocking beer. One person was noticeably absent of course, even though he'd never planned on coming—Reid. It made her feel empty in a way that was impossible to describe, but she knew she could tap into that. Use it for good. Just like she had that morning during her drive. The timing was perfect considering the song she was about to play. So she closed her eyes and let the music take over.

Willow opened her eyes when she finished the song. Bailey and Gabe clapped, which was fairly embarrassing. It was like having her parents present at the school talent show. "Did it sound okay out there?" Willow asked. "Monitors are good up here."

George gave another thumbs-up, then walked away. Willow packed up her guitar and headed back to her dressing room. Gabe and Bailey arrived a few minutes later.

"I love that song, Will," Bailey said. "Is it new?"

"Yep. I started writing it last week."

Bailey eyed her with suspicion. "Feeling inspired?"

"You could say that." Willow cleared her throat, wishing she could talk to Bailey freely. "Can one of you do me a favor when I play that song tonight? Can you record a video of it on my phone?"

"I can," Bailey offered. "How will I know when you're going to play it?"

"It'll be the first thing I play."

Willow's set time was scheduled for eight and the stage manager had made it clear in no uncertain terms that if she was even a minute late, she'd have Willow's head. Which was why Willow arrived ten minutes early. As she stood in the dark behind the curtains that hid the wings of the stage, she was struck by the murmur of the crowd. It was loud. Louder than before.

"You're up," the stage manager said, looking at her phone.

Willow walked onstage, toward the single spotlight dead-center. In the distance, someone whooped. Somebody hollered. Someone else whistled. She was pretty sure that was Gabe. He had an ear-shattering whistle, just like Faith. Willow took a deep breath. Thoughts of last time intruded again, but she was so tired of feeling defeated. She wasn't going to let tonight go down like that. She'd promised Reid she would try her hardest. And if she was going to set her dream aside, she'd give everything she had tonight. One last time.

You've got this. She reached for the microphone and adjusted it on the stand. "Hi. I'm Willow." She squinted into the spotlight. "I'm going to play a few songs for you."

The crowd offered enthusiastic applause, of course because they were excited about Sierra, but it was a decent start. Willow strummed her guitar a few times, closed her eyes, and made a little wish to the universe—that she'd be okay after this was all said and done. She leaned into the microphone again. "This is for Reid. It's called 'About Time.'" Then she did the thing she'd known how to do since she was a little girl—she sang. And she sang and she sang and she sang.

Song after song, she won the crowd over a little more. Now, she'd done that plenty of times, but the important part was that she hadn't done that here last time. By the end of her twenty-five minutes, she took a bow and soaked up the appreciation, but she wished more than anything that Reid could've been there to witness it. He would've been even more proud than he was the other night at Station Eight. He would've hugged her afterward. He would've given her a kiss on the head. And it would've been imperfectly perfect, just like they always were together.

Guitar in hand, Willow walked offstage with her head held high, the opposite of her last exit from that same stage. She navigated the club's corridors backstage, receiving well-wishes from several members of the crew.

"Great set."

"Good job."

"Love your music."

She smiled and said thank you, then ducked into her dingy dressing room. She set down her guitar and collapsed on the couch. Bailey and Gabe arrived a minute later.

"You were so amazing tonight, Will," Gabe offered first. "Get up here. Give me a hug."

"You really were awesome," Bailey said.

Willow slowly rose from the couch and hugged Gabe, then Bailey. "Did you get video of the first song?"

Bailey handed over Willow's phone. "I did."

"Who's Reid?" Gabe asked.

Willow wanted to blurt that Reid was what was missing from an otherwise perfect night. "A friend."

"I know him. He's a good guy." Bailey slid a smile in Willow's direction. "Good guy."

"Thanks. Both of you. Thanks for being here and for being so supportive." Willow realized that she needed to say a bit more. "And thanks, Gabe, for setting this up. I really appreciate it."

"Well, I didn't want you to quit," Gabe said. "And Mom and Dad don't want you to quit, either. I told them."

"What did they say?"

"Mom started crying. Dad was flabbergasted."

"Mom cried? Seriously?" Willow could *not* believe this. "Why didn't they call me? Try to cheer me on?"

"I told them not to," Gabe said.

Willow's sights flew to Bailey, who held up both hands to claim her innocence. "Why?"

"You're always telling me about how much pressure you feel from them. I was trying to insulate you from that. I told them to back off and let you figure it out."

Willow shook her head. "But you didn't back off, did you? You booked me this show without even asking me about it. You put me in a corner. I had to say yes."

"But isn't tonight what you've always dreamed of?"

This was an impossible question to answer. Yes, she'd

dreamed of this, but it turned out that her dreams didn't match the reality. And maybe that was life. That was basically what Reid had said the night they talked about their burnout. "Yes, tonight was amazing, but it isn't that simple. This is one night. One performance. If I went back to it, I'm guaranteed to bomb at a different show. I get so tired of hustling all the time for every little break. It's exhausting."

Gabe paced the room. "Don't quit now. I talked to a friend of mine and he can connect you with an unbelievable manager. That's what you've been missing. Some firepower. He can get you in with some big producers. Maybe you go to Nashville or LA. Record some demos. See where that gets you."

Willow wanted to scream. *Where was this unbelievable manager three years ago, Gabe? Why didn't you step up to the plate for me then?* Because the reality was that Willow was tired. The fire of creativity definitely still burned hot in her belly, but her enthusiasm for everything else? The business part of the music business? It wasn't there.

Bailey perched on an armchair and smiled hesitantly. Clearly she was picking up on what Willow was feeling, which came as no surprise. Bailey had always been in tune with Willow, and vice versa. "It's not like you have to make some big decision right now," she said.

"Of course. I'm not trying to pressure you." Gabe stood next to Bailey and looked down at her.

Funny, but that no-pressure talk felt like pressure.

"I just didn't like the fact that you'd decided to shut the door on the whole thing completely," Bailey added. "I get that you might want a break, but to say that you weren't going to do it at all? Ever? That seemed a little harsh."

The choice had been harsh. But it had been coming for a long time. "I have a lot to think about."

A tall, skinny man with a bushy mustache and two full sleeves of tattoos knocked on the doorframe of Willow's dressing room. "Willow Moore?"

"That's me."

"Hi. I'm Sierra's road manager, Brian." He took a step into the room. "Sierra always tries to meet her opening acts, but she's been on the road for three months now and it's taken a toll on her voice. She wants to save it for tonight. But she still wanted me to say thank you for opening. She stood in the stage wings for the end of your first song. She liked it."

Wow. When Willow had dreamed about one of her favorite artists listening to her music, she'd imagined it quite differently. Zero fantasies were built on anyone merely *liking* the *end* of a song. But it was something.

Gabe strode over to Brian and thrust out his hand. "I'm Willow's brother, Gabriel Moore. She's about to sign with a new manager, so I'm filling in for now. Is there any way we can get Willow on some of Sierra's dates? Maybe a future tour?"

Brian looked completely caught off guard. "Uh. Maybe. Possibly. Give me your cell number and I'll let you know. No promises, but I can see." He handed over his phone. "Add in your contact."

"Will do." Gabe tapped away at Brian's phone. "Thank you. Again."

"Sure thing. Good luck." Brian turned and disappeared into the hall.

"See?" Gabe looked at Willow, rubbing both hands together like an evil genius. "Things are happening. I can feel it."

There was a time in the not-so-distant past when Willow would've bought in to what Gabe was saying, but it simply didn't feel right anymore. "He said he'd let you know. He also said no promises."

"You don't know what might happen, Willow," Gabe said.

Willow turned to Bailey for support, but her best friend was looking at Gabe like he was the smartest person on the planet. "Then I'll repeat what Brian said."

"Which part?" Gabe asked.

"No promises." Willow got up and put her guitar in its case.

"I can live with that," Bailey said, apparently returning to earth.

"Fine," Gabe said, seeming like it wasn't fine at all.

Willow picked up her guitar. "Cool. Now can we please go get some pizza? I love Old Ashby, but I need me some New York City love."

Eighteen

Willow rolled over in bed and stared at her old alarm clock. It was 4:32 a.m. Apparently her body had acclimated to her Flour Girl wake-up time. *It's Sunday*, she told her brain. *I don't have work today. Go back to sleep.* But it was no use. As comfortable and familiar as this bed and the sheets and the comforter were, she couldn't sleep.

Willow rolled onto her back and stared up at the ceiling as her eyes slowly adjusted to the light. Off in the distance, somewhere in the city, an ambulance approached. It hadn't been that long ago that she'd missed the sound of sirens. Now it was just another noisy part of the city. Had she been so nostalgic for New York when she first went to Connecticut because she was feeling untethered? Because she didn't feel that way anymore. She definitely felt tied to something—her new life. To Flour Girl. To Faith and Ella and Isaac. And especially, to Reid. Just the thought of him made her smile in the dark. It made her feel optimistic about the future, even when so much was up in the air. So much was undecided. Did that mean she loved him? She was pretty sure it did.

"Let me guess," Bailey whispered. "You can't sleep."

"Oh, my God, yes." Willow flopped to her side to face her best friend.

"Shh." Bailey sounded like air leaking out of a balloon. "Gabe is sleeping."

"I know. I can hear him snoring."

"You should be exhausted. Too amped up after your show?"

"Not exactly."

"Then what?"

Willow drew in a deep breath, searching for the words. There would be no good way to say this without Bailey feeling some degree of betrayal that she hadn't been consulted. "I have to tell you something. And I'm not sure how you're going to feel about it."

"Please tell me you aren't thinking about staying here for the rest of our two months. We're more than halfway through, and my class is going so well."

Willow didn't want to be pissed off, but *that* was the place Bailey's mind went to? "No. I'm actually thinking about staying in Connecticut. Like not leaving."

"You like your job at the bakery that much?"

"I do. I'm good at it. I like being good at something."

"How much does Reid have to do with this?"

"A lot. I won't lie."

"What does he say?"

"I don't know. We haven't talked about it. He said that we shouldn't make promises to each other." Willow hadn't been a big fan of it when he'd said it, but it sounded even worse out loud.

"Sounds like you shouldn't get your hopes up."

"Then maybe it won't work." Her stomach sank at the thought. "But you know, I'm going to try. I want to try. And my best friend lives there, so that could be pretty next-level."

"I tried to get you to visit me in Connecticut a bunch of times and you always made me come here. So I hope you can see how this sounds a little out there. And the fact that you're planning on making this big life change because of a dude?"

All of that was absolutely true. And Willow felt more than bad about it—she felt terrible. She'd acted selfishly and self-centeredly for a long time. It had come from the relentless pursuit of her dream. When she was chasing that one thing for so long, there'd been no balance in her life. It'd been so easy to have tunnel vision. Nothing had mattered more than her goal. And that was the start of the problem. "This is me becoming a better version of myself, okay? It starts with making a change."

"It *would* be nice to live in the same place again."

"See?"

"What about the apartment?"

"The lease is up in September. Maybe the timing is right."

"Whatever you want to do, I support you," Bailey said. "What do you need from me?"

"Can you help me bring some stuff down to the car?"

"In the morning? Sure."

"Now is morning."

"What are you two talking about up there?" Gabe's groggy voice sounded from below.

Willow and Bailey giggled like girls caught staying up late at a sleepover. "Nothing, *Dad*," Willow replied.

"Willow's going back to Connecticut," Bailey said, flipping on a light. "Get up. We're going to help her load the car."

"I thought we were all going to go out to breakfast." Gabe's head popped up from the stairs up to the sleeping loft.

Willow climbed out of bed. "Sometimes, plans change."

When Willow pulled into the driveway at Reid's, she spotted him in the yard doing Tai Chi. Just seeing him made her smile, even when she wasn't sure how he was going to react to the decision she'd made. It was a big one, and he'd been the one to say they shouldn't make promises to each other. But if she wasn't willing to be completely vulnerable with him, love was sort of a moot point.

She hopped out of the car and jogged across the yard, past the garden beds. The morning sun was magical, but then again, so was this property. Everything about it filled Willow's heart with joy. "Reid!" she yelled.

No response came. Just like the first time.

She slowed down to a quick walk and thought about texting him to announce her arrival, but then she saw that his phone was on the ground. "Reid!" she called again. Nothing. *Damn those earbuds.*

Willow wasn't about to scare him like the last time she'd encountered this scenario, so she gave him a wide berth and started walking around to the far side of the tree. All the while she studied his graceful movements, in awe of him. She was overcome with this sense that she was coming home. That was all she'd really wanted—to come home to warmth and someone she loved. She loved him. She did. She knew it in that moment, just liked she'd known it dozens of times before then, even when she wasn't brave enough to say or even think the words.

And she couldn't wait to tell him. So she started flailing her arms.

It only took a second for him to see her. That was how good she was at flailing. He pulled out one of his earbuds. "Willow. What are you doing? You're back? What time did you leave?"

She ran up to him, smooshed his face with both hands, and planted a kiss on him. "I left way too early. I had to get back here. I had to talk to you."

A deep crease formed between his eyes. "I'm not sure what that means. Does that mean the show went well?"

"It did. And I owe it all to you. I got up on that stage and all I could think was that I wanted to make you proud. Even though you weren't there. Does that sound weird?"

He grinned and rubbed her cheek with the back of his hand. "Not at all. It's very sweet, actually."

She pulled her phone out of her pocket. "Bailey recorded a video of me playing my new song. I can't wait to show it to you. I finished the lyrics in the car on the way to New York."

He picked up his own phone from the ground, then gestured toward the house. "Cool. Let's go inside to watch it."

He started for the front door. "You must have been inspired in the car."

"Actually, I cried for the first twenty minutes," she admitted as they walked up the stairs together.

"What? Why?" He turned to her when they arrived in the foyer, deep concern painted on his face. "Were you that scared of doing the show?"

She peered up into his kind, warm eyes. "I cried because I knew that I loved you." She grasped both of his arms, hoping like hell he wasn't going to think that she'd lost all touch with reality. "I love you, Reid. And I know you have a lot of stuff you need to work your way through, but so do I. And personally, I think it was very shortsighted and more than a little bossy of you to tell me that we shouldn't make promises to each other." She was practically gasping for air by the time she reached the end of that very long thought, but at least she'd gotten it out.

"You're right. You're absolutely right."

"Which part?"

He reached for her hand. "The part about promises. It wasn't even shortsighted, Willow. It was a lie. I've known I loved you for a while now."

"Really?"

"Yes. At first, it didn't make sense. Do people fall in love in five weeks?"

"Some people fall in love in five minutes."

"There's a chance I fell in love with you in five seconds."

"I do not think that's true. You were not very nice to me the first time I interrupted your Tai Chi."

"True." He laughed quietly. "Honestly, I don't really care what the timeline is. And I know you're supposed to go back to New York at the end of the month, but I really do love you and I'm willing to do whatever it takes to make this work. I've been thinking and I'm okay with long distance. It won't be easy, but we can do it. I know it."

That was pure music to her ears, albeit not her plan. "I'm not going back to New York at the end of the month, Reid. I brought a bunch of my stuff with me. I realize that's a lot to put on you, but I can move back into the cottage. I can get an apartment in town. We can take it slow."

"Slow? You want to take it slow? That ship has sailed. You've seen me fall apart. You know all of my secrets."

"All of them?"

He nodded eagerly with a clarity in his eyes she wasn't sure she'd ever seen. "Yes. Everything." He leaned closer and kissed her softly. "I love that you're staying. More than you'll ever know. Faith will be really excited to hear it, too." He started for the kitchen. "Come on. Let me make you breakfast to celebrate."

"Yes. Please. I'm so hungry." Her heart was pounding fiercely, but only out of pure, unadulterated, helium-balloons-and-cotton-candy happiness. "There is one thing we'll need to work out."

"What's that?"

"Just as you predicted, a door opened last night. Or it opened early this morning, actually. When my brother finally looked at his text messages."

"What kind of door?" he asked, opening the fridge and pulling out some eggs.

"Sierra Smith's road manager invited me to join her for a few dates on her European tour. It's not a lot, but I'm trying to look at it as an adventure."

He pulled out the cast iron pan and set it on the stovetop. "Whoa. That's huge. Did you walk through the door?"

"I did. I'm hoping you can come with me. It's in September."

"Oh, wow. That sounds amazing. I might have to play it by ear on that one."

Willow didn't want to be disappointed, but she was. "What's going on?"

He slipped a pat of butter into the pan, then started cracking eggs. "I have my own stuff to catch you up on. I agreed to do the garden at the school. And I'm thinking about hiring Isaac to help me part-time. He's really interested in learning about gardening and it would be nice to have him around. He's a good kid."

Well, if that was going to be his reason for possibly having to stay behind, she could more than live with it. "Oh, my God. Reid. That makes me so happy. Both parts, but especially your dad's garden."

"I know. It's about time I finally said yes to that project."

She grasped his arm. "Hold on. What did you just say?"

"It's about time I finally said yes to that project?"

She could hardly believe that he'd said the exact phrase that had come to her in the car. "'About Time' is the title of my new song. The one I told you about. Hold on. Let me play it for you." She pulled out her phone and started the recording for him. Her heart was thundering again, but she was resigned to that being the normal state of things when she was around Reid. She didn't look at the screen because she'd never been able to watch herself on film. But she did listen, and she heard herself say the words, "This is for Reid. It's called 'About Time.'"

He looked up at her and she witnessed the moment when he teared up. "You dedicated a song to me? Even though I wasn't there?"

"I hoped that you would feel my presence. That you would know I was thinking about you. Somehow."

He held his finger to his lips and redirected his attention to her phone. She loved seeing the look on his face as he watched the recording—all of that affection and adoration? It was for her. All for her. When it was finished, he set aside her phone and pulled her into his arms. "It's so good."

"You were the inspiration. And everything that's happened between us. It's about how time is the one thing we need most and the one thing we don't have enough of. So we have to make the most of it. By putting ourselves on a path that makes us happy."

He smiled wide. "Staying in Old Ashby is the path you really want?"

"All that time I was chasing my dream, I forgot to live my life. I have a life here. And I don't have to give up anything. I can still have my music. I can have a job I love at the bakery. And more than anything, I can have you."

He drew in a deep breath through his nose and pulled her close. "And that all makes me happy."

"Good. I'm glad."

"I should probably tell you now that I lied when I told you that you know all of my secrets."

"Oh, no. Now what?"

"I finished up the cottage last night, and while I was there, thinking about you in New York and thinking about how much I loved you and hoping that we could somehow find a way to be together, I actually felt my dad's presence. So I talked to him. About you."

Now it was Willow's turn to tear up. It was about the sweetest thing she'd ever heard. "What did you say?"

"That I met a woman that I was sure he was going to like."

"I would've loved your dad, Reid. I know you're just like him."

He smiled. "Not exactly the same. But he's in here." Reid patted his chest, right where his heart was. "So. Europe in September. That's big. What do you think will happen after that?"

"No clue. And I've decided that I'm just going to focus on enjoying the process. Zero expectations other than having fun playing my music. For that same reason, I'm going to talk to Ted at Station Eight about the residency. I think that will be fun. It'll be an outlet for my creativity, no pressure."

"See what happens. I think that's the perfect attitude."

"Good." She leaned against the counter, looking at Reid, realizing that although she was starving, she'd rather have him. "Do we have to have breakfast right away?"

"I thought you were hungry."

"I need you to do something." She wrapped her arm around his waist and pulled him closer.

"What's that?" he asked, narrowing his eyes but still managing a sexy grin.

"Me." Willow popped up onto her toes and delivered a long, slow kiss, just like he deserved. "I'm the one thing."

★ ★ ★ ★ ★

Look for Bailey's story coming in Spring 2025!